ELIZABETH HARROWER was born in Sydney in 1928 but her family soon relocated to Newcastle, where she lived until she was eleven.

In 1951 Harrower moved to London. She travelled extensively and began to write fiction. Her first novel, *Down in the City*, was published in 1957 and was followed by *The Long Prospect* a year later. In 1959 she returned to Sydney, where she began working for the ABC and as a book reviewer for the *Sydney Morning Herald*. In 1960 she published *The Catherine Wheel*, the story of an Australian law student in London, her only novel not set in Sydney. *The Watch Tower* appeared in 1966. Between 1961 and 1967 she worked in publishing, for Macmillan.

Harrower published no more novels, though she continued to write short fiction. Her work is austere, intelligent, ruthless in its perceptions about men and women. She was admired by many of her contemporaries, including Patrick White and Christina Stead, and is without doubt among the most important writers of the postwar period in Australia.

Elizabeth Harrower lives in Sydney.

FIONA McGREGOR is the author of five books, her most recent novel *Indelible Ink* winning the *Age* Book of the Year award. She writes essays and reviews, and is working on another novel. She is internationally known as a performance artist, completing the epic *Water Series* at Artspace, Sydney, in 2011. fionamcgregor.com

ALSO BY ELIZABETH HARROWER

Down in the City
The Catherine Wheel
The Watch Tower

The Long Prospect
Elizabeth Harrower

Text Publishing Melbourne Australia

textclassics.com.au
textpublishing.com.au

The Text Publishing Company
Swann House
22 William Street
Melbourne Victoria 3000
Australia

Copyright © Elizabeth Harrower 1958
Introduction copyright © Fiona McGregor 2012

All rights reserved. Without limiting the rights under copyright above, no part of this publication shall be reproduced, stored in or introduced into a retrieval system, or transmitted in any form or by any means (electronic, mechanical, photocopying, recording or otherwise), without the prior permission of both the copyright owner and the publisher of this book.

First published by Cassell & Company, London 1958
This edition published by The Text Publishing Company 2012

Cover design by WH Chong
Page design by Text
Typeset by Midland Typesetters

Printed in Australia by Griffin Press, an Accredited ISO AS/NZS 14001:2004 Environmental Management System printer

Primary print ISBN: 9781922079480
Ebook ISBN: 9781921961762
Author: Harrower, Elizabeth, 1928–
Title: The long prospect / by Elizabeth Harrower ;
introduction by Fiona McGregor.
Series: Text classics
Dewey Number: A823.3

This book is printed on paper certified against the Forest Stewardship Council® Standards. Griffin Press holds FSC chain-of-custody certification SGS-COC-005088. FSC promotes environmentally responsible, socially beneficial and economically viable management of the world's forests.

CONTENTS

Aces from Hell

by Fiona McGregor

'THE front door of Thea's flat was ajar so Lilian gave it a push and went in, her eyes on swivels.' So begins Elizabeth Harrower's second novel, *The Long Prospect*, first published in 1958. It is an auspicious invitation, hinting at malice and incursion, morbid curiosity and humour. Lilian, little despot of a little world, barges through the lives of all the characters, setting traps and settling scores. Counterpointing her destruction is the coming-to-life of her granddaughter Emily, neglected by all but Thea and later Max, at different times Lilian's boarders. The industrial seaside town of Ballowra, a fictionalised Newcastle, is the setting.

Harrower's writing is devastating. The prose is exact, spiky, a chiaroscuro of dread pace and bright voice. You laugh and cringe at the same time. The psychological precision is relentless. It's like watching keyhole surgery: Harrower's gaze is so penetrating you can feel her looking through the pages, down the years, at us. And she is.

Snooping into the novel with Lilian in the first pages, we learn that Thea has a lover, Max, but he is married. Thea boarded with Lilian for eleven years before moving into her own flat, that interwar symbol of scarily independent youth, particularly for women. 'I thought I'd come and have a look at your *flat*,' Lilian announces weightily when Thea catches her eaves-dropping, as though it is an equal transgression. Vexed by the loss of control of Thea and without a man of her own ('if you had any spirit you had to battle with them, belittle them, and learn to enjoy it'), Lilian delights in Max being Catholic and unable to leave his wife for Thea.

Years later, when Lilian gets the opportunity to offer Max a room on his return to work at the steel-works, the stage is set for her to weave another of her wicked webs. Others around her, like Rosen, her hapless lover-cum-boarder acquired after Thea's departure, are bent on their own petty revenges. Cameos like Billie, drawn as savagely as a German expressionist portrait, complete the gallery. Chance delivers Lilian some aces from Hell, and she plays them like the devil.

Emily Lawrence observes all with the raw clarity of a child. Her mother, Paula, a petit-bourgeois remit-tance woman, was packed off to Sydney by Lilian due to marital discord. At different times from their different abodes Paula and her husband, Harry, drift into Ballowra to perform parental duty in a less-than-cursory fashion. Society is not impervious to the unconventional arrangement; Emily even loses a friend over it. She is ambivalent when her father visits. 'Just the same, it was immensely embarrassing to have a stranger as an intimate relation,' is the tart observation. Emily is as thin-skinned as her parents and grandmother are thick-skinned, but is intent on survival, too fierce for self-pity. Her isolation is terrible; she can be arch, manipulative, utterly self-absorbed in the way of a child. But she learns.

There are moments of reprieve. In one hysterical scene, Lilian takes Emily out of school for the day so they can go to the pictures and have an afternoon tea party. Lilian entertains her with song. 'And Emily pressed her to tell again how, if she had not had her tonsils removed at the age of eighteen, she might have been another Melba..."You owe your life to my tonsils," she said, and then she sang some more.'

Lilian makes the sort of remarks that today's psychotherapists spend years addressing. When Emily is bereft at Thea's departure, Lilian goads, 'her interest sharpening as...Emily began to cry..."That's right! Cry, cry cry! Your bladder's too near your eyes, that's what's wrong with you, Emily Lawrence. No wonder she wouldn't stay to say goodbye. I don't know who would."' The cruelty is dreadful, and incessant.

It is no surprise that Emily falls for Max when he comes to board. By now she has survived twelve years of bullying and humiliation at the hands of her sadistic grandmother. Love-starved, she has already had crushes on a teacher, Miss Bates, and Thea, and when Max treats her with respect, including her in discussions about literature and science, it is enough to send Emily to the moon.

> Emily and Max had taken up a dialogue that had no end, leaning across the table like antagonists—Max speaking slowly, listening, watching her, smiling and sending up clouds of smoke, Emily, serious, blotting up facts, ideas, and more than anything, a manner of thinking.
>
> Leaning back in his chair when Emily had carried one of the ideas he had thrown forward to a triumphant conclusion, he would say, 'Perhaps. But look at it from this angle, Em...'
>
> And she would be, at the same time, dashed and fascinated to see the many, many angles to the problem, the ifs and buts and qualifications without which no answer was possible.

For his part, Max endures a trial by mob. Hounded by Lilian's sanctimonious cabal, subjected to moral opprobrium for his friendship with Emily, he is proof that mere gossip wreaks ample damage.

Harrower moves through the terrain of prepubescent love unencumbered by prurience and sentimentality. Her formal studies in psychology are evident; she is an expert in human behaviour, and her analysis of it underpins everything. Yet the writing is aflame with emotion arising from the characters' quests and ordeals. And we are always aware of the author's service to her craft. Harrower is, as the cliché has it, a writer's writer.

The Long Prospect survives the decades also for its evocation of place and time. The ACIL steelworks, where Thea and Max work, belches black smoke across the pages, its 'shuddering machinery' punctuating Lilian and Thea's conversation in the fateful opening scene. Always beyond is the glittering ocean. This is the Australian coast in summer: 'The vast sky of a vast unmisted land shone bright and hard in the light of the afternoon sun.'

I've read critiques of Harrower's work as an exposé of misogyny, but that is reductive, if not defensive. Her women can be as sadistic as her men, her men as dignified as her women. What she exposes is the will to power. Its politics, its battles, its terrible atrocities rage within the domestic realm—and the world remains indifferent. People get up and keep going, scarred and flayed, their comrades pretending nothing has happened. 'People simply existed and things happened to them for no reason,' Paula thinks, with more profundity than perhaps even she recognises.

Here is another myth to be scotched: that we revisit books as often as restaurants. Rubbish. We don't have the time. But I have reread *The Long Prospect* a couple of times, and I keep finding new insights, finely faceted as jewels, packed into its sentences. I keep laughing and cringing. I notice another masterly fold in the structure. Its conclusion is both tragic and a merciful escape—it is an ending of ashes, like that of Harrower's later novel *The Watch Tower*, from which a phoenix may arise.

The Long Prospect

CHAPTER ONE

THE FRONT door of Thea's flat was ajar so Lilian gave it a push and went in, her eyes on swivels. This was the first time she had been here but Thea's name was printed on a card next to the bell so there could be no mistake about it, any more than about the building which, on its cliff-side road, was hardly more to be expected *there*, and hardly less conspicuous, than a transplanted Sphinx.

To Ballowra, for Ballowra, the building, and the choice of the building as a dwelling place, seemed pretentious. Since its birth Ballowra had been—you might say on principle—low-lying, single-storeyed: in everything, that is, but steelworks and factories.

Ignoring the lift, walking upstairs with one ironic eyebrow cocked ready to greet Thea, one drooping disdainfully, Lilian had reflected on the truth of her late husband's saying. The exact words of it were in the grave with him, but she remembered it as a complaint against the commercial types from Sydney who were even then coming up and building up and making money—spoiling the place, he had incredibly said (for what could spoil Ballowra?) with their great department stores and blocks of flats.

That someone *she* knew, that someone who had boarded in her house for years, should have aspired to and achieved the tenancy of one of these quaint apartments struck Lilian as more than comical—it was ludicrous. It was as if Thea had suddenly claimed for herself some marvellous talent.

'God in Heaven!' she softly exclaimed as she walked through the small passage into the sitting-room.

What she thought of the room was neither here nor there and had nothing to do with her cry. The thing was, she had registered her disapproval of Thea's unnatural act in coming here: that done, she more tolerantly looked around and crossed to the wide windows. There, below, and straight ahead, was that much-praised view of the sea. A lot of water, yes, but nothing to make a fuss about. She had once said, 'For all I care the Pacific can jump in the lake.' It had been a success. On the strength of that success she now relaxed her mouth at the Pacific and admitted that it was blue.

Turning, her eye took in with less and less attention flowers, books, ceiling, floor...

Now that her first curiosity was assuaged, she had begun to wonder at Thea's continued absence. There had been doors to the right and left, she remembered, as well as this central door she had chosen to enter.

She took herself again to the hall and listened, frowning. She meant to charge and reprimand Thea for her carelessness in leaving her flat unguarded, and in order that her reproof should have authority, she wanted to keep combined the full surprise of her physical and vocal presence. Therefore she was silent, but she thought, I might be Jack the Ripper for all she knows, and here I am, inside.

A few quick steps carried her heavy, erect figure to the kitchen—little more than a gleaming cupboard of white and dark blue—where the sight of dishes, two sets of dishes on a tray, in a moment overrode the more immediate effect made by the dazzle of fitments and paint.

Thea was solitary: *she* was unexpected. Affronted by the mystery of the dishes, Lilian went back across the hall towards the other door, almost shut, presumably the bedroom.

As she approached it a voice was raised and Lilian stopped dead. Then with a fall to something like disappointment, she realized that Thea was speaking on the telephone. She let out a breath. But then, again, at a note in the voice, at the tone, her face twisted incredulously. She had never heard anything like it. And that was Thea, whom she knew.

Tense, eyes fixed, Lilian listened, her mouth quivering with anger and excitement and a curious kind of pleasure. Absorbing it all, directing content, manner and implications to their appropriate ends, she decided that the really annoying thing about it was that but for this accident she might never have found out.

Another small, galling but unadmitted factor in her reaction was jealousy, for at this time she had not met Rosen, and Olly had had his day.

Now Thea was speaking again, and there was her voice...

When at last the receiver was replaced on the stand Lilian was unprepared for it. She gave a jump. She had banged the front door and turned with a smile to meet Thea before she knew what she was doing. Several long seconds passed in silence and astonished surmise strained the smile to a grimace.

'Lilian!'

Defended by a poise that Lilian had never shaken, Thea stood in the doorway and was eyed by her uninvited guest with the usual mixture of awe and derision. A woman by temperament thoughtful, generous and feeling, Thea was accustomed to being suspect by the majority that was her opposite.

'Did you expect someone else?'

'No. Not even you. I heard a noise. Was that...? How are you?'

'Anyone might have come in. Luckily it was only me.'

'What do you mean? Sit down over here.'

'The door. You should be more careful. I read last week—'

'Why? It's so hot,' Thea excused herself, turning to light a cigarette. 'There might have been a breeze.'

'But there isn't.' Lilian protestingly flapped her gloves in front of her face. 'Billie and Gladys and I and a few others were round at the Horizon this afternoon, so when we broke up, and I was practically next door—I knew you'd be home from work—I thought I'd come and have a look at your *flat*.'

'And what do you think of it?' said Thea, standing at the windows. When Lilian continued to watch her with cold, amused grey eyes she knocked some ash from her cigarette and said, 'But you haven't seen it yet, have you? I'll show it to you.' She added tonelessly, half lifting a hand, 'This is almost all there is.'

Another silence came over them. At length Thea said, 'And how is Emily?'

'Wondering what's hit her now that you're not there to spoil her,' said Lilian ironically of her granddaughter. She said, more slowly, looking round the room, 'The house is empty now with only the two of us, but I see why you had to have your flat. I see *now*.'

Unable to relax so far as to sit down, Thea nevertheless seemed to grow easier, though there was about her still an unfamiliar, uncharacteristic distractedness. Behind Lilian she touched a cushion on an empty chair. 'I must see her soon. You do like it, then? A room of this size is rare in a new building.' Seeing by Lilian's smile that she had mistaken her meaning, she said, 'The position? The view?'

'Oh, the view!'

In Greenhills, the most western suburb of Ballowra, farthest from the coast, from her house on the side of a hill, Lilian could see three provision shops on the opposite corner, two roads at right angles, hundreds of corrugated iron rooftops, and smoke from acres of steelworks.

Nevertheless she said of the cliffs, the long curved beach, and the Pacific, 'Oh, the view!'

'Then what? What do you mean?' Thea smiled, disarmed by her scorn, her attention finally canalized, concentrated on Lilian.

Lilian tilted her head. 'Who's Max?'

There was the slightest pause during which their eyes held together stilly.

'Why do you ask? Did you overhear our conversation?'

'I heard what *you* said,' Lilian declared. 'Luckily it was only me. You shouldn't leave your door open. Who is he, anyway?'

By Lilian only the broadest of gestures and words were comprehended; for that reason, very little that was natural to Thea ever came into play against her. That, in Lilian's company, passivity and non-retaliation were the sole defences of integrity she had long ago learned. She had agreed to pay the enervating toll exacted by the stopping-up of spontaneity.

She therefore stood, and holding at bay the idea of Lilian's witness, said indifferently, 'You must have heard me mention his name.'

'He's at the works with you? Is he a chemist, too?'

'You could call it that.'

'Something atomic?' Lilian hazarded, looking suspiciously up at her. 'Trying to ruin our weather, is he?'

'Happily, no,' Thea said, with the ghost of a smile, and felt free to walk to the mantelpiece to discard her cigarette: having done that her position became devoid of purpose.

Outwardly controlled, she eyed a small vase of petunias with blank resistance, and waited for Lilian's next remark which was, 'Of course, he's married. I made out that much. Will he get a divorce?'

'There's no question of it.'

'Ah!' Lilian dug her heels into the carpet and bounced farther back on the sofa. She said shrewdly, after thoroughly studying Thea's figure and pose, 'What's the trouble, is he a Catholic or something?'

Seeing in Lilian's unsuccessful speculation a means of halting the catechism Thea almost warmed to her. 'Yes.' She sat down in an armchair and added, forestalling further questions, 'Tonight, as you probably heard, he's flying to Melbourne.' She said it with the air, casual yet candid, of one telling all.

Lilian was nonplussed. Her other questions, banished by the previous moment's intense receptivity, could not be recalled. She cleared her throat. 'It's a good night for a plane,' she remarked.

'The forecast says fair weather.'

They did not speak again of Max.

When Lilian was leaving, Thea came after her to say, 'Tell Emily—tell her I'll come to see her soon.'

Thea had known Lilian Hulm and lived in her house for eleven years, ever since the year of her graduation when the opportunity offered by A.C.I.L. for research had brought her from Sydney. In those days there were no flats; a moat of steelworks and factories surrounded hills and plains of drab bungalows and shops. Cinemas, hotels, reared up from the encircled plain like small cathedrals. At night the sky glowed dusky red with industry.

For a newcomer, a single woman, accommodation meant a room in a stranger's house in whichever suburb was nearest to her place of work. That Thea had at the beginning chosen to stay with Lilian indicated no more than the convenience of the house, and the lack of an alternative; that she continued to stay was the measure of her detachment.

Lilian Hulm, handsome, twice-widowed, forty-seven, had had boarders in her house—sometimes one, once as many as three—ever since her first marriage at eighteen.

For two years before the death of her first husband, Paula's father, she had been the mistress and landlady of Jack Hulm—a personable man twenty years her senior. Now *his* widow, free of ties and financial worries—he had left her a row of houses and three taxis—she was searching in an intuitive but none the less methodical manner for his successor.

It was of bygone and potential candidates for this rôle that she talked tonight.

Thea had to hear again the old story of Olly's defection. She was told, incidentally, about the woman across the street who had bunions, and Jill having trouble now that she had reached that certain age. She was told that Billie Duncan no longer slept with her husband; that Moira Digby along the street owed ten pounds to the grocer, that at forty-two Janet Olafson expected her first baby and no one could guess who the father was. Olafson was at sea. Thea was taken, in detail, through Dotty's mother's operation for gall-stones. And an ancient interesting haemorrhage of Lilian's own was recalled in passing.

In return, Thea did not mention Max. She did not give her opinion of the United Nations' resolution on the European crisis, or ask for Lilian's. She did not say that she had last night, with great pleasure, rediscovered Housman. Neither did she attempt to summarize what she knew of the work of Jung, nor try to convince Lilian of its great value. That she and Max had dragged themselves from bed at dawn to walk on the empty beach, and smiled now to remember their subsequent exhaustion, she did not say. And about Emily, whom she suspected of not being properly fed, she did not ask. The hostile irrelevance of Lilian's reaction was all too predictable.

It was several months since Thea had been to Greenhills. Her visits now were always arranged to coincide with Max's periodic trips to Sydney or Melbourne for meetings. But tonight, in spite of his absence, she was depressed by the senselessness of time so spent. Inevitably, she and Lilian had shared a web of associations: they knew the names of each other's friends and relations, recognized each other's clothes, brands of toothpaste, soap, and cigarettes. Each knew what would not amuse the other. The routine of Lilian's daily life was as familiar to Thea as her own. And, too, it had not been possible to live in her house for years, through vicissitudes which had included two deaths, two weddings and the birth of her granddaughter, without having come to respect some part of her immense, uncompromising gusto, and the sheer size of her most wrong-headed qualities. Thea understood Lilian, but discerned the point beyond which her understanding did not go: Lilian, on the other hand, pronounced on *her* with the confidence that comes of ignorance and physical propinquity—but without intentional malice. This was the sum of their relationship. Tonight, to Thea, it seemed insufficient reason for her presence.

In a small agony of restlessness Thea felt it insupportable that they should remain as much as acquaintances. Communication so arid should long have been abandoned. But in the past, living in the house, there had not been this necessity to sit face to face for the purpose of entertaining and being entertained, and if there had been, it was not impossible that she would then have responded without the sensation of disintegrating boredom and reluctance that now assailed her. Then, alone and disengaged, she had had endless tolerance and patience. Now, she could not bear for the length of an evening, the fall to tedium, flatness, and the exchange of personalities. And it was a delusion to think of her presence or absence, her interest or distaste, in terms of selfishness or generosity: anyone over the age of twenty-five with normal hearing would have served Lilian as well.

Her coming tonight was an act of hypocrisy—one that had not gone unpunished, she wryly thought. And she suppressed a sigh, for this brief return to the past made her long for the present, long for Max, long for their life together, as sharply as if all were unattainable.

Her eyes drifted abstracted over the room she had known to satiation—white walls, dark picture rail, plain beige velvet sofa and chairs, two round mirrors, the big chiming clock, ten o'clock. A pink racing guide poked out from under a cushion. Ten o'clock.

Lilian was saying, 'The thing about Olly is he's got a bit too big for his boots. They're all the same. Put a few pounds in their pockets and before you know it they're telling you what to do. He's threatening me—*me*, mind you—that he could get off with that Mrs Rufus, you know, her with the mink coat, that he could get off with her any time he likes. Well, you can imagine—'

Standing behind a high black chair which was at an oblique angle to the wall, Emily slowly ran a small forefinger along, up, along and down the narrow aperture between the spars. Slowly, round and round, the finger went while she stood, eyelids drooping with sleep, staring at Thea. At the same time, mechanically, with tongue and teeth and breath she formed a soundless chain of words, worked a hundred soundless Theas into an incantatory chain to link her to the woman in the chair.

Since dinner she had been there. Three times she had resisted the appeal of Thea's outstretched hand lest her grandmother should be reminded of her existence and send her away. But still she was near, seeing, listening to Thea...

Again Thea stretched out her hand and looked at her, and again the child glanced away.

'So I said to him, "Mr Olly Porteous, I've put better men than you—" What are you doing standing there? How long have you been there?'

'A while,' Emily said, reluctantly.

'A while, indeed,' said Thea, smiling, recognizing in the child the reason for her continued association with Lilian. 'She's been very quiet. I don't wonder that you didn't notice her.'

Her grandmother said, not unproudly, 'Oh, she knows how to behave when there are grown-ups in the room. Don't you? Don't you, Emily?'

And Thea remembered that Lilian had been brought up to be seen and not heard. The result *there* had been such that, looking at her, though she was dismayed to have the formula applied to Emily, Thea had to laugh.

'Oh, Lilian!' she protested. 'I thought I had convinced you long ago—'

She was disregarded.

'Well!' Lilian said irritably to the child. 'Can't you answer when I ask you a question?...Don't you think she's a great silly lump of a girl for nearly seven, Thea? What do you think of a girl as big as that who won't open her mouth when she's spoken to? Oh, she's as stupid as all the Lawrences!'

Salt waves of mortification washed over Emily. She met the scorn in her grandmother's eyes and then bent her head to look at the carpet. No one could like a great lump of a girl. No one could not agree with a voice so positive.

Yet, miraculously, the towering mountain that was Thea—suddenly beside her—could be heard to say, 'She's my most favourite girl of nearly seven. I love her.' Turning to Lilian she said, 'The most clever, too! Did you see her school books, tonight?' She leaned down. 'Sleepy? It's late for you to be up...I know it really is too bad to have to go to bed when things are happening out here, *but*, Emmy...and I'm going very soon.'

Rising, Lilian pointed an imperious finger at the door. 'Take yourself off this minute! You should have gone hours ago without being told.' Scarcely giving herself time to draw breath she said, 'What do you say?'

'Yes, Grandma.' Emily clutched at another chair as if to anchor herself to the room. She could not bear to go. But slowly, as she watched the two women, her fingers uncurled.

'I'll help her,' Thea said, but Lilian cried, 'No, no, no, no! She can get herself off. We'll have a cup of tea. I'll put the kettle on. Now say good night to Thea or she'll think you've got no manners and she won't come to see you again.'

The confusion of having the slow, full stream of Thea's attention—all of Thea's concentration—on her was great. She looked up and adored. When she said goodnight it would be over and Thea would go. Thea would go, and would she ever come back?

She was all at once enfolded, engulfed in warmth and softness: she could have died in the embrace—anything to stay with Thea. But a moment later, inadequate, wriggling away, she giggled shrilly, called good night in a high false voice and, arms outstretched, twirled in dizzy circles to the bedroom, laughing stupidly.

'Well!' said Lilian, not displeased. 'After all you used to do for her. You used to be a great favourite. I noticed tonight she wouldn't go near you.—Oh, the kettle!—Yes, you always spoilt her. But they forget. They change.'

Sitting back in her chair Thea gazed heavy-lidded at her hands without answering. When Lilian still hovered over her, shifting her weight from foot to foot, fiddling with a china ornament at one moment, putting it down the next to squint along the length of a table for smears or dust, Thea felt rather than saw the sharp glances that investigated her face. She said, 'And how is her mother? How is Paula? Have she and Harry come to any decision?'

'Oh, them!' Lilian straightened up. 'Paula's all right. She still likes Sydney better than Ballowra and she sells a few hats now and then. She says she wouldn't come back here for all the tea in China, but nothing would get her out to Harry in Coolong, either. The latest idea is that if and when he gets a transfer to Sydney, they might set up house again and take Emily, but I wouldn't be surprised if they got a divorce before then.'

'It's come to that?'

'Well, you know what they were like together.'

With a snort of laughter Lilian went out to the kitchen and Thea was left with the spectral figures she had defensively conjured up. She had known Emily's parents well.

Paula, Lilian's only child, a solemn girl held in thrall by her mother, had, in a moment of revulsion following the discovery of her mother's relations with Jack Hulm, turned outwards to the importunities of Harry Lawrence, a local boy who worked in the local bank. He was attracted by her calm good looks, by her mysterious stolidity, and a belief that she was not like all the other girls he knew.

Their world was Greenhills, their literature and philosophy Hollywood. Young, unthinking, they were nevertheless conscious of having transgressed; until they married, their fear was genuine. By guilt they were estranged before they properly knew each other.

When Emily was born—having come to believe himself trapped—Harry reacted violently. The thought of a son had been his one consolation.

Half drunk, he refused to visit Paula, or to apply for a birth certificate. According to Lilian's version, he would not listen to reason and he would not talk sense. The christening ceremony to which he was forcibly driven by her was a fiasco.

Thea, living in the house, was unwilling observer of it all.

For so impatient a woman, Lilian was tremendously patient with Harry and Paula. It was not until Emily was three that, wearied at last by brooding silences and razor-sharp quarrels, she advised them to find a house of their own. Taken aback, apologetic and mild, they moved to a small bungalow in the next street. This was the period on which the success of the marriage depended.

A year later, Harry's transfer to a town in the outback, Paula's refusal to accompany him, and Emily's semi-permanent removal to her grandmother's house made clear the result.

Lilian bought for Paula a half-share in a hat shop in Sydney. And there, in the city, as far as one could tell, she had been content in her quiet humourless way to sit with the resignation of a decoy duck in a fun-fair allowing things—life, in this instance—to be thrown at her. As at fun-fairs the missile most often missed, and she was left in much her original varnished, undamaged condition.

Recently Thea had heard from Lilian that there was talk of a reconciliation. Harry visited Paula at least once a year, during his annual holidays; they corresponded infrequently but regularly, and it seemed that a kind of friendship had grown up during their separation.

It now appeared, however, that nothing was settled, that probably another year would pass before they reviewed the situation again. In the meantime, for both Emily and her grandmother the position was less than satisfactory: this had been obvious from the beginning. Lilian had her own occupations—chief among them, living her own life—and they took all of her time and interest.

Though on occasion she displayed her granddaughter with an appearance of pride, the impression was that she would not have been dissatisfied if the child had ceased to be between performances. And, to a woman like Lilian, a constant reminder of her age could not basically be anything but unwelcome.

While Thea was there Lilian had been able to avoid her responsibility without so much as knowing that she did so: now it was simply shelved. If more properly the responsibility belonged to Paula and Harry Lawrence, there was the fact that Lilian herself had failed one of them. But who had handled Lilian? And who, that person? How far back must one go to find the root of human imperfection? Thea wondered. And in which direction first?

'She's a good girl, Paula, but she's funny—you'd sometimes think she hated Harry to hear her talk,' said Lilian, charging in, laden.

She stooped to plug the kettle in at a point next to the electric fire—slightly dusty and defeated by the long non-activity of summer.

'In fact'—she straightened up, hand to her back—'she hates all men. So do I, so do you, eh, Thea? Still you've got to have some around.' She gave a boisterous laugh. 'What do you say, eh?'

'I've sometimes wondered why you don't go to stay with Paula,' Thea said too quickly, and knew at once that she had been unwise. It was not even true. She could think of nothing that would be more disastrous for either.

Her instinctive purpose had been to distract Lilian from associations that might lead to a conversation which, with Lilian as one partner, could only go too far.

She had, at least for the time, succeeded. Until the tea was made, Lilian angrily set forth her contempt for the city in which Paula lived, and for all that vast crowd to whom she was unknown, over whom she had no power. Illogical and dogmatic, she was carried on by her irritation.

Knowing herself guilty, Thea bore the outburst as well as she could, in silence, and when Lilian challenged her with a jerk of her head, and clattered her cup on the floor, Thea said, 'Of course you're right. I don't know why I said it.'

Thwarted, Lilian seemed to deflate. Her head slowly restored itself to an upright position. 'Well of course I'm right. More tea? Oh, yes, you will!'

Burrowing towards some sharp little revenge against the woman opposite her, Lilian poured the tea, brooded over the steaming flow for a few seconds, then she brought out, putting the pot down decisively, 'What about you? You stay, though there's nothing to keep you any more.'

Thea took the cup. 'I'm used to it. I don't mean to stay for ever. I like my job. Friends.'

'Other jobs.'

Thea passed this off with a faint smile; in answer, Lilian's face curved maliciously. She shook her head.

'And let's see—if I'm forty-seven you must be about thirty-three.'

'I seem to have missed the connexion.'

With a laugh and a comfortable rearrangement of cushions behind her back, Lilian said, 'You should go off to the big city and find yourself a rich old man before it's too late.' She met Thea's eyes without a flicker. 'This—this Max—this chemist man—what's he going to do about it?'

Unbelievably his name had not been mentioned between them since that day months ago when Lilian had heard it for the first time. True, she had had few opportunities: what made it remarkable, however, was that her restraint had been not only unwilling, as it only could be with Lilian, but, too, imposed on her from the outside—by Thea.

Sitting upright in her chair Thea said with ironic calm, 'About what, Lilian? About what? Please don't worry about my future. I'm sure there must be other problems of more interest to you.'

She cast about for her handbag, glanced at her coat which lay across the sofa.

Lilian took this without expression, transfixed by a kind of blank satisfaction in having brought off her experiment. Now she exploded back to life, 'Catholic! Catholic! What does that matter? It's just an excuse.'

She longed to know, but even she baulked at asking if she was his…? Did they ever? Did being a Catholic make any difference there? She yearned to know. Looking at Thea told her nothing: she had an adult, experienced look, an aggravating look of enduring stability, fulfilment. She did not look like an old maid although—and here Lilian could have kicked her feet in a flourish of triumph—the fact was, she was.

Thea stood up. 'It's time I went home.'

Half lying back in her chair, Lilian eased her fingers under the edge of her stiff corset where it cut into her skin and, with a grunt, jerked it down a fraction of an inch. She went on, slightly distrait after the exertion, 'You're a fool to stay on his account if you think this is such a rotten place. It doesn't sound as if he's ever going to be much good for you.'

Thea realized she was tired. She knew that to Lilian she presented a constant challenge, that the other woman could not desist from efforts to demolish her. Though she felt no anger, Thea was tired by it, and strangely saddened. There was something touching in Lilian's attempts to wound: in them she exposed herself more than she knew, was more human than she knew.

Just the same, the impossibility of defending Max to her, of so much as saying his name in her presence, collided with Thea's resistance to hearing him attacked, by Lilian, for idle amusement, and incapacitated her.

As she felt her way into her coat, Lilian turned her head to observe that she was apparently unmoved. With grey anarchic eyes she looked at her, then she smiled and said, impatiently, 'Oh, what you need's a man—not a Catholic—a fine woman like you. You shouldn't waste any more of your life mixing cough-drops and bombs and waiting for his wife to die.'

There was a sudden silence in the room, then from the steelworks some two or three miles away came the giant shuddering of machinery. The air throbbed with noise. Then the room was silent.

It was impossible to know what reaction, if any, Lilian had expected. She was unable to think before she spoke, and therefore unable to plan ahead. But instinctive presumption and lack of feeling led to her displaying a callousness which in itself, distinct from what was said, appalled the heart.

'Good night, Lilian. I'll ring next week about Emily.'

'Now you don't have to get touchy just because I mention what's-his-name's name, do you?' She followed Thea at a little trot and confronted her at the door, her eyes brilliant with expectation.

Thea sustained the neutrality of her expression. Inside her gloves, her hands felt dry and curiously weak. 'Good night.'

Lilian took a deep breath and shook her head. 'You'll come to grief. The trouble is you don't know men. They're all rotters. If this Max wanted you it wouldn't matter whether he was a Catholic or a Chinaman.' She felt a bubbling insatiable desire to prod and prod and prod.

Thea walked across the veranda, down the steps, along the path, finding her way by habit. The uninhibited Lilian cried, 'Well, remember!'

If Emily had looked from the bedroom window to the dark deserted road, she would have seen the darker figure of Thea, her wonderful Thea, leaning against the fence: Thea who was the only one in the world she loved.

Between this visit and the last there were some picnics arranged by telephone, Emily despatched in one of the taxis and collected by another—glorious days during which she briefly bloomed with happiness.

The next time Thea came to Greenhills some months and aeons later, Emily was at school. By four o'clock, when she came home, Thea had gone and it was only when she heard her grandmother talking to Dotty in the kitchen that she learned of the visit.

Questioned, Lilian said, 'Here, grate these carrots for Dotty. —Yes. She came in for five minutes to say goodbye. She left Ballowra this afternoon. She probably won't ever come back. Oh, it's high time she got away. There's nothing for her here.'

Emily gave a whimper and backed away. Dotty looked round in surprise.

'Well, what's the matter with you?' her grandmother asked. 'What does it matter if Thea's gone?' she persisted, her interest sharpening as, at her repeated questions, Emily began to cry. 'My goodness! Blubbering because Thea's gone away. Well, well, well! All this about Thea and she didn't even stay to say goodbye to you. She wasn't worrying herself about you, don't think it!'

Though she thought Mrs Hulm was going a bit far, Dotty couldn't help smiling to herself as she took over the carrots and grater.

On and on went the inexorable voice, amused, sarcastic.

Sobbing fiercely, Emily stamped her feet to make it stop: she waved her clenched fists.

'That's right! Cry, cry, cry! Your bladder's too near your eyes, that's what's wrong with you, Emily Lawrence. No wonder she wouldn't stay to say goodbye. I don't know who would.'

Sick with inexpressible shock and loss, provoked to frantic hatred of her grandmother, Emily ran out of the house—eyes, nose, mouth streaming, hands clapped over her ears.

Lilian called, 'You'll go to bed at five o'clock with a dose of castor oil, you little monkey!'

But Emily, out of hearing, lay on a narrow strip of dried grass and weeds by the side of the house, mourning into the ground, not thinking of Thea, but alarmed to the heart by the knowledge of her absence, made by it more vulnerable than she had ever been.

CHAPTER TWO

WHEN PAULA came back into the room Mr Rosen had gone and she gazed at his absence.

'I told him to go for a walk or read the papers in his own room for a while,' Lilian said. 'We don't want him hanging round every minute you're here. He's a real old woman, anyhow. I can't be bothered with him.'

So there had been a quarrel? No, not so much as that, a few words. Lilian had spasms of conscience during which she was not at ease alone with her daughter and her lover. This was one of those occasions. In a silent exchange taut with gratitude and respect, mother and daughter acknowledged the rightness of her feeling. But at that moment, seeing the figure of the new boarder passing the open doorway, Paula sought to extricate herself from his hurt. 'Oh, Mum! I think he heard you!' she whispered.

When he was past, Lilian condescended to become aware of the possibility, but added no soft words to her judgement. Loudly she said, 'Close that door, Emily. There are so many people wandering round this house...'

And Emily, who did not like Mr Rosen, ran willingly, grinning at the joke, to give the door a bang. *She* was on the inside, one of a trio, *related* to her mother and grandmother: no one was pushing her outside.

Returning to her pose on the round leather hassock, she looked conspiratorially at the others, eager to go on with the fun of Rosen-baiting if it suited them. But nothing happened. Lilian cleared her throat, lifted the newspapers that were lying at her feet and rustled through the pages yet again, sifting, searching for a last sensation.

It seemed to Emily that the dismissal and the dramatic bang that she herself had been allowed to contribute should have led to something more than this. She watched, and elation turned to despondency as Lilian threw all except one paper down, and her mother reopened the novel she had been reading on and off all afternoon.

It was agonizingly quiet.

The electric fire, with both bars turned on, burned Emily's face and threw pink-orange light feebly into the darkening room. She gave an exaggerated sigh and clasped her face in her hands.

Paula raised her head and looked at her in silence for a moment as if the effort of breaking into speech was more than she could contemplate. She was gagged by the wintry Sunday dimness and warmth.

'Haven't you anything to do?' she asked repressively, at last.

'Nope. Nothing to read or anything.'

'Don't say "nope".'

Lilian intoned, her eyes on the paper, 'Did you see this about the man who strangled—'

'Yes. I read it,' Paula said quickly, repelled and bored at the prospect of listening to Lilian's portentous delivery. She was beginning to subside into her book again when she remembered Emily, felt the exasperating weight of her eyes and expectations. She said, trying not to lose contact with the printed page in front of her, 'We'll have to see Santa at Christmas time. Perhaps he'll bring you some books.'

'Will he? Will he? When'll it be Christmas, Mum?'

Paula sighed, moved a foot away from the heat of the fire and said, 'Oh...about six months.'

Emily pulled a face at the carpet and Lilian, catching the last words, said, 'What's six months?'

After another drugged pause, Paula said, 'Christmas.'

Lilian stretched her arms out and was temporarily hidden as she turned a page. From behind the rustling barricade came, 'Well, what about it?'

'*Oh!*' Emily cried, and in tones of long-suffering explained, while her mother read on in passive gratitude. Emily sighed again.

'Books? Books? What do you want more books for?' her grandmother asked. 'You've got a cupboard full of them out there.'

'They're old. I've read them a million times,' said Emily sulkily.

No one answered.

Some minutes passed during which Emily supported herself by examining her thin gold bracelet and twisting it round her wrist. By now, though it had an almost mystic value for her, she seldom remembered to connect it with Thea, from whom she had received it: simply, it was her most valued possession; it was a comfort.

For further minutes she counted and mentally redistributed the scrolls on the white plaster ceiling, and then she dreamed about Miss Bates. After that it was time for the clock to strike. She watched the hands and listened for the whirring of the mechanism that would signal the imminence of an event.

On the hour it gave an elaborate performance—one sufficiently prolonged to disturb both Lilian and Paula. Blinking across the glowing darkness, pressing fingers to their eyes, they told Emily to put on the light.

Paula yawned and smoothed her hands over her fair hair. She was so far distracted as to turn her book face downwards on the arm of the chair. Emily took in the signs of a renaissance with exhausted relief. The day had been endless.

The silent eagerness of her forward-leaning pose debilitated the two who observed it. She had been carefully ignored. Now someone said, 'You should have your bath.'

She protested half-heartedly, waiting for insistence. When it came she jumped up. 'Well, will you...? Mum? You said last night you'd see...'

Again her mother appeared unwilling to commit herself and there was an indecisive silence which might have augured anything. It lasted too long.

'You're mean. Lots of girls in my class's mothers do and they're home all the time.' She despised herself for asking, loathed her petted voice.

Lilian said, 'A big lump like you! Go and wash yourself and give your mother some peace. I want to talk to her. She's working hard in Sydney for you all the time, so when she comes to see us—'

But Emily had stopped listening. She scuffed over to the door, breathing deeply, emotions stormy and incoherent. Looking back over her shoulder as she turned the shiny white handle she cried, 'Well, I don't care! I don't care!'

The grown-up faces were impassive. Paula said, 'Don't forget to clean your teeth. They don't look as if they've been touched since I was here last month.'

For the second time that afternoon Emily banged the door, but now she too, like Mr Rosen, was outside in the free cold spaces of the house.

It was quiet. It smelled of polish. There was a chill lack of desirability about the room she had left, and about those she might enter—a bleak and rigid lack of warmth that penetrated the future as well as the present and past. She swept her arms over the cold papered wall in longing for something, something...Not, she knew, letting her arms fall, for her mother to wash her.

Waking up now that the lights were on, Lilian took off her spectacles and rubbed the deep marks on the bridge of her nose. In the instant between jumping up and flopping down, she thrust the folded papers under the cushion on which she sat.

'She's all right. She always plays up a bit when you're here. Other times she's as good as gold—ask Dotty. We don't know she's in the house half the time.'

Good as gold. It was a phrase which, applied to Emily, roused Paula's scepticism. 'As long as she is. I don't want her to wear you out.'

'Do I look it?' Lilian's expression dared Paula to have found signs of decay.

She shook a tired, submissive head in answer to her mother's rhetoric. She had so trained herself that any treacherous thought was blocked at its subconscious source. For the most part her thoughts about her mother were of a mythical nature—pure and reverent. For after all, she would think, *à propos* of she knew not what, she is my mother, my own mother. And the curious connotations of that 'after all' were never probed.

A certain physical resemblance between the two was, as it were, fended off by enforced differences of temperament. On the never-to-be-developed soul that was her daughter's Lilian's fierce vitality had grown stronger. Whom she attracted she stultified and distorted without effort or conscious intention. Now, what was in her electric, in Paula was static: evidence of this was subtly caught and exemplified in mouth and eyes and lift of brows.

Paula had early accepted the idea of Lilian's permanent, unlimited prerogative in every department of life. There was little for *her* to be but an adjunct, and in matters of doing, she assumed she would be informed, in due course, of her duty.

At more than one remove from reality she was always to exist with the most intimate changes in her affairs appearing like objective phenomena: facts to be noted.

For the past few years alone in Sydney, alone for the first time, she found if not contentment, at least a most desirable order and simplicity in her existence.

With quiet competence she organized her share of the tiny shop that supported her, and for the rest, she fixed her large grey eyes on a point in space and let the objects and people who chanced on that point into focus—no more than that.

Long ago she had willed herself to forget the ancient reason for that sudden and disastrous call to Harry Lawrence. It was not possible that her mother, who was her mother after all, should have been found to be less than she, Paula, had always supposed her. Dear, dead Jack Hulm who had married her mother had been a good friend, and later a husband, and could be safely enshrined in memory.

The strangest thing was that Lilian should have felt herself obliged, since Paula had grown up and left the house, to play her rôle of mother seriously. Indeed, it seemed not so much a matter of obligation as of choice. And the fact that she sometimes tackled her lines in a tentative fashion might be accepted—in her—as proof that she was no less sincere than Paula, to whom the image and its preservation were all-important.

Alone together they were nervous, as if each feared the dissolution of the inner script and her own exposure, speechless, staring naked eye at naked eye.

With the belated recognition of Paula as a person, Lilian brought to their relationship the nervousness inherent in all but the most brutal or most true. But Emily, watching, saw only the exaggeration of warmth and feeling, and what was not genuine she condemned.

At the same time, surprised and scornful as she was that they were satisfied by mutual deceit, she envied them, for she found satisfaction in neither. They did not act for her—a child and not quite human—they were themselves, and what they were was not sufficient. They spoke to her from unreason and were frightening. Having no way of expressing her intuition in lucid thought, she simply knew that they were amateurs. This perception brought with it a sensation of complication being passed from ignorance to ignorance; of complication handled by indifference; of complication on the verge of being dropped to the ground where it would inevitably shatter.

'Well, what's the news from Harry?' Lilian asked now, briskly.

'Harry?' A faint grimace dug a dimple in Paula's cheek. She stared at the fire. 'The same. No sign of a transfer.'

'So!' Lilian exclaimed, less than intelligently. She tried to round up her thoughts. 'And you certainly won't go out there to him,' she said approvingly, though she had, in fact, no idea why this was so.

'No.' Paula sounded, at the same time, vague and evasive. She knew no more about her decision than her mother: she had taken it ages ago, just like that, and she was not going to change her mind now. If there had ever been conscious reasons, they were forgotten, but conveniently supposed to have been impassable, had grown through time to be sacred. Nevertheless, in place of these sacred, forgotten reasons she was disinclined to tell her mother that she could not endure the thought of a small hot country town, far from the sea, with Harry and Emily; that housekeeping, and responsibility, and bridge—any change—would kill her in a month. She instinctively knew, but would not acknowledge, that there would be too much *wanting* for her to cope with.

When Lilian said, snorting a little, 'You should just get a divorce and find yourself someone else to give you a nice home,' the reprieve from questioning enforced animation and a degree of honest bitterness in her reply.

'I wouldn't want anyone else if I did divorce him. I hate them all.'

Lilian knew she meant men. She had heard this before, but with an easy, admirable assumption of interest she leaned back in her chair, fixed her eyes on Paula's face and prepared to hear again an oration that had become a fixed piece for her daughter during the last two or three years.

Tolerantly, feeling that Paula would be brighter company for the delivery, Lilian listened. But as usual, she had in memory and anticipation watered down Paula's intensity. Reintroduced to it, behind the placid silence she maintained, Lilian came up against an uneasy blankness in herself. She knew that she did not agree. As far as men were concerned, no one would more willingly admit that they were faulty—aggressive, rough, thoughtless. And Paula had, beginning with her father and ending with Harry Lawrence, come up against some weird specimens...Still! What did it matter?

To Lilian, who had competed with and excelled them in most of their faults, and who knew how to baffle and reduce them in a peculiarly feminine way as well, it all added to the zest. No, she could certainly not agree. Pursing her mouth as she listened, she wished that Paula could see the immense possibilities for amusement in the situation. It was all right to *hate* men—any woman in her right mind did—but if you had any spirit at all you had to battle with them, and belittle them, and learn to enjoy it.

Having wound up, vehement, confused, and confusing, Paula sat, for the moment, deprived of sight and hearing, but presently the stimulant worked, and she said quite brightly, as if it followed, 'So we'll let things stand as they are for a while.'

And, as sincerely as she had advocated divorce, Lilian said, 'I think you're right. Emily can keep on at school here, and you can get on with your little shop.'

They exchanged a serious, devoted look.

'Harry still sends the money?'

'Oh, yes, yes.'

Feeling lazy, but more than usually vital and aware of well-being, Paula rose, intending to inspect Emily's teeth, but a vivid change of expression on her mother's face, a sort of coming back to herself, made Paula turn to the window where Lilian had just seen Mr Rosen walking along the path by the side of the house.

A big pale man, he could not bear, even indoors, to be separated from his hat, for his sandy hair was thinning fast and he was vain. His perpetually hatted presence had the effect, it seemed to Paula, of turning any room into the waiting-room of a railway station.

To see the diffident smirk that the great creature turned on the window behind which he knew Lilian to be, made Paula draw in a silently exclamatory breath and turn away for the door. A kind of dreary frustrated discouragement took possession of her.

The apparition at the window was stayed, electrified by a gesture from Lilian who, holding him, as it were, by one finger, called to Paula—by this time in the hall.

'I'll tell Mr Rosen to get the car out and collect a few people for a little party for you tonight.'

It was not yet a statement.

Paula drew her eyebrows together in mutinous negation at the thought of the people Lilian was certain to assemble. She wanted peace.

'Don't do it for me, Mum,' she called back. Then on an impulse she returned to the room with a sudden false subsidence which it was hoped would surprise Lilian to accidental surrender. 'Yes, get them if you like. I don't mind. It's nice to be quiet when I come so that we can talk, but if you'd like to have them in, yourself...I don't mind...'

There was an occupied pause. 'Oh, some company'll do you good. You're too quiet! I'll just send him.'

The self-conscious grin that Rosen had been regretfully wasting on a pane of glass was restored, as Lilian turned, to its original extreme of doting subservience. Enjoying themselves, the two conducted a farcical scene through the closed windows, Lilian all hands and eyes, he seeming to melt downwards into the ground, from the pinnacle of his hat, seeming to melt with admiration for Lilian.

Abruptly Paula went away, her face stony. In the bathroom she found that Emily had not, after all, been able to bring herself to violate her nightly routine by cleaning her teeth, so with considerable force Paula undertook to do it for her. It was a relief just then to encounter Emily's sullen glares: they loosed her authority, turned her from a daughter to a mother. As a dutiful mother she had a right to wield a toothbrush firmly round the mouth of her disobedient child. They stood clamped in a tight untender embrace until the operation was over, Emily squawking with rage.

Later, when Emily lay in bed, face to the wall, Paula dressed to meet the visitors whose raucous whoops were even then resounding through the house. Fastening the last of the small black buttons on her dress she remembered to say, 'You can turn round now.' She went over to the dressing-table to look at herself and dab scent on her throat and hair.

Tomorrow, Monday, she would have to go away again. Already the customary sense of helplessness and smouldering desperation was swamping over her. She would have to say goodbye again, as she did every two months, to her mother and Emily. As the taxi drove away she would want to cry, would feel she ought to cry, but would not, would know that they would not. Turning the corner she would tremble with something she took to be fatigue for they would not cry and she was guilty of relief at going.

Paula sighed and rubbed her arms. The question of responsibility for Emily's life, or even for her own, she had never tried to solve. People simply existed and things happened to them for no reason. The miraculous thing was that she did not consciously want to die.

'You're happy here with Grandma, aren't you, Em?' she asked, going to the bed.

'Yes,' Emily said, non-committal, giving an inward squirm of apprehension. After a second she added, 'Some of the time.'

This was, and was not, what Paula wanted to hear. Awkwardly she teased, 'You won't want to leave to come to Sydney one of these days?'

That awful, marvellous scent was as dizzying as anaesthetic: Emily could remember it from long ago. 'Oh, yes,' she answered weakly, strained and mortified to feel her reliable calmness driven off. 'When?' She bit at the top of the sheet and eyed her mother.

'One day,' said Paula comfortably, satisfied that she was at least interested, and she started to move away, but Emily clutched at her and cried with an excitement that was only half-feigned, 'And will Dad be there? And will it be like it was before?' She wailed, 'I want a mother and father like everyone else.'

This was a familiar line. Years ago she had said it and meant it; now she only put herself off, made herself sick, made herself wail again, miserably conscious that though she might be acting, there was a coldness somewhere about things that was reason enough for misery.

With the cool and slightly exasperated air that her helplessness engendered Paula said, 'Do you miss your father?'

'No.' She gave a sycophantic giggle into the bedclothes. 'He needs his head examined, Grandma says. She says he was a pig to us. She says all the Lawrences—' Her mother's non-response was apprehended by her and she stopped, wondering if she was required to abuse Lilian. She was most willing.

She thoughtfully puffed out her cheeks and looked at the round yellow light that dangled from the ceiling.

Silent for a moment, Paula straightened the cover over her. 'You were happy then, weren't you? When there were just the three of us?'

Emily plaited her toes in embarrassment. She wanted to giggle hysterically. This was sloppy. What had she said? Happy? It was a word that left her nowhere to go. She was nonplussed by it, did not properly know what it meant. But behind her, from where she had come there were intimations of something—she didn't know what—a row of trees, a sandy beach, a face, a voice, a thin gold bracelet, the minute examination of stones and earth and bits of leaves. It was no good. No catalogue, however full, included what it was she longed for.

She could not speak. Paula endured the clutching arms for a moment, then with an impatience that was only just apparent, released herself and went to open the windows before switching out the lights.

When the taxi turned the corner Lilian said, 'Well!' and went inside. The vacuum cleaner, propelled by Dotty, roared up the hall to the open front door. Emily's arm dropped: her eyes clung to the corner. She felt nothing. She was shrivelled, indifferent.

Alice stared at her, smiling.

'Chasings! Let's play chasings!' she cried to Alice, and at once they began to pound down the quiet cement footpath.

High overhead smoke was blown from the thundering steelworks by a sea wind: it blew towards the plains of the west.

Approaching, levelling, passing the two puffing figures, came the baker's van; its tyres added yet another elaborate pattern to the surface of the damp clayey road.

Reaching the old wire fence that proclaimed the unbuilt spaces beyond, the country, Emily and Alice stood panting and giggling. But Alice never blinked, or looked away from Emily's face. She had a hard, old-fashioned air, a deathless curiosity.

She said, 'Don't you mind about your mother going away and leaving you?'

Emily flashed her a glance. She pointed, 'There's a mushroom!'

They climbed through the sagging strands of smooth wire and plucked the small creamy hummock. Their four hands and eyes examined it.

'It's only an old toadstool.'

Scornful, they tore it to pieces; they jumped on the poison-pink fragments that fell to the sparsely grassed earth. Emily spat into the palm of one hand, washed them both and wiped them on her skirt. Alice did the same.

They sat then on the lowest loop of the fence and wove themselves up through the wires. Suspended thus, Alice worked the heels of her shoes into the clay. Emily copied her. Three magpies flew low across the paddock in front of them.

'Yes, but don't you mind about your mother?' Alice said, turning her thin freckled face on Emily. 'If *my* mummy—'

'No!' Emily joggled her heels on the ground. 'I'm lucky. I don't have to do anything I don't like the way everyone else does. I'm lucky. I don't care.'

Dotty went out to the side garden to pick some mint for the sauce. Monday was always busy for her but today, what with Paula to get rid of in the morning, and Emily on holiday, tearing in and out over the polished floors with her damp shoes, and Mrs H. not giving her any help because she had to go and have her hair done for tonight, it had been—what?

Winter sunshine soothed her as she bent over the pungent green bed. She pulled another sprig of mint and shook her head. There was no word to describe what today had been.

Tonight, with her thin black hair washed and screwed in silver curlers, a bag of caramels by her side and her monthly treat—a magazine of true love stories—on her knees she would feel each shiny polished table knob inside her head, round and hard; with the whole clean house inside her head, she would read the choicest story with detachment. And some of them, Dotty admitted, disapproving, *were* choice. But then in America, of course, anything could happen...

Dotty and Ma Brown lived in a little cubby-hole of a house two streets away on the money and food and clothes paid her by Mrs Hulm. A girlhood spent, during the depression, in a camp for the unemployed among the hills behind the steelworks made Dot think of herself now as lucky. Then they had lived on bread and dripping, and her brothers had gone rabbit-hunting all day long: there were no magazines and caramels then, no pictures twice a week. As soon as there was work the boys went away from Ballowra and never came back. All very well for them but Ma never seemed to get over it: she was always sick.

Straightening up, Dotty pushed back her hair and, turning to survey the garden, saw Emily lying flat on the grass, peering through the thick black roots of the hedge to the footpath. Sniffing the mint she went back into the house.

Emily put the fourth stick of chewing-gum in her mouth and worked on it. She felt the dry, powdery peppermint stick moisten and expertly added it to the—by now tasteless—wad of the three previous sticks. With her neck stretched and her chin on the ground, swallowing was, if not dangerous, difficult, but vigorous chewing somehow added to her courage and she needed it. She was waiting for Miss Bates.

Through the gnarled black roots she watched the feet go by. Presently, having swallowed the last thin peppermint-flavoured drop of moisture, she resigned herself to the steady monotony of chewing plain gum.

A pair of dirty white sandals passed. Only two out of ten for them, she decided.

The warmth of the sun made her think for an instant of swimming. She was riding in on a breaker, weightless, buoyant...

Suddenly she glowered. A pair of red sandals were coming down the hill and she knew who was in them—Joyce Hoskins whose father was a headmaster. Noiselessly the pretty red sandals went past. Six—well, perhaps six and a half—was all they were worth out of ten.

Smitten by a pang of bitter envy, Emily tormented herself by calling up scenes to illustrate Miss Bates's fondness for Joyce. For while she, who lavished on Miss Bates so many hours of daydreams, was treated only to the general benevolence that the dullest in the class received, Joyce was singled out for all those kind and intimate words, Joyce alone caught all those special friendly smiles.

Emily quite wondered, as she brooded into the coarse grass, that she did not lose patience with Miss Bates. But that obvious impossibility made her smile shyly, self-consciously, and chew a little faster.

Her third year at school had brought her to Miss Bates: a second year together in fourth class had hardened this—for Emily necessary—attachment into a pleasant obsession. It employed her thoughts; it gave her emotions something to do. While there was contact it would not fade. One-sidedness was its only flaw; she had known what it was once to have something back. Someone once—was it Thea?—had liked her and said so.

Miss Bates's especial charm was that she was logical. The marvellous inevitability with which reason appeared in her least pronouncements gave Emily an almost sensuous thrill. And to be subject to firm, if bulk, direction, was mysteriously of deeper satisfaction than all the amorphous freedom allowed her by Lilian. Truly, the days of the week from nine till three-thirty were bliss!

Hearing the clip of high-heeled shoes on the path, she peered through the roots with frightened eyes and saw the small black kid shoes into which Miss Bates tapered like a genie into a bottle. Oh, undoubtedly ten out of ten for them! Were there ever such shoes!

With a moment's abstracted wonder at her own powers of deduction in correctly timing Miss Bates's appearance here, she ran, bent up, casting furtive glances over her shoulder, to the front gate and waited until she was past. Then, chewing and swallowing, chewing and gulping, she eased herself on to the path and began to trail her plump blue-coated teacher. Meticulous, she had provided herself with a prop in the shape of a rubber ball; with this in her hand, if discovered, she hoped to appear natural.

Plop, plop, plop. The ball bounced from the palm of her hand to the footpath and back again. Plop, plop, plop. And there was Miss Bates turning the corner just ahead.

She could hardly have told, if questioned, why she had today decided on this vertiginous piece of detection. To be found out, reprimanded, would be punishment so acute, so painful and undermining that if she had stopped to imagine the possibility she would surely have desisted.

But the impulse, the daring, and the blocking of prudence, had come together in one parcel, and she was carried on now by a high wave of scientific disinterestedness.

The teacher was not a local person; she boarded somewhere in the area—this much Emily knew and no more. She had been worn for months by a dreadful—because unsatisfied—curiosity concerning the private life and personality of the jolly, kind, dependable Miss Bates: at school so firm and mild and sweet, at home—what? Where?

Hundreds of idle hours minus company or occupation had given up thousands of versions. Gazing at ants and grass and earth, she had roamed with Miss Bates through stories gay and tragic. The sticky clay road had opened to reveal to her enthralled eyes such harrowing death-bed scenes as *East Lynne* never knew. In her most desperate moments, suspended on the gate, craftily sucking a clean patch of sun-warmed wood, she would see herself a brilliant hypnotist exposing to Miss Bates's shame-faced bewilderment the real, repulsive little Joyce Hoskins, and the real, endearing little Emily.

An advertisement in a Sunday paper advised her to write for a free prospectus of a course in hypnotism, but when it came with a long letter and a request for five guineas she felt the whole enterprise to be low, unfitting. Miss Bates would be so disappointed if she knew. Besides, who had five guineas?

Nevertheless, her daydreams alone, without the miraculous intervention of hypnosis, served to create a middle plane of existence—neither dream nor reality—where, with Miss Bates as constant companion and guide, with Miss

Bates's hopes and expectations to be fulfilled, behaviour had a standard and the world reliability.

Bouncing the soft green ball, Emily turned the corner and saw Miss Bates, about fifty yards ahead, open the gate of an old-fashioned bungalow and go along the path. This was the street where Dotty lived. It was well known to Emily. Even so, having saluted it as the happy dwelling-place of Miss Bates, she was at a loss.

The end of the journey was something she had not envisaged. Her one intention had been to discover where Miss Bates *was*—if such a marvellous creature was anywhere—when she was not at school. That had seemed the limit of desirability. Now she could not help but feel that some more positive satisfaction should be wrung from so enterprising a deed.

What—she threw the ball past the house and fled after it, terrified—what if she could think of some way to get in? Knock and ask for something—an aunt, a scooter.

Miss Bates would come to the door, cry, 'Emily, my dear. I was lonely. You must come in and have tea with me. An aunt? A scooter? I'll help you find them afterwards.'

She might even say, 'I'll be your aunt, my dear. In fact, I *am* your long-lost aunt. And you may have the scooter I rode when I was your age.'

No. No. Emily cancelled that. She could not bear to be too optimistic. She stooped over the gutter for her ball and started a slightly more probable conversation.

Recklessly she threw the ball back in the other direction and tore past the house again, glancing at it with such alarm that the brief image received by brain and eyes made her heart bang with shock.

In a daze, she began to hit the ball first with one hand then the other. Dazed, she watched it drop and leap, drop and leap.

On either side of her the squat dull houses sat behind their weeds, rough grass and battered flowers. The yellow road chalked a dividing line between. Above, white smoke streaked the cooling blue sky and the lurid setting sun was wintry, frozen.

She was cold, her courage ebbing. This was the real world and she could not knock. Over there, behind that façade of brick, carved wood and tiles, was a Miss Bates—a short plump Miss Bates with tightly waved fair hair shooting back from her tanned, pink-cheeked face, with round bright eyes behind glasses. No longer the friendly guide, she had become in an instant a stranger, an authoritative stranger, about whose life and circumstances nothing could be wanted to be learned.

Chilled by the black and white of reality, Emily looked for the last time on the windows of the house, and ran.

In the safety of the familiar kitchen, sitting at dinner with her grandmother and Mr Rosen, she listened like a convalescent to their attempts to communicate in code. They seemed so nice. She felt so indulgent towards them. Mr Rosen's ponderousness was balm; Lilian's ignorance of her escapade (which made it seem that it had never happened), her lack of expectation that she, Emily, should do or be or say anything, was as soothing as hot milk by the fire.

Rosen solemnly cut a piece of meat and ate it. He said to Lilian, glancing at her over his rimless glasses, 'She asked me to return. You'll appreciate that it was very'—he paused, and stressed—'embarrassing for me, Lilian, at the gates of the works, like that. Everyone saw her.'

'She's stupid!' Lilian said, and Rosen flushed. He looked at Emily but she composed her face to a degree of childish non-comprehension that reassured him.

He said heavily, 'She's not *you*.'

'Ha!' said Lilian, helping herself to more sauce. 'And when do you go?'

There was no sound but the hissing of the boiling kettle on the stove. The three ate stolidly.

Miss Bates! Miss Bates! Sharp needles of memory pricked Emily till she was crouching persecutedly over her plate, wincing as if at a nagging tooth. Remember what you did! the voices sang in her ear. Remember!

She dragged herself away. She *would* listen to Mr Rosen. It must be that Mrs Rosen, that little woman with the grey hair, wanted him to go home instead of staying here with Lilian. She considered the idea without feeling or opinion. Had George been with his mother when she waited at the gates? George was twelve and had red hair. He was Mr Rosen's only son. In the days when the whole family used to visit Lilian, Emily and George had gone to the pictures while the grown-ups had parties. On the way home they ate hamburgers and talked about outer space, and wondered whether there were people on Mars. She liked George.

Reaction wrapped her in a cocoon of weariness and she went to bed with a willingness that might have made even

Lilian suspicious, but Gladys and Billie came early, bringing their newest friends, and another party was on the way.

Very shortly, shrieks of laughter preceded the arrival of more guests. The customary noises of community singing, solos, square-dances, and the clinking of bottles and glasses lulled Emily to sleep.

A flashing figure in a straight dress of thick navy satin, Lilian commanded her willing guests to silence and applause, kept them noisy, kept them moving. The crowd around her in the composite was a restless, harmless amoral creature with winy breath and slippery eyes, an over-mobile mouth, and hair that dipped to a forehead which, as the night went on, grew shiny and flushed.

When Billie had for the third time done her celebrated imitation of bagpipes, guitar, and violin, they left the house and drove in a string of cars to the chromium-plated Ballowra Bowery, overlooking the sea. In a private room they mixed drinks, ate oysters and quarrelled, changed partners and returned from an absence on the beach, the women to smear soft lipstick on mouths suddenly pale, the men to blow noses on fishy handkerchiefs, have another drink, and pat their friends on the back with the generosity of self-congratulation.

Quite suddenly Emily was wakened by the weight of silence in the house. Incredulous, she listened, going cold with premonitory awareness of her solitude.

Oh, it had happened again! The house was in darkness and empty of all life but hers. The mechanical ticking of the clock on the table, simulating life, made her bound from the bed and hurl herself across the room to where she knew the light-switch must be. She knocked herself without feeling against the sharp corner of the dressing-table.

Now the room was an island of light. Outside the night was spectacular with the stars of the south, but moonless; here the rest of the house had yet to be stormed and illuminated. A ferocious expression her only defence against intruders, Emily flew from switch to switch through the house, a streak of red and white pyjamas.

She knew what had happened. They had gone somewhere else to finish the party. And here she was, alone in this brightly-lit oasis with windows through which she could be seen, and seen to be alone. She stood, curled fingers touching her lips, tears held cold in her eyes.

Lilian's insatiable interest in real-life murder stories had done its work on Emily. She had for years been treated to a reading of all the more unpleasant crimes from the Sunday papers, and, when *they* failed, to reminiscences of the famous crimes of Lilian's youth.

Old men with beards pursued small girls through blackberry bushes, strangled them, and remained at large. Small girls were put in bags and drowned. There was apparently no limit to the number of atrocities to which they might not fall victim. Even the avoidance of the most likely situations for murder left them very exposed indeed in a world that seemed bent on the destruction of their species.

Lilian had come to take for granted the frequent nightmares from which the child woke rigid and screaming. She was mildly gratified to think that they showed her as being 'highly strung' and, consequently, ran Lilian's mind, of noble stock. But other manifestations of the nervousness that she herself had bred and nourished were seen as a taint most surely stemming from the unmentionable side of her parentage.

Now the house hovered round Emily with evil intent. She was trapped, encircled by it. As the impression of hidden malevolence grew stronger, she went into the hall; from there she could watch every doorway.

Then slowly, a moment later, with an accumulation of speed let loose, she made for the front door, threw herself against it and struggled with the lock. Sobbing, she ran down the gravel path.

At once all was different. Up on the gate, if it was cool and black and quiet, it was safer, much safer, than that hideous lighted tomb behind her. Now if they all poured out in pursuit she could fly down the quiet hill calling for help, and people would hear her and come.

For a moment she looked at the stars, let the sight of them soak her; for a moment in the place where she had been was simply black air and a vision of stars.

A hiccough brought her back. She began to make the gate swing to and fro and was, for a time, occupied by the sensation of swinging bravely on a gate in the night. But shortly, feeling cold, the sadness of her position made her cry.

Aggrieved, but scarcely more than that, she grizzled into the flaking paint of the gate and mumbled to herself that her mother would not like this. Miss Bates would not like it. They would be angry if they knew that Lilian had left her alone when she was so frightened. Other people didn't leave people at night. It wasn't nice to have girls swinging on gates so late at night. She would not do that to anyone even if she hated them. It was so mean. But no one cared about her, not really...

From midnight till three o'clock in the morning she stayed there, crying a bit, talking a bit, sucking the gate on the patch reserved for sucking, and falling into day and night dreams. Miss Bates might really be her mother? There were few distractions; occasional cars and no late pedestrians.

When at last Lilian's car started up the hill, Emily ran, as she had for the others, to the corner of the garden from which she could see both roads. Recognizing it, she ran into the house and turned out all the lights.

She was in bed, shivering, in an ordinary room in an ordinary house by the time she heard the garage doors swing open. Stretching in bed, rubbing her cold feet together, she listened to the noises of the return, a small smile of relief on her mouth.

Lilian and Mr Rosen came in the back door and up the hall to the bedrooms, whispering. There was a confused scuffle, a disagreeable noise which Emily identified as someone being sick. There were more whispers, then raised voices.

Complacent, disapproving, she drifted towards sleep. They were home and someone was being sick. It was all normal again, all routine. Tomorrow she would see Miss Bates.

CHAPTER THREE

AS HE left Jack Stevenson's old weatherboard house, Harry Lawrence pondered on yesterday's decision and marvelled at it. So there were to be no courts, no witnesses, no legal documents—in short, no disturbances in his life. Three days of talks in coffee shops, harbour ferries, and the zoo, had resolved this. For the indefinite future he and Paula had exchanged firm promises to try again to live together.

Neither could have told why they leaned to the side of non-action, but to both, after twelve years of marriage, many of them apart, the abstract idea of their partnership was solid and immovable as a mountain. The failure earlier to make the separation legally permanent had carried them past the time when it could ever become so. For while the living, warm and fleshy, even—when encountered face to face—slightly shocking, three-dimensional creature who ate and walked, might have been exorcised by a few words from a judge, that old idea each had of the other gradually took possession of the future and was not to be eradicated.

Dislike, warped passion, non-comprehension—nothing could outweigh the inner, unconscious, fabulously romantic idea of marriage—themselves the hero and heroine: to part would have been to live life deprived.

Due to return to Coolong tomorrow, his leave at an end, he had come last night to Ballowra to pay a duty call on Emily and her grandmother. As was his custom on these infrequent occasions he stayed over-night with the Stevensons, old friends, and for many years next-door neighbours.

Passing the red-brick house where he had been born, he felt nothing. Some family of strangers lived there now. He saw the old bamboo trees by the side fence thrashing in the hot wind. For no reason he could think of they reminded him of his mother and the old days more than anything else about the place.

He continued down the hill, noticing the changes that had taken place since his last visit, gradually worked on by that recurrent, surprised regret that infects those in their thirties and forties when confronted with places, or people, or thoughts from the past—from a past so recently present, and present to those who remembered no past, for who would be younger than twenty?

After years in the country, this subjection to industry, the smoky sky, the matured deterioration immanent at the birth of such towns as Ballowra left him oppressed and indignant. He was unwilling that it should be so bad.

Below him, acres of flat land were covered by low wooden houses in front of which swayed sappy knee-high grass. Paint was lavished only on the giant advertisement hoardings that bestrode the numerous vacant allotments. There were no trees. The steelworks which, at a great distance, surrounded the rise where Harry stood were the only reason, and, he was forced to suppose, justification, for the existence of Ballowra.

Once, for Harry, the depressing plain had been printed with names and emotions: there was the wide white storm-water channel where he and his brothers had played; the picture-show into which, without money for tickets, they had contrived an entrance; there was Russell's hotel, the most substantial building for miles round, on the corner at the bus terminus. Around these landmarks were situated Joe's place, Al's place, Eck's place, Paula's place, and finally, one labelled 'home.'

Pausing at the edge of the footpath until a horde of grey-clad, black-faced men swept past on bicycles, Harry felt a kind of appalled relief that he had at least escaped that. He was not a doctor: there had never been a chance of that, but he had managed to get into a bank. He was not quite to be discounted, to be put on a level with those anonymous creatures who pushed in a crowd through the heavy morning air, going home from night shift, or afternoon shift, or some other shift he was pleased not to know.

He crossed the road and lifted his left arm in order that he might be reassured of *something* by the sight of his new wristwatch. With an effort of concentration he read the time. Self-consciously he rubbed a tanned well-shaped hand over his moist upper lip, and starting a conversation with himself about the coastal heat—so different from Coolong—he strolled down the main street of Greenhills.

Here on his right was a garage with no visible customers. On either side of it was a patch of land traversed by paths. After that came a few houses, soon to be demolished according to the signs, and farther ahead, the shops, two-storeyed, impressive, on both sides of the street. At Russell's corner they ended, and more houses and West Greenhills began. Among the houses on the farthest edge of the maze was Lilian Hulm's.

Earlier this morning Harry Lawrence had visited the cemetery which, conveniently, was on the crest of the low hill above his old home, and the present one of the Stevensons. He had even done some work on the grave plot of his mother and father. He supposed that none of his three brothers had seen, or ever would come back to see, their graves. They had left home years before to roam about the country from town to town, taking jobs when and where it pleased them. They, too, could be dead for all he knew. The inconsistent piety which had led him to the cemetery did not carry him so far as to make him care if they were.

Just the same, as a man who actively believed in God—'I am Church of England'—Harry was, in most companies, though not unique, certainly among the few. And, after this morning's sacred task, as he walked down the deadly, littered street, buffeted by a hot wind, he was rather more conscious of this than usual.

The smell of over-ripe fruit, fried fish and new leather composed the dusty air. A double-decker bus lazing at the terminus overslept the time-table: its driver, leaning out of the window, was suddenly recalled to the idea of time and motion by the sight of a cart and horse returning to the dairy. With a jolt of alarm—for he was normally conscientious—he was inside and off so quickly that the conductor had to swim the blue stream of the exhaust for twenty yards before he could jump on.

The audience—it was Saturday and the men who were free from furnaces and boiling steel stood outside Russell's—said, 'Ha!' and turned away to listen to the few among them who spoke—about work, about horses, and what would win this afternoon. They rummaged abstractedly among their teeth and listened, disappeared into Russell's for some beer, and came out again to stand and stare at the housewives with their shopping baskets, and the girls adangle with earrings and bracelets and curls.

The young unmarried men, conscious of their unaccustomed whiteness and thickly brilliantined hair, grinned knowingly at one another as the girls passed, and made audible comments, but were permitted no further licence. They were all reserved, at seventeen or eighteen, by the girls they would eventually marry. To be seen in intimate, necessarily provocative, conversation with another girl would have been to invite a vendetta.

The older men were dour, with a look of uncharitable hardness about their eyes. Self-enclosed, past the age when living is itself sufficient incentive to go on living, with atrophied capacities for thinking or feeling, they worked grimly towards old age and death. Their wives flirted with the tradesmen, looked for lovers, and their children feared them. Preparing for a picnic or a dance they would be silent suddenly at the entry of their father into the room. Was he drunk? What would he say?

This attitude of humourless endurance, natural to a few, had been imposed on most by parents like themselves, surroundings of monotonous ugliness, participation in wars the young could not remember, and by a brief education delivered with so little relevance to circumstance and ability as to be incomprehensible.

Recalling the healthy, weather-beaten faces of Coolong, the clear, tremendous sky that arched the miles of open country, Harry felt he knew where was the better place to be.

He fancied that he recognized a few old neighbours, school-friends, and he walked stiffly by. He told himself that it was because he was anxious to have the visit to Emily over; in fact, he was embarrassed, sensed the uselessness of talk, knew there would be nothing to exchange but antagonism. To prefer the bush to Ballowra was to be an outcast, a bushwhacker. To come back clean-handed, well-dressed, from the bush was not good.

Passing the terminus, he lengthened his stride.

Farther along the street ahead of him, going in the same direction, Emily and her friend Patty, having spent the money given to them by Lilian, were on the way back to their paddock.

Emily wore a salmon-pink *crepe* dress of Lilian's which drooped unevenly from calf to ankle: on her feet were flat brown sandals and red socks—high heels had been abandoned before the expedition to the shops. Patty's dress was green: it was gathered across her thin chest and held by a bone brooch shaped like a canary. This had come out of a Christmas cracker. On her feet were white sandshoes. Emily's long brown hair and Patty's blonde curls were garlanded with small wild roses of pink and white which every spasmodic canter caused to slip farther from their restraining pins until they tumbled over ears and brows in gay, untidy confusion. The effect was, aesthetically, not what it had been when they set out.

With metronomic regularity Patty waved a newspaper parcel between herself and Emily, and each in turn extracted from the torn end of the packet a long golden chip. The grease made their orange lipstick, contributed by Dotty, run; and while the bright daubs on their cheeks remained intact, the colour went oddly with the dull flush brought on by heat and exercise. Puffing with the exertion of running, eating, and communicating, they sucked in long draughts of humid air and giggled at nothing, for these were the long summer holidays.

As he approached the two figures, a frown superimposed itself on Harry's carefully bland forehead. Quickly passing the girls and turning to stand in front of them he knew that undoubtedly one of them was his daughter Emily. After a moment of stupefaction he sought to counteract the impregnable frown by forcing a laugh. It came out rasping and unmirthful and did nothing to mitigate the haggard displeasure with which Emily regarded him. Nevertheless she held her ground.

'Well, aren't you going to give your father a kiss?'

She blinked up at him. He leaned down and she stretched up an unwilling neck: mistiming her salute, she made a little smacking noise with her lips when she was an inch away from his cheek and they separated, daunted.

With an unmeaning chuckle, her father said, 'I'm taking you back to your grandmother's. You'd better tell your little friend to run home,' and Patty was off, shooting up a side-street before Emily was forced to look at her.

Deserted, she had no choice but to walk by her father's side, glazed with awkwardness, wondering why in the world people had to have fathers, and why they had to come out of the footpath on hot Saturday mornings when people were just enjoying their holidays and doing no harm to anyone.

She made several fumbling passes at the roses on her head, and hoped—but pessimistically—that her father would approve of, even admire, them and her.

They both stared at their feet as they walked, glanced severely at the trucks and cars on the road at one side, at the bungalows quietly stewing in the sun on the other.

Finally bringing himself to look at the flower-strewn head beside him, Harry said, 'This is a fine costume you've got on! Did your grandmother know you were going down the street like that?'

She resentfully looked up, her glamour shattered, herself ridiculous. 'I don't know...Yes,' she muttered.

Her father's eyes slid from the painted, hostile face.

'Your neck's dirty!' he exclaimed, catching her by the arm, making her stand still.

Emily was rocketed by indignation to fabulous altitudes. She swayed on the far heights of the globe. Oh, what a thing to say! What a thing for a father to say! She yearned for the moment when she could tell Lilian.

The two stared at each other with fast-breathing, close-lipped resolution. Harry clenched his teeth, grabbed the girl's hand and started off again very fast, and she, with as much eagerness and determination, ran alongside.

The cream-painted gate, the hedge, and behind it on the corner, set in a pond of grass, the red-brick bungalow with its many additional verandas and decorative pieces of fretted woodwork—home—was now in sight.

Judging the distance, Emily pulled her hand free from a clasp uncomfortably damp and familiar. She lifted the trailing skirt to her knees and turning to her father with an excruciating assumption of friendliness, cried, 'I'll just tell them you're coming,' and fled head-first to the house.

'Emily!'

An answer streamed after her but she kept running.

This unprecedented defiance made Harry hasten a step or two and open his mouth to call again. But the exertion demanded by anger and command—in this heat—and the problematic success of any such attempt, arrested him. He slowed, closed his mouth and looked at his watch again.

Her throat and chest scorched with breathlessness, Emily scrambled up the stone steps to the veranda and skidded into the hall.

'Grandma! Grandma!' she gasped, trying to read the walls for indications of Lilian's whereabouts. She thundered towards the kitchen. 'He's coming! Daddy—Dad—my father's coming! He'll be here in a minute! Grandma, he said my neck was dirty!'

At the door of the kitchen where they collided, Lilian absorbed—what she had before merely seen—Emily's startling appearance.

'My God!' She drew a deep exasperated breath. 'Isn't that just like the thing.' She glanced at the open front door. 'And he said your neck was dirty?'

'Yes, and it isn't!' cried Emily, triumphant. She had told on him.

Lilian led her to the daylight at the back door and scrutinized.

'It isn't, is it?'

After the slightest pause Lilian said, 'What a thing to greet his daughter with after all this time! It must be more than a year since he was near you. I'll have a thing or two to say to Harry Lawrence before I'm through.'

Emily fished the roses from her hair and looked at Lilian with beaming admiration. She had a champion. She was defended. A moment later, remembering the need for stealth and speed, she got her grandmother back into the kitchen: from the front door her father would have seen their two figures outlined against the strawy grass of the back lawn. What fatal gesture she expected from him, she hardly knew, but her hopes were infinite.

'Listen!' she hissed to Lilian, and, bending forward, open-mouthed, they received Harry's shout, 'Anyone home?...Lilian?'

Guiltily the woman and child backed away. 'Harry!' Lilian bellowed. 'Wait just a minute! I'll be there in a minute.'

She straightened the skirt of her thin shantung suit and briefly examined her face in the unflattering surface of an egg-lifter. At the same time she delivered orders to Emily to wash and dress and have a glass of milk and—here Mr Rosen wandered in from the garden where he had been unenthusiastically pushing the mower—sing a little song for Mr Rosen. Full of piety and obedience, Emily disappeared into the bathroom, and with much the same expression Mr Rosen went away to put on a tie and take off his hat.

'Well, and how's the world treating you, Harry? Come in, come in, come in and sit down!'

'Oh, same as usual, you know. How are you getting on these days?'

'Oh, you know me, always the same. Nothing changes here.'

They both laughed.

Harry said, 'I saw Paula when I was in Sydney. We've—er—we're going to stick it out together, we think. So maybe next year we'll be able to take Emily out of your way.'

Lilian lifted her arms in a dramatic gesture of approval. 'Well, I'm glad for your sakes. I'm very glad to hear it. Sit down—anywhere.' She waved a hand at the dark empty chairs of velvet and leather.

They looked cool to Harry, like caves. The sun was at the other side of the house and in here, through the open window, he could smell the fresh-cut grass. A small illusion of cool air beat with tantalizing gentleness about his flushed face.

'Whew!' He found a handkerchief and blotted his face and head. 'Gets you down, doesn't it? I'm sweating like a horse.'

'It's not the heat, it's the humidity.' Lilian explained his discomfort to him as though the platitude had just been thought of, and Harry, who was prepared to take seriously any words that had a remote connexion with his well-being, looked interested and even impressed to hear it.

When Lilian reappeared, after a moment's absence, with a glass of cold beer, he felt a rush of affection for her that quite outdid anything he had felt at the sight of Paula or Emily. She was a good sort, all right. One of the best.

'Paula knew you were coming up?' she smiled. 'She didn't tell us.'

'No?' Harry looked dense.

'You might have stayed or something.' Lilian smiled again with sheer annoyance. 'Oh, well!...You've seen Emily. She's grown, hasn't she?'

'Yes. Too right.' Harry made other affirmative noises until Lilian allowed him to shut up and drink his beer by starting off on a monologue, a tapestry of *non sequiturs*. Harry drank, listened, and nodded, grateful to be talked at.

He was a lazy man. He was lazy with the physical laziness common among Europeans who live in hot climates; unthinking, with the masochistic laziness of an adult whose mind has gone inadequately trained; but the lack of moral and emotional force might have been said to be an inherent limitation, rather than a wilful or accidental withholding of effort. For these reasons he looked forward to promotion and transfer in the future with more stoicism than pleasure. He was constrained to dangle before his own nose the prospect of material gain and prestige, when he thought of the future, to assuage the fear in which his lethargy went. For these reasons he sat comfortably uninvolved while Lilian talked and wondered whether Paula had told Harry that Rosen was living with her, and what he would say when they met.

Harry *was* one of the family, in a way, and he was a man. When he was present his opinion had to be thought of, especially now when Rosen was beginning to irritate her.

The unlikelihood of Harry's forming an opinion, and the even less likely extraction of unfavourable criticism from him at this time, when he was beholden to her, she easily overlooked.

In the kitchen, Emily glowed with soap and satisfaction. For once she was confident that she had the interest of the adult world; better still, she was attacked and defended. And Lilian would win. There was no obligation to feel more than contempt for her father, but since he had been the one to provoke this situation of interest round her—though she could not forgive—she withheld further censure.

A little weak, a little pampered, she sat at the table and held between her hands, untouched, a glass of milk. The glass was full and perfect. With a vague idea that it would be a kind of cannibalism to ruin its perfection she pushed the glass away, for the moment, at least, renouncing it. And gazing at this symbol of her own completeness she added up her value yet again.

On the opposite side of the table Mr Rosen sat smoking. He said, 'Your grandmother promised me a song, Emily. How about it? And don't spoil it this time by giggling in that way. Playing up. Sing properly and don't laugh.'

As long as the songs were Irish or Welsh (he himself claimed to be one or the other) he had no objection to hearing several.

Emily grimaced. She could not leave the house and perhaps miss something important; on the other hand the pathos of Mr Rosen's glances was nauseating. From past experience she knew he would cover his pale-blue eyes with his fingers as soon as she began to sing, and all at once it seemed worth the effort to cancel them from view.

Lilian, who had been listening for a song as the signal to break up a conversation which even she had begun to find opinionated, led her son-in-law to the door of the kitchen.

It was an old-fashioned, high-ceilinged room painted in dark brown and cream: a single white-shaded light swung in its centre over the chenille-covered deal table. Four blackish wooden chairs were pushed in at the table, two more stood against the wall. The curtains, of some thin white stuff, billowed in the hot draught that ran between the open door and the window. From the blue mottled gas-stove, faint smells of the Saturday roast were beginning to drift. Some flies buzzed near the ceiling. Level with the top of the big green refrigerator a bare, high-powered light globe was stuck in a socket in the wall. Sunshine fell diagonally across one-half of the room.

With a curiosity to know whether or not she could make Mr Rosen cry, Emily had chosen to sing the most plaintive ballad she knew. But gazing through the door at the zinnias and the ivy-covered wall of the garage, at the width of pale sky, she forgot to notice him. She was soothed by the high mournful notes, by the colours, and the pleasant lack of thought and conjecture. Only when, accidentally, her eye came to the empty milk glass, did she unknowingly use her voice to such effect that Mr Rosen's eyes filled. And she knew there had been a loss. An old, sad loss.

'Ah!' sighed Lilian. 'That was lovely. Hasn't she got a nice voice, Harry?—Now up you get. Your father's taking you to the pictures.'

Lilian introduced the two men while Emily absorbed this news. She wound her arms and legs round her chair, stunned by the outcome of the battle.

She stared at the big, familiar-looking stranger and heard herself say boldly, 'What are we going to see?'

'And how have you been getting on at school?' Harry asked when they sat in the bus. 'Are you set for high school after the holidays?'

'If I pass. The results'll be in the paper any day.'

'And will you?'

'Mrs Salter says so.'

'She your teacher? It used to be a *Miss* Someone, I thought.'

Emily looked blank. She thought back. 'Oh, Miss Bates! That was years ago. Two years ago.'

Harry persevered automatically: the day was so quiet and hot and meaningless that he wanted nothing but to sleep. It was a fine kind of torture to see empty seats across which he might horizontally have stretched, and yet to remain vertical. He forced himself to ask, 'And what was this one like?'

Smoothing her fingers over the nickel frame of the seat in front, Emily said disingenuously, 'All right.'

But the truth about Mrs Salter and the part she had played in her life for the past two years could not have been conceived by her father whatever the tone or answer had been.

Separated from Miss Bates, Emily had floundered in an alarming void until, sinking under the weight of her unused affections and undirected aspirations, she attached herself to the one new adult in her world—Mrs Salter, a woman in her early thirties, shrewd, dimpled, with devastating smiles, sarcasm, and a dislike of children who were anything but normal.

Now, to Emily, it was merely an interest from which she had very simply recovered—by separation. For these were the long summer holidays, dividing childhood from adolescence, dividing primary from high school, three weeks, dividing her from Mrs Salter. Now she could think calmly, kindly, even with patronage, of Mrs Salter with whom she had for two years sought and failed to ingratiate herself.

An air of diffidence, almost automatically assumed, marked Emily from the first day as a target. She seemed to Mrs Salter a born target. The fact that—pushed by fascination and fear—she worked well and gave no opening there for criticism made the pleasure of pinning her down on points of attitude, expression, and personality, the more subtle. With Emily Lawrence, and a couple of others who were dunderheads, Mrs Salter quite exploited herself as a satirist. The rest of the class laughed hysterically. She had no need of a cane to keep order.

Aware, even at the apex of her malaise, of its absurdity, of the peculiar self-betrayal she daily exacted of herself,

Emily nevertheless persisted in thinking of herself as entranced. With fanatical persistence she fed the idea of devotion to Mrs Salter: she *would* be attached to someone.

During visits from Paula, and days at the beach with Patty; through laughter and screaming quarrels with Lilian she was inwardly never deflected from concentration on the image to whom she sacrificed, by whom it was a pleasure to be rent and mortified.

For in everything she did, Mrs Salter was reliable: and what could not be proved she did not say. She surveyed her pupils with bright watching eyes—eyes alive with conscious intelligence, eyes that drew conclusions, behind which there was thought. The unknowable ramifications of grown-up thought in Mrs Salter's head attracted Emily hypnotically. She was planet-struck by the extensions of life she sensed in her.

But today, miraculously, when her father, reluctant to leave a subject he could share with her, repeated, 'So she was all right?' Emily looked at him with mild astonishment, was compelled for a moment of something like boredom to reconsider her verdict, and felt a small surprised memory of warmth. Poor Mrs Salter!

Emily saw her standing at the gate that Thursday afternoon, after the examinations and the party: she had said goodbye to them all for the last time. She, it had seemed, was doomed to stand there for ever, while they, suddenly freed and optimistic, went on and on, growing up but never old, gaining strength and power.

With a happy, sentimental, spiteful sensation in her chest Emily said goodbye. It was over and she was resigned.

As for the declarations that Mrs Salter would never hear, she could but feel that they were her loss. She had never felt herself so invincible as at this moment of extraordinary change, at this incredible going forward.

Sitting beside her father, she remembered enough to remember that it was a pity. Something to do with Mrs Salter was a pity. She had smiled at them as if she was sorry to see them go—even her—just three weeks ago.

'Yes,' she said vaguely.

They both swayed slackly as the bus started up again. Someone climbed the stairs. The vast scattered buildings of the steelworks, black and grey, ranged alongside them—barbed-wire fences, scrap-iron, disused carriages, smoke. An American car turned in at the entrance gates, passed a garden, stopped at the office block.

Harry looked away. 'What else's been happening to you all this time?'

Emily sucked at her bottom lip and scanned the interior of the bus. Against the ever-present background of obsession little stood out in the immediate past. She could think of nothing except the new facts she had learned at school, and that she and Patty had broken into an old deserted convent a week before and had been frightened stiff ever since. *That* she would keep to herself.

'Patty and I went for a hike on Sunday,' she finally offered.

'Oh? Where to?'

'Oh...' She waved an arm in the direction of the trunk road. 'We went along the road as far as the crematorium. That's three miles there and three back. There's a radio station, too. You're allowed to go in and look at it, so we did. But you can't,' she warned him, 'go into the crematorium. But we wouldn't, anyway.'

Harry nodded, and, when he saw that she was about to start again, said hastily, 'Who's this Patty? You used to have a friend called Alice, didn't you?'

Emily gave him a pitying look. He didn't know *anything*. She gave him an edited version of the change-over.

It happened that on leaving Miss Bates's class, Alice had been relegated to the B grade as a result of a falling-off in her work. The two girls, who had become friends circumstantially on their first day at school, were separated for the first time.

Humiliated, Alice had reacted against Emily and threatened to find a new friend. Rebuked by her father, told by her mother that Emily, with fewer advantages—no mother, no father, no proper home-life—had yet been able to succeed where she had failed, Alice resolved that the loss of her friendship was insufficient punishment for this paragon—though even that, she knew, would be a blow. *She* was all right: there was a new girl in her inferior class this term, a pretty new girl who wanted a friend. Emily would be the odd one out. Everyone was paired off.

For a few weeks the old partnership held together—Alice cool, Emily hectic with perturbation. It was not Alice she wanted; it was the symbol of social success and security; it was Alice, the stable landmark she had known for years; the protection against a charge of unpopularity—simply, that is, the useful bulwark that most youthful friendships are.

To this end, she daily drained herself of her sense of what was right, what was fitting; there was even a sense of what was dignified that had to be sacrificed—as it turned out, in vain. Emily's temporary successes only hardened Alice's determination to break away.

The climax and the end came one day when they sat eating lunch in the shed at school. Another parental lecture the night before had finally decided Alice.

In a clear thin voice she said, 'My mother says your mother and father'll get a divorce. You'll be an orphan. It'll be in all the papers. My mother says I ought to have friends who have nice homes like me.'

Emily was conscious suddenly of tears waiting under her lower lids. She had not armed for this attack. They were in the midst of a contest, yes, but this was out of the blue, irrelevant, and surely, not true.

'They will not.'

'My mother says they will.'

There fell the cold rain on the pitted asphalt; there stood the red-brick school with its high grey windows; beyond it, a fence, a road, a line of houses. On her arms there was cold damp air; round her there were girls who smelled of the food they had eaten—bananas and onion and garlic sausages. Through the wall of skirts and legs she could see the wooden floor of the shed, and at the entrance, the garbage tin, stuffed with crumpled papers, crusts, and fruit skins.

The girls stood watching and listening with mindless curiosity. Emily and Alice, knowing this now to be their last encounter, smiled tightly at each other like small-mouthed animals.

'*June*'s going to be my best friend now and my mother's glad. She says your grandmother's a disgrace and that Mr Rosen living there isn't respectable. She says—'

The bell rang for assembly and they stampeded from the shed, clasping lunch-boxes, throwing up knees and feet, tearing across the wet playground.

'June! June!' screamed Alice. 'Wait for me!' She threw a backward glance over her shoulder at Emily and sped to join her new friend.

The dull wet afternoon was spent on art. On rough grey paper the children drew with coloured chalks which infiltrated fingernails and fingertips. Untalented, unconcentrated, into her circular red apple and her bright banana, Emily drew it all—the stab of fear, the beating heart, the tears that stayed, the smile, that awful smile she had worn, it now seemed, all her life.

Automatically thrilled by the silent tigerish passing of Mrs Salter up and down the aisles between the desks, Emily squeaked away with her chalks, and remembered *knowing* Alice as an individual. There had been an unemotional knowing, a recognition in some part of her mind or nerves so calm as to be objective, that Alice was a small girl with sharp teeth and an animal lack of feeling. She had rejoiced in the audience, wanted to create a sensation, would gladly have spilled blood for effect.

Drawing the apple and banana, Emily made no effort to put her feeling into words, but the memory of it came to her and she felt it again. She looked at the fruit on the table, the stick of chalk in her fingers: her eyes went momentarily to the grey windows, then passed to the grey page in front of her.

Divorce? An orphan? To be as different as that from everyone else? And Lilian and Mrs Rosen? Remember the day Mrs Rosen came crying and Lilian chased her away? Remember George looking the other way if he saw her coming?

She hurled herself and her bag through the kitchen door that afternoon and pelted Lilian with questions. If she was tactless, Lilian was too outraged by the impudence of her accusers to notice.

She vehemently denied the likelihood both of divorce and of Emily's becoming an orphan. And what was it, she wanted to know, that Alice had said about Mr Rosen?

A quiet afternoon by the electric fire with a book had brought Lilian to a readiness to be roused that Emily and her story touched off at once.

Stomping to and fro across the room, glaring belligerently at everything in sight, Lilian abused Alice, her mother, her father, and all their relatives for many generations into the past and future.

They could be had up, going round saying things like that about people. And coming from *them*, anyway, it was pretty good.

'When I first knew that family—that was when your mother was just about your age—do you know what they were?'

Having heard before, Emily knew, but she shook her head.

'They were flat broke. The grandfather was round here every day asking if he could cut the lawn for us. I used to give him a basket of food to take home to them all. If you gave him money he drank it though his wife didn't have a loaf of bread in the house or a decent pair of shoes to her feet.

'She was round begging me not to give him even a sixpenny piece. Ah, yes! Of course, they don't remember any of that now. All set up in their nice big jobs, they don't remember.'

'But, Grandma—but Lilian'—Emily always found this perplexing—'*why* were they hungry?'

'It wasn't just them,' Lilian corrected her with a threatening nod, 'everyone was.'

'Us?' She narrowed her eyes. A different answer from the one she was invariably given would not have surprised her.

'No, we were lucky.'

'Well, why were they...hungry?'

Faintly harassed, Lilian at length said, 'Well, you see, there was no work for the men.'

'Why?'

'Why?' Lilian frowned. 'Because there wasn't, that's why.' Then, for her own benefit, for it puzzled her, too, she added, 'You see there was the Great War and then the Depression came and then...'

Emily squashed her face between her fists and was silent.

After a tentative pause, during which Lilian gathered with relief that she was to be questioned no more today, she said, rallying, 'So don't you worry your head about those ones and all their talk. My goodness, you should feel sorry for them for being so stupid. They can't help it, the...'

This sudden reversion to personalities found Emily unprepared. She could not so quickly rise to Lilian's magnanimity. But when she had thought it over for a minute or two it struck her as indeed most gratifying that pity was the reasonable return for Alice's spite. It was what she had suspected at the time.

'Come on!' Lilian cried. 'We'll make ourselves some afternoon tea and have a party. And there's no school for you tomorrow. We'll have a day off and go to the pictures. What do you say?'

After a feast of iced fairy cakes and tea, Lilian sang—as she sometimes did when she wanted to be particularly amusing—a series of music-hall ballads remembered from her childhood.

And Emily pressed her to tell again how, if she had not had her tonsils removed at the age of eighteen, she might have been another Melba. If that had happened, she never failed to point out, Emily would never have existed. 'You owe your life to my tonsils,' she said, and then she sang some more.

She was very funny, and Emily, who loved to be entertained, laughed and cheered her on until they were hoarse and weak with giggles.

Wiping their eyes they looked at each other with the harmonious affection of shared, unmalicious amusement and laughed again. Mr Rosen, coming in from work, was baffled by their happy hysteria.

He made a few bewildered attempts to join in, but finding the tide of Lilian's interest against him he went away to his room.

But he had reminded the others of time. After she had done a few imitations of him, Lilian wanted to be alone to get dinner and to fall into the state she called thinking.

She faced the idea that she might eventually have to return Mr Rosen to his wife and let her reputation rest: for the present it was a thought to be kept available for use on those occasions on which it suited her to frighten him.

For Emily the problem of finding a new friend was easily solved by the presence three houses away of Patty, whom she knew by sight, a Roman Catholic in a Protestant neighbourhood and consequently isolated. Unutterably relieved to have found each other they talked one afternoon and vowed, the following week, to be friends till they died.

The repercussions of the distant break-up with Alice were still at work in Lilian. More and more frequently it occurred to her to remember that she and Rosen were locally criticized. For some time past her chief interest in Rosen had centred round her ability to humiliate him. He, for his part, was able to irritate her without trying, by acting in company like the master of the house, and unwisely trying to exhibit his non-existent power over her.

Recently the possibility of bringing, not competition, but a levelling agent, in the shape of another boarder, into the house, had been appealing to Lilian. It would be a perpetual reminder to him that whatever the situation was between them, he was there as a paying guest and his privileges, if peculiar, were not unlimited.

Lilian was resentful that she should be labelled, because of someone for whom she now felt only a spasmodic interest, as less than respectable. And, too, she had all along been aware of Paula's frozen disapproval. The performances of mother and daughter had been intolerably strained by her unorthodox behaviour, were so far from expressing what each truly felt that their meetings teetered on the edge of farce.

Last week, after a quarrel, knowing only that she was irritated with Rosen, and plagued by a compulsion to ingratiate herself again with Paula, Lilian wrote to say that she was looking for news of someone suitable to take in as a second boarder.

With deceptive casualness Paula had passed on this information to Harry. *His* mind turned on his own affairs. He imagined that people were always coming and going in Lilian's house; he guessed, also, that Rosen was Lilian's friend—a euphemism for something which, in Ballowra, had no other name—and he was less than interested.

But to break the silence back into which he and Emily had fallen he said, 'Old—er—what's-his-name—how do you get on with him?'

She got on with him as well as she got on with the dining-room table, or the grandfather clock, so she said, 'All right.'

'Look out!' her father said. 'That's the Royal, isn't it? This is where we get off.'

She saw his tweed shoulders preceding her down the stairs of the bus and said to herself, that's your father.

CHAPTER FOUR

DURING THE holidays Emily turned twelve and some time, but at no identifiable time, after that she woke to a world that made what she had known before seem one-dimensional. She was collected in one place, made subjective and aware of it: made capable of objectivity. Overnight she had become all-seeing and all-wise. She had become the sounding-board for thin waves of intuition by which she incredibly, sometimes shockingly, and often to the dismay of her heart, knew what was true and what was not.

Battered by ceaseless messages from an autonomous translation centre she looked away from shuttered adult eyes, overcome by a conviction that they lied not only to her but—what was infinitely more alarming—to themselves.

Had she accidentally become a hypnotist, that she knew so much? Had her eyes developed X-ray vision? she wondered. No, it was more miraculous than that, something more sober and terrifying than that, that had happened to her. A palpitating new world of extraordinary richness and complexity had sprung round her. She and the world had been reborn.

Through the hot summer days she lay on the grass and watched the clouds, and wandered along the river trying to probe the mystery of the fabulous being she had become.

If a universal miracle had taken place, someone, she thought, would have to mention it sooner or later, so she waited and watched.

She studied Lilian and Mr Rosen, dropped hints to Dotty while she dried the dishes. She gave Patty opportunities which, had she known the language, she could not have failed to understand. Reluctantly she concluded that whatever had happened, she was in it on her own. No one else had changed. They still lived from day to day, and meal to meal, and talked about the price of peas and tomatoes. They talked about Gladys's Tom getting drunk and breaking one of her teeth ('His inside must be pickled in alcohol,' Lilian said); and about Mrs Hodges who was so stuck-up suddenly having hysterics in the butcher's shop and being taken off in an ambulance ('Swearing like a trooper,' Lilian said). And they talked about the floods last winter, the people whose houses were flooded out for the third time in the season ('Waves crashing over their chimneys, poor souls,' Lilian said). And they made love, and made themselves sick on cheap wine.

The application of her belief that the truth of a situation, pointed out, would be self-evident, taught Emily that nothing was easier to resist than reason, and sent her to the river to think again. It sent her out at night to lean against the wall and watch the sky until she saw stars jerk a hundredth of an inch or a million years across the blackness. By day she lost her eyes in the spaces where she knew the stars to be.

Particles of dust hovering in shafts of sunlight were atoms which, with her new vision, she was not surprised to see. Ants and birds, tadpoles in the shallows of the river, she gazed at with a kind of still intensity as if quite suddenly her concentration might help to bring about a second miracle to supplement the first and make the universe completely comprehensible.

At length she hit on what seemed the only answer to the enigma of differences between people and, especially, differences between herself and everyone else. There must be a series of lives to be lived, and age, real age, depended on the number of lives, not the number of years in the past.

When the pride of discovery had diminished, the conclusion that she was a few lives ahead of everyone else she knew made her feel not so much superior as marooned. Where were *her* people? Where were the others like her, to keep her company? And where was she to look for help or information? She might, she felt, have been told something before being dropped off in Ballowra.

She longed to be in a climate of effort where people strove, where mathematical precision would eventually arrive at the answer to all questions, and where warmth and kindness and love were everywhere, but mainly over her.

What she chiefly suffered from—like a champion swimmer without a coach, or a pool to practise in—was the lack of a teacher and situations in which her capacities might be tested to the limit. She felt the need of spiritual exercise and testing, and she wanted it to be scientific. She wanted, not to do good for others, nor for herself, but simply to exercise for their own sakes the qualities that lay like wasting talents, the qualities that *were* her talents.

To these unformulated feelings was added a corrosive desire for fine behaviour, from those around her, in everyday encounters. She sent prayers into nowhere that Mr Rosen should keep his mouth closed when he ate, that teeth and ears should not be examined at mealtimes, that Dotty should not belch, that Lilian should not utter words in anger that made even adults look peculiarly depressed. She wanted for them straight shoulders, clean skin, alert, seeing eyes. She wanted dignity, discrimination, and the cessation of war against the gentle virtues she admired. She provided constant amusement for her grandmother and friends.

It was only necessary, she had discovered, for a person, place, or thing to be admired by her, to become the object of hilarity and scorn. They'd even laugh at Shakespeare, Emily thought, and when Mrs Salter and the head talked the way they did there was clearly something to him. But if she so much as mentioned Mrs Salter and Mr Wills in support of an argument they minced her up with smiling sarcasm, and laughed at the teachers, and laughed till she and the teachers shrank to dwarf-size. She burned with anger hot and gusty as a bushfire—an appalled, helpless kind of anger. For no one wanted to be just, and that still seemed—in spite of her theory of life and age—so unaccountable and alarming that her strength evaporated. They'd even laugh at God, she thought.

She had no feeling for Shakespeare or God: if they had, she could have listened like a stone. But not to what they *did* say.

Baited, she retired to patch up and comfort her treasures. She learned to be silent under provocation—for no one was twice allowed to desecrate what she valued. Suppressing herself to explosion point, she continued to agitate the air with pleas for at least an external change in the direction of nobility. A noble Lilian, a noble Rosen, everyone to be perfect!

Lilian sat at the kitchen table and began her letter to Paula. She loathed writing but she knew by the unusual silence from Sydney that Paula was annoyed with her, so here she sat.

> 'I've done what I said,' she wrote, 'and got someone into the spare room. Mr Watts at the chemical works heard I was looking for someone so he came to *inspect* us all and then took the place for this man who was coming up from Melbourne. Max his name is. He's quite a big-wig at the works so we'll have to watch our step. We'll be having all the heads around the place coming to see us. (Ha-ha!)
>
> 'He used to work at this place here before, then he went home to Melbourne, and now he's back again for about a year. But that's just by the way. The funny thing about it is that he's the Max Thea used to know. (I knew that before he came. Mr Watts and I had quite a little chat.) But he didn't know that this was

where she used to be until I told him, and of course he didn't know that I knew what I did. But we had a talk about her, he keeping his distance and me mine, if you know what I mean. The thing was, if they wasted any time talking about us, she would have called me Lilian. It was the name Hulm he didn't know. He remembered Emily, though. Thea's Emily he called her if you please, and then looked as if he could have bitten off his tongue. I said what a good memory he had considering how long it was since Thea went—'

Lilian paused, wondering if she had been too frank, if she had given anything away. These were some of the facts, if her arrangement did somehow counterfeit the tone of the meeting. She was reluctant that Paula should see she had been impressed; on the other hand she was unwilling to prejudice her against him. He was here to propitiate her as much as for any other reason.

Lilian drowsed idly over the blotting-paper and dotted it with tiny spots as she remembered Rosen's discomfiture on being introduced. The whole thing had been news to him. He was horribly put out. She smiled indulgently. It was doing him good already. He was jealous! As if...She opened her eyes and looked at the wall rather bleakly. It was not for that reason she had got another man into the house. If it had been, she would have chosen differently.

She drew herself up and, sitting straight in her chair, scrawled several boxes on the blotting-paper with the decisive air of one signing a cheque. Only the stiffness of her corset and her disdain for the blank paper in front of her kept her from slumping over the table again as she sat thinking of the new boarder. His eyes, like her own, were grey. They had held her flickering eyes and caused in them a baffled stillness of which she was unaware.

Aggrieved at that first meeting to feel that she had not made her impression, she was impelled to staccato bursts of laughter, to a puzzled, defensive attempt to get through to him. But her wit was over his head, she concluded. He was not one of her men. But he had been, she recalled on an upsurge, and thought she would repeat the thought to Paula, a thorough gentleman. If Rosen would only behave like that, she began to think, and then she could have giggled. If she had been looking for a thorough gentleman, she would never have landed herself with Rosen.

Perhaps it was because Max was a Catholic that he seemed so different. Lilian paused over the thought. Was he? Incredibly, she seemed to hear now, over the years, an equivocal note in Thea's admission. Perhaps it was not true. She sat breathing away, thinking about it gloomily, abstractedly; then she thought: well, as long as he doesn't hang any bleeding hearts on the walls, I don't care one way or the other. Those holy pictures gave her the creeps. Gladys had her house practically papered with them, and the things that went on there...Lilian honestly wondered how she could. She was sure she would feel put off.

With a shiver she picked up her pen and wrote at great speed:

> 'Just after that, Emily came in from the pictures and I had to go out and I've hardly seen him since. You'd think,

though, that she had known him all her life. Still, it's dull here for him after the big city and she keeps him busy.

Have you forgotten the road home? Why don't you come on Friday night? Ring and let me know or send a telegram. Rosen can meet you at the station.

Your loving Mother.'

'Thank God!' she said aloud.

For the third night in succession Emily had been to the Rialto where, on Wednesday, she had seen the archetype of her aspirations—someone apparently famous, of whom she had never heard. In what kind of a fog had she been living, she wondered, that she had never known the extraordinary range of subtlety people had it in their power to command. This was how people should be—witty, wise, compassionate, and clever.

On Thursday she had difficulty in keeping her delighted smile concealed. She neglected Patty, spent several shillings on film magazines, and locked herself in the bedroom to examine each one from comma to comma for a word of information about the actress on whose behaviour hers would henceforth be modelled.

She found a small biography and read with veneration till she had it by heart. Not American, twice married, no children. No children. She smiled with hard satisfaction. Dramatically she sighed and leaned against the wall. No children.

The magazine learned, she sat gazing at the carpet, facing facts. By distance, fame, and *her* silence, this one could be kept safe from sneers. But oh, what a distance to admire from! Advantages and disadvantages went hand in hand, it seemed. After Friday *she* would be gone from Ballowra, and though she was making another picture, according to the magazine, it would be months and months before it came...

On Thursday night she committed large tracts of the dialogue to memory, and tore a poster, advertising the film, off a wall. It was a bit ragged round the edges and had a hole in the middle where the glue was thickest.

On Friday she practised the dialogue, fitting it into her conversations wherever it would be least remarkable. For all her care, a few people were startled by its irrelevance.

Tonight, Friday night, she had been there for the last time. Now she flew home through the dark streets, plunged in a fantasy in which life-size portraits on the walls of the room gave way to visions of a private cinema and trips to Hollywood. She stowed away...

Unbalanced, she had caught at what she took to be a lifeline; something that took her a step further away from a life she had no use for. She went home, stretched with a nervous, not happy, exaltation which fell, inevitably, on reaching the gate of her own house. Both she and her exaltation were diminished in the steps that carried her inside.

She heard voices in the sitting-room—Lilian's and a stranger's—and with automatic curiosity started to walk past the door, looking in.

'Oh, there she is!' her grandmother cried. 'Just the girl we've been talking about. Come in and say hullo to Mr—' She turned to the man beside her. 'I can't think of you as anything but Max, I'll just have to call you that.'

With her eyes fixed first, unnaturally, on her grandmother's, and then with equal unease on the stranger's, Emily got herself over to Lilian's side, sea-sick with the swaying conflict between tongue-tied shyness, and a frightening sensation that an impertinent remark might come out, accidentally, and shock them all.

The man spoke to her and she mumbled something back. Then she knew she was being fondly extolled, 'My only grandchild...' Hearing, but not listening, she looked at the man from under her brows with oblique, fluttering glances. Lilian's human bulk and warmth and peculiar musky smell at her side.

Under the light, the man stood, nodding occasionally, listening to Lilian, looking now and then at *her.* He was tallish, not solid, rather thin. His hands were brown and sinewy.

Her eyes darted again at his face, half in shadow, took in the high forehead, the thin bony structure; with impersonal interest she looked at a mouth that told her nothing. His hair, she saw, had begun to recede a little on either side of his forehead.

The voices still went on. She looked again at the man, idly, with more ease, at his eyes, and saw with a shock of profound surprise that his grey eyes were turned on her, and more than looking at—*seeing* her, saluting her with a kind of serious friendliness as if he knew her. She throbbed with surprise and alarm, looked away, to Lilian, to Lilian's diamond watch, to the armchair. No one ever looked as if they *saw* her.

Cautiously she charted an upward course again for her eyes. He was talking to Lilian. He looked nice. She liked him.

'Wake up!' said Lilian, with a laugh. 'I said, where have you been?'

'The Rialto, Grandma.'

'That's the third time this week, isn't it? What do you think of that, Max? Three times to see the same picture.' Preparing to go, she said, 'All these young ones need their heads read, I think. Pictures, pictures. It's all they think about. And a pile of magazines in there...'

Emily waited for an attack on *her*, quite mistaking, in an upsurge of guilt and loyalty, the perfunctory nature of Lilian's remarks and interest. She was amazed when the voice trailed off as if her grandmother scarcely remembered what she had been saying.

Beneath this surface reaction, she felt, but would not remember, a submerged shamefacedness at the mention of pictures and magazines, as a toddler might who had been reminded in company that it still used a dummy. She was unadmittedly ashamed of what, an hour before, had been a kind of claim to fame.

Outside, from some point among the furnaces and foundries, a whistle signalled the change of shifts.

'It's time I wasn't here,' Lilian said. 'You'll be all right, won't you? When you've unpacked Emily'll make you a cup of coffee. It's one of the few things she *can* do, and she'll give you a hand in with your things.'

'No, indeed! I'll have them in in five minutes. But as for the coffee, Emily, if you don't mind, later on...'

'No, no, no!—Emily! Did you see those cases by the door?'

'No.'

'Oh! She can be awful stupid when it suits her. Well, they're there! Now just start bringing a few things into the spare room—into Max's room.'

'Is he...?'

'He's staying.'

'Don't let me keep you late, Mrs Hulm. I've held you up already.'

Pleasant though he was, it struck Lilian that he meant to have his own way. A kind of inward surprise, a fraction later, registered itself on her face. Recovering, she waved her hands with a show of indifference or incomprehension, and started for the door, laughing, only to stop and say, one finger aloft, 'Lilian! Not so much of the Mrs.'

By the time she left the house, the stranger had his coat off, the sleeves of his shirt rolled up, and, Emily watching at a distance, had transferred the suitcases to his room.

Now he unfastened the padlock of a chest and, lifting the heavy lid, scooped up two armfuls of books. Emily goggled, came forward. 'I'll take some.'

They made several trips from the dark veranda down the lighted hall to his room and, when the chest was emptied, carried it in.

Satisfying herself that the man, withdrawn, methodical, was occupied with his unpacking, Emily gazed over the room—at the assortment of luggage, the heaps of books. Loving sensation, she abandoned herself to the alternate gusts of exhilaration and compassion that swept over her.

His bare brown arms worked over his luggage; she saw the white shirt, the tie hanging down as he leaned over something on the floor.

But her job was over; it was her business to get out of the room and leave him in peace. Reluctantly, hands behind her back, she began to inch her way out—but not altogether silently; she wanted him to notice.

'Going? You don't have to. Stay and look at the books if you like.' He was abstracted, but he still *saw* when he looked, and meant what he said. She was convinced of that.

'All right.' Willingly she dropped to her knees and began to lift the books, reading the titles, opening some, handling all with respect. He was stuffing things into drawers, and hanging things up. She sat on the floor and started to work systematically. Absorbed, she was silent for a long time, but suddenly she said, 'What's this?'

'What've you got?' He came over. 'Oh, that. Latin. You haven't seen it before?'

'No. I might soon be doing it, though, Mrs Salter says.'

'Who is that?' he asked, and Emily told him more, in a few words—with a curious mixture of willingness and fear—than she had ever told anyone. She finished up, showing him the book again, 'Can you read this, though?'

'I know that one fairly well. But most of the others—no, unfortunately. I've forgotten it all. There isn't'—he zipped up a bag and put it against the wall—'there isn't enough time.'

Mentally, Emily shrugged and raised her eyebrows. He was nice, this man, but what did he mean? Time. That was one thing there was too much of. He was, after all, a bit nuts like all grown-ups.

With cagey, critical eyes she watched him roll down his sleeves and stack one empty bag inside another. He noticed her again, and said, 'Don't wait to ask if you want to take any of those any time.' He paused, and looked at her for what seemed a long time, in a serious, searching way—yet as if he knew her. It was a bit confusing and embarrassing, especially in view of what she had just thought about him, and especially when he didn't look exactly happy about it. She wriggled and fiddled with some books, then, spotting a dark red box from which the man at that moment lifted a raincoat, said, 'Oh, is that a gramophone?'

With an effort he responded to her expression of repressed delight. He said, 'Do you know how to work it? Would you like to play something? I wonder what?'

She couldn't think. 'Yes, but you say. I don't know. ...Are you going to stay here?'

Plugging in the machine, he told her where he had come from and what he would be doing in Ballowra. Because he was more than tired he gave a heavy sigh, half groan, half sigh, as he knelt beside the girl on the floor to explain how to use the machine.

And Emily, kneeling there, listening to his voice, watching his hand point to a piece of mechanism, turn a knob, suddenly felt at a great distance, was conscious of his unconsciousness of her, of his mechanical concentration on the task he was performing for her, and she felt a wave of compassion for him. She felt a small physical reaction on her spine to the suddenly strange, living humanity of the man beside her.

'Yes, yes, I see,' she nodded dreamily. 'I understand.'

The music started. The chairs were littered, so Max sat down on the bed, then leaning forward, lifted a packet of cigarettes and his lighter from the dressing-table.

If there was one thing he had not expected this morning, on the plane, he thought, it was that at half past nine he would be in the room where Thea had lived, in the house with people she had spoken of, the child she was fond of.

Whatever record it was he had chosen, he never knew.

A spiral wall was woven by the music—a tower from which Emily leaned at leisure, to gaze out over strange lands and fancies. She listened to Wagner's trumpeting with a quite incongruous sensation of peacefulness. There was a man in the house, with a man's different voice and look. The vitiating femininity of life in the house was balanced; authority rightly centred.

His head wreathed for an instant in smoke, the man listened with eyelids reflectively lowered. He was not young. There were lines on his forehead. He had at the same time a look of sorrow, and a look of humour. Now and then he raised an arm as if it were stiff, or troubled him.

Into an extraordinary quiet, Emily finally said, 'I think it's finished.'

And not smiling at being caught, but not angry either, she thought, he stood up and ground out the butt of his cigarette in a green glass ashtray. He forgot to mention the music, but frowning, said to himself, 'I'd like to leave the rest of this for tonight.'

Emily scrambled to her feet. Reminded of her, he said at once, with an inexplicable change to cheerfulness, 'What do you think, Emily? Do people call you Emily or

Emmy? Either? Both? Anyway, what do you think, yes or no?'

She was hypnotized by his confidence and his interest. She shook her head more in wonder than answer.

He gave her a quizzical look. 'No, we don't do it?'

'I'll make the coffee,' she said breathlessly.

In the kitchen she went from cupboard to sink to stove. The man found cups and saucers, competently cut the raisin bread and stood by the griller while it was toasted. He was not far away now, but talking as if she were grown-up, about her, about himself, giving himself away to her. She was his. She knew that she would always have to be what he expected her to be. She knew it with a feeling almost of sadness. It was a journey's end.

At the same time, she was lifted off the ground with a high childish glee at being taken under the wing of the enemy—the adults—into the enemy's camp. She yearned to tell one of her tribe—Patty, anyone.

Sitting at the table, drinking coffee, Max said of the kitchen, looking round, 'I wonder if I might borrow this room some nights when I have work to do. The light's good. Table, too.'

Emily looked from it to the big globe, mildly. 'Yes, I do my homework here.' She pushed her hair away from her face, swallowed some toast and blurted, unintentionally, into the silence, 'I'm glad you're staying here.' Her eyes filled and she giggled. She picked up her cup and drank a frantic mouthful or two.

Max shook a cigarette from the packet into his hand. He leaned on the table easily and smiled at her. 'Thanks,

Emmy. It's nice of you to say so.' There was something reassuringly level about his look, or the set of his eyes. Illuminated for an instant, by the flame of his lighter, they were bright grey.

'By the way, did you carry in a telescope?'

'Was that it like a bicycle pump? Well, I did. Was it a telescope?' All the rest and a telescope, *too*, her tone implied.

But there was relief in her voice. This first meeting, this being with Max was rushing past her. She could remember nothing, here and now, of what had made her grateful for his interjection, she only knew that she had now to think about a telescope. Realizing this, she marvelled. How she had longed to see the heavens close! Should she ask?

All at once it seemed incredibly foolish to risk alienating this man by presuming too far on his offered friendship. Had she not been warned often enough of the dangers of going too far with adults and tiring them? And that when she had not gone a quarter of the distance she had gone tonight! For what hadn't she told him!

'One night next week—the moon isn't up, yet, tonight—if you're interested, we could have a session with it.'

'I've read about the moon—all about it—in a newspaper,' she said, pale with confession. 'I might like to be an astronomer one day.' With each secret piece of information, she handed over part of herself, was lighter for the delivery, lightheaded.

'Well, there's no reason why you should not be.'

'What do you have to know to be one?'

'For one thing—mathematics.'

'Oh, then I won't.'

He laughed. 'Don't be in such a hurry! I might be able to help you—but not tonight,' he added, seeing her change of expression.

They smiled, then gradually, again, Emily was overtaken by the idea that she must be cautious. Apologetically she got herself from the table and began to collect the dishes.

In an effort to tone down the man's memory of what Lilian would surely have branded cheekiness, and forwardness, she moved about the room almost stealthily, and spoke, when driven to it, in monosyllables. And trying to immunize herself against a possible future rebuff, she pretended to believe that he had used her as a stop-gap and would drop her when an adult came.

Contrary to her fears, no one disputed her claim to Max, and after that first night there were no further preliminaries to their friendship. The others simply recognized that he was not for them. His physical presence among them was a phenomenon, to which they accustomed themselves with the ease of savages, as if he were some extinguished comet dropped out of the sky: to keep off the fear of the unknown, training themselves to think of him as part of the natural formation of the land.

As far as Emily was concerned, his coming and her growing-up, relegated her early idols, from Thea to the model actress, to barbaric—albeit revered—pre-history.

It might have been expected that nothing less than all of his attention could satisfy her craving, for, finding herself valued, she could keep no feeling from him to bestow on those whom she was bound by convention to honour. But his manner was the opposite of intense. There was no place for her fierce possessiveness in a relationship which, by its ease and lack of patronage, denied her nothing. And somehow recognizing that her childishness might mean a diminution in him, her unrestraint was yoked by a kind of scrupulous chivalry.

The test was not so severe as it might have been. Max had few, and no visible, ties. The vital times of his life were in his past. But this was her great time and she rose to meet it.

The picnic was over and now they all dispersed—not that it mattered: it was the relieved dispersal of incompatible parts, there was no fragile unity to be shattered by the homecoming.

It had not been a real picnic. It was the first time these six had been out together—a command performance—and they had all sat for hours, jammed tight, bathed in petrol fumes and the smell of warm leather. That was discouraging, not to say nauseating, to begin with. Apart from that, what had the day contained?

There was the sea below, a cliff—some incalculable feet above which hovered the miraculous end of a rainbow—where Emily had contrived to isolate herself for some seconds before they all came up. And how full of meaning might that not be? A rainbow arching the sea. But *they* had taken it calmly enough, of course, walking stodgily up to it, scoffing at it as if to say 'mirage' or 'go away'. But that could have been jealousy; they were obviously unwilling to believe what they could so clearly see. It outstayed them on the cliff, though, and that seemed to prove something.

Apart from those few minutes, and the eating, which went well, the day ground animation and ease to death.

Rosen, having taken in too much of the tripe in the Sunday papers, Lilian said, but more affected, Paula thought, by the amount of beer he had taken in, was argumentative, contentious, busily occupied with foreign affairs, bent on baiting Max and provoking him to the defence of something—in Rosen's view—indefensible.

It was sultry. Rosen drove the car; next to him sat Dotty, and next to her, Lilian. In the back, Emily sat between her mother and Max. It was one of those days, Lilian said, when everything on wheels was on the road. The cars crawled bumper to bumper to the five beaches of the district. And Rosen talked until a series of well-placed questions from Max brought about his self-immolation. There was a short silence for which everyone was grateful.

Lilian cried, 'Well, now, cheer up, everyone! This is a picnic, not a funeral—though God knows I've seen livelier corpses than some of you. Emily, pass round the chocolates. Put on the wireless, Dot, and don't get us a sermon, either—we've had enough of them for one afternoon.'

There was a bustle in the car, but, her task performed, Emily sat amazed at Max's questions. He had listened to all of them, her mother and Lilian, as well as Rosen, and asked them questions as if he wanted to know what they thought. It was impossible to accuse him of insincerity, yet how could he question them as if he thought they were sensible?

Paula had not approved. Even though she disliked Rosen she was shocked to hear his opinions questioned. A kind of numbed look came over her face, and when Max had taken up her remark, forcibly expressed, about the White Australia policy, she had quite hated him. The idea of discussion was anathema to her. Surely it was not done to disagree, however mildly? Good manners surely prevented you, if you could not agree, from contradicting someone in cold blood?

Hearing the arbitrary, dogmatic statements come, as if from voices in the air, Emily wondered if it was fair to be interested for any reason.

No, she decided, it was not really fair, and then there was the oddness to be thought of, and the blind, voiceless signals between the other heads. Emily felt the chill of their messages on her skin, their hostility, their drawing together. United against the stranger, the party found its second wind and there was much merriment and politeness. They finished the whole box of chocolates.

Max endeavoured, after his first error, to make Paula enjoy the day, for there was something pathetic in her air of youth, and age, and coldness and disillusion. But it was no good. He had exposed himself. She could see that under that nice-seeming manner he *thought*, and wanted to *talk*, and stir things up. It quite made her shake when people were like that. Only drunks were like that—but he wasn't a drunk. The only thing left for him to be was peculiar. He fitted no classification she knew. He was peculiar. The more she repeated the word, the more she gloomed over it, and was convinced of it. He was definitely peculiar. Mr Rosen shone in comparison. Up to a point he tried to keep to the rules. He knew that there *were* rules.

The blue and yellow-green of the day passed, and the white clouds and the white foam of the waves, and the rainbow. They drove away from the sea and the cliffs into the semi-bushland on the outskirts of the town where new houses by the hundred were being built.

Lilian extorted appreciation for everything—gum trees, houses, Chinese vegetable gardens, and dogs carrying sticks. Dotty glued her teeth together over a square, hard chocolate and sat entranced by the problem of keeping her knees out of the way of the gear handle. She read the number plates of the other cars. The others responded dutifully to Lilian's clamour.

If it had not been for the living presence next to her of Max, Emily would, she felt, have rolled up her eyes and died when her grandmother called yet again, 'Look! Quick!'

The roads were so dusty that they had to keep the windows up, and the windows were so dusty that they could not see through them. It was a positive pleasure to get home away from the main roads and sightseers and petrol stations and dark gum trees. The house was cool and clean, the garden was quiet. That was the picnic over.

Now, barricaded in the bedroom, called in to sit beside Lilian and watch her mother pack, Emily sighed.

Paula folded her dressing-gown and put it in the case. 'This is better without all the men, isn't it? Just the three of us. We've hardly had a chance to talk since I came up.'

Lilian stood up and began to comb her hair; she agreed that there was nothing like being with the family, even if it was only a small one. It was much nicer now, she said.

Silently, Emily listened. If to be bored, if to be isolated, if to be unnatural was better, then this was better.

Paula and Lilian could think of nothing to talk about but trains—a subject suggested by Paula's journey tonight—so they recounted to one another the details of all the train journeys they had made for the past several years. There was the time of the bush fire; the time a man pulled the communication cord; the time in the box carriage when the floor was so filthy; there was the time in the sleeper when the woman below snored all night.

Emily pulled a biscuit out of her pocket and stuffed her mouth full.

'You'll have false teeth before you're fourteen,' Paula told her.

'Don't care.'

Her gesture of disassociation made the conversation impossible. She was looked at with exasperation. She munched drily.

Turning back to the mirror Lilian screwed her face up, stretching the skin tight, now over her chin, now round her nose. She scraped off a smut.

At length Emily said, 'Max is teaching me to play chess. And the other night I saw the moon through his telescope, and the stars. It looked—'

'Your mother doesn't want to hear all that,' Lilian told her, but to Paula she said, 'He keeps her amused though.'

'You'd think he'd have other things to do.'

'I'm going,' Emily said, and went.

'The things that kept him busy when he was here before aren't here any more.' Lilian dragged a powder-puff over her face.

'What do you mean?'

'He used to be Thea's fancy man, you know.'

Paula's disapproving head came up from the suitcase, her face pink. '*He* was? Was that what you meant in your letter? How did you find out? You never told me. I didn't know she…'

'What? That she had a boy friend? Didn't I? I thought you knew years ago,' Lilian lied. At that time, years ago, it was a touchy topic. There had been some awkwardness with Paula over Olly Porteous at the time and for mixed motives Lilian had kept her discovery to herself. 'Yes, you wouldn't think it to look at him, would you? Though I don't know why. Just the same he had our Thea on a string for two years. Then off he went to Melbourne and off she went to Sydney.'

Standing, shaking her head slightly, Paula hardly knew whether she disliked most her mother's expression, her choice of words, or the fact that it was not possible in this house to condemn the existence of men who might be termed 'fancy'.

'I saw Thea last week.'

Lilian swung round. 'No! Where? What was she like?'

'Oh!' Paula frowned as if she was suffering some minor kind of anguish. 'I just bumped into her in town. She was just the same.'

'What did she say? How did she look?'

Hunting round for her possessions, Paula conveyed the unimportance, to her, of the meeting. 'She asked about you and Emily. Nothing much. She was by herself. She looked the same.'

'Married?'

'No, I—oh, there's my brush—no, I don't think so. She still works for one of those big chemical companies. A different one.'

'Well, did you get her address? Are you going to see her again? It'd be some company for you.'

'I don't *need* more company, Mum. Yes, I've got her address and phone number but I'm not going to bother to ring her. If she wants to ring me—well, she can. But—I don't know—' Paula looked at her mother for help and concluded lamely, 'She's a bit like him.'

'Well, what if she is? You always got on all right.'

'I know. She's nice enough.'

'Well? Why not go along to see her if she wants you to?'

'She's just not like us!' Paula said, seeming almost defiant.

Lilian took this with the downcast lids of a realist. One must not expect too much, she seemed to say.

'I know what!' she said. 'Bring her up here next time you come. They haven't seen each other for years. Don't tell her he's here, of course. Let it be a surprise.' She gave another short exclamation of amusement. 'That'd put a spoke in Emily's wheel, wouldn't it?'

Paula stared at her. 'Oh, Mum,' she said at last, her voice wobbling with reproach, 'what a thing to say! I certainly wouldn't dream of bringing her here, and fancy saying that about Emily! She's only a little girl.'

'Oh, you're too fussy! It was just a joke,' blustered Lilian. 'You're getting as bad as them—no sense of humour. Anyway, I don't see what harm it'd do. She's not married and he's still mooning around like a lost soul. Maybe they'd have learnt some sense by now.'

'But it's nothing to do with us. We can't start interfering. Besides'—Paula raised her brows—'it's more than three years since she went away. They'll have forgotten, and he's still married, you said. And they're not all that young, even.'

Lilian was submerged in hostility. 'Not young? They're not all that old, either! In their thirties and not young, she says!' At the door she added, 'They're a good deal younger than me, but I think some of us dodderers've still got more life in us than a lot of you young ones.'

'Oh, Mum, I didn't mean that. You're not old. I only meant...'

'*You!*'

And Paula was left to take this to heart while her mother went to the kitchen and started to slash the rind from a pound of bacon.

When, very shortly, Paula went to help prepare the meal, they exchanged a glance of truce.

Through the open window Paula could see Max and Emily on the garden seat. With a sweep of his hand he drew a plan on the lawn, in explanation for Emily, who bent over her knees and stared at the grass with what seemed to Paula sycophantic attention. Then her daughter's face was raised, a sunburst of comprehension.

Thea's fancy man. Paula turned away and cracked an egg into a blue china bowl. Sometimes she wondered about her mother. She changed that. Sometimes she wondered about Emily, getting worked up about some stranger or school teacher, some stranger whom she would learn soon enough would not walk five yards to help her when she needed help. Call them strangers, call them friends, it all came to the same thing: only families mattered. But Emily was young. Paula had to keep reminding herself to excuse her on that account. Thea's fancy man, she thought.

In some way, Paula connected the danger of trusting strangers with her own unfortunate marriage. Harry Lawrence had, after all, been a stranger, and was so still: he was no blood relation. And he, like all the others, men and women, had let her down. Only her mother she *would* believe in, and Emily, too, when she was old enough to co-operate.

'Would you like me to make some scones, Mum?'

Outside in the pink evening light, Emily resisted the knowledge that Max wanted her to go in to her mother. Nothing had been said. She looked down at an ant that was making off through the grass balancing a big crumb of biscuit. She looked up at Max.

'I'm going,' she said, unresentfully, and started to drift across the lawn.

'Oh, it's you!' Paula gave her a long look and slapped at the dough vigorously. 'Decided to come in, have you?'

'What are you making?'

'Scones. Do you want some dough to play with? You used to make scones, remember?'

Emily ate a piece of dough. 'The rats used to get them all, you used to tell me. Did you throw them away?'

'They were awful old things. You had them black as the ace of spades before they went in the oven.'

Brushing her floury hands together over the sink, Paula sneezed. It left her shattered, self-pitying, and in need of a handkerchief. Irresolute, she glanced at Emily but could not ask, as she wanted, that a handkerchief be fetched from her case.

Aggrieved to have no response to her unspoken question she went up the hall, Emily chasing her and then skipping ahead.

It was unbearable to say it, but pushing open the door of Max's room, Emily said, 'Look at all the books! I can have as many as I like. It'll take me years to read them all.'

She was pierced by an instant antagonism in her mother and the forced liveliness of her tone abated. It was useless. She fell silent and watched while Paula, half irritable, half curious, turned to look into the square nondescript room where he slept and kept his belongings.

Books there were indeed—hundreds of books overflowing from the startled varnished shelves, books on the chairs, books on the floor.

Paula was unable to hide her reluctant admiration for their quantity, but she mistrusted the implications of their possession. They seemed excessive, and she loathed excess.

Emily absorbed her mother's reaction. She said, 'He's going to get some more bookcases.'

'So he should. The place looks like nothing on earth.'

Tears burned Emily's eyes. She leaned against the wall in the passage. Why all the hate in the air? she wondered dolefully.

Stumbling into the dark bedroom to find Rosen and Lilian in whispered conversation, Paula came out again more quickly: Emily was where she had been, a trembling hand was laid on her shoulder.

'Ring and ask for a taxi at seven, please, Em,' Paula said shrilly. 'And—oh—have you got a handkerchief?'

'What's that?' said Lilian, coming up behind them. 'The taxis'll all be busy. *He'll* take you to the station.'

Paula made an unseen gesture towards the kitchen, meaning that the scones must be thought of. 'He's driven a lot today. Just ring for a taxi, Em.'

The visit had been an appalling failure. No one and nothing had been on her side. The situation between Lilian and Rosen had still to be endured; she would not believe that there was anything wrong in it, but it was offensive to see one's mother enamoured of a pompous fool who had deserted his wife and son. And Emily could scarcely spare five minutes from the company of a man whose reputation was such, according to Lilian, that one might have expected her to refuse to house him, to talk to her, Paula, her mother, whom she saw so seldom. The only one who had put himself out at all for her was that man, but she had seen through him. He wanted her to be friendly.

In the face of the obstinacy and cruelty of her mother and Emily she felt so helpless that she would have cried if she could. But Paula could only brood.

Amorphous, chill and cloud-like, her presence filled the house during the last hours of her stay. When she had finally gone, the two left behind who belonged to her were heavy with a sense of their own inadequacy, of their complete failure to be ideal.

Lilian had not the heart to torment Emily, nor would she have risen to provocation. They were at a loss—that is, for half an hour or so, and then Lilian cried to Rosen, 'Get out the car. We'll go and see what's happening to old Olga from the Volga. Sunday night, she's sure to have something on.'

And during the same half-hour of recovery after Paula's going, Emily returned to herself as the tide returns to an empty beach, giving meaning to what was before an enigmatic waste. With the intruder's withdrawal the defensive camouflage—pertness, childishness, the *child*—was submerged, and there appeared the youthful human creature who had lately come to life through being known to be alive.

CHAPTER FIVE

THE ALARM clock gouged the darkness of Lilian's room, but not the deeper darkness that enclosed her. It rang for Emily, who vaulted from bed, horrified by the noise, the boredom of sleep, and the overpowering musty airlessness her grandmother chose to sleep in.

Between the sheets, Lilian unconsciously expanded, adjusting to the greater freedom, perhaps as pleased to be alone as Emily was to stay no longer close to a body older than her own.

Out of the room, Emily went to the kitchen at a run, dragging on her dressing-gown, breathing deep draughts of the morning air that swept through the house, her eyes unsticking themselves. She beamed in the door at Dotty.

''Lo, Em. Give Max a shout in a minute, will you?'

'I'm going to, Dot.'

In the bathroom she brushed her hair, cleaned her teeth and so lavishly soaped herself that her skin went smooth and shiny as scented marble. The mild flowery smell preceded her into Max's room, beginning another day in which he would be.

She stood motionless while her eyes went over the familiar room; it was sunny and smelt of damp grass for the window was wide and the curtains drawn. No amount of light disturbed Max. He slept profoundly, and was guarded by an expression so austere that the smile faded from Emily's face. As she drew nearer to him she felt her heart beat with awe and terror, yet she could not do other than move closer to the side of his bed.

'Max,' she whispered. 'Max. It's time to wake up.'

He came unwillingly to life, pushed his straight hair till it stood on end and automatically threw an arm over the edge of the bed to grope in mid-air for cigarettes and matches. Then he woke up, saw Emily, and grinned at her in such a way that she was instantly reassured. It was him. He had not changed.

She smiled down at him. 'Hullo.'

'Hullo, morning glory. Time to get up, is it?'

'I'll get you a cigarette, then will you race me to breakfast? I'm washed.'

'That far ahead? Then no cigarette. I'm handicapped enough.'

In the kitchen, which last night had seemed to concur with the idea that it was a study, the lately self-effacing gas-stove wheezed with activity: on it bacon sizzled, under its griller the toast was allowed to burn and sent up acrid fumes and blue smoke. But everyone liked burnt toast.

The percolator, once part of a still-life, bubbled vociferously on the stainless-steel draining board and sent delicious coffee steam into the room. Milk boiled on the stove. Every inanimate device rejoiced in its reinstatement and all joined, in a noisy and appetizing way, in proclaiming this the beginning of a good new day.

Here, last night, and for many nights back, when textbooks were closed, Emily and Max had taken up a dialogue that had no end, leaning across the table like antagonists—Max speaking slowly, listening, watching her, smiling and sending up clouds of smoke, Emily, serious, blotting up facts, ideas, and more than anything, a manner of thinking.

Leaning back in his chair when Emily had carried one of the ideas he had thrown forward to a triumphant conclusion, he would say, 'Perhaps. But look at it from this angle, Em...'

And she would be, at the same time, dashed and fascinated to see the many, many angles to the problem, the ifs and buts and qualifications without which no answer was possible.

As they walked on soft black evenings round the familiar streets, with Emily carefully lengthening her step to Max's long one, they talked poetry, history, astronomy, art, psychology, politics, sense and nonsense.

Concerning life and people the girl was uplifted by something like fear to find that not only were her inclinations not invariably fantastic, but sometimes well thought of, and that on the same side of the fence were Max and people whose names he honoured. It was marvellously cheering. And to know that she, Emily Lawrence, whose name alone—Emily Lawrence—could sound like a phrase meaning stupid and lazy, was thought to be worthy of Max's thought, made her eye herself in the mirror with an altogether new respect. And because she was no longer expected to strive and care for herself alone—to be healthy, to work, to succeed, to be clean and much more for her own sake alone—from matters of simplest hygiene to the most complex matters of thought within her youthful capacity she made great efforts and progress.

Through the open door of the kitchen, and through the window, sunshine came, lighting conflagrations on the yellow china, on Emily's hair, piercing the honey, falling also on the clock, which all were constrained to watch.

'Last night I saw Max's laboratory,' Emily told Dot. 'I did an experiment.'

'What happened?'

'Nothing much,' she said airily, but Max said, 'Don't believe her, Dot. A great deal happened without a single explosion.'

Spreading honey on her toast, Emily smiled, and chanted a Latin conjugation. She played it silently over on the fingers of one hand. 'I know it.'

'You're a genius. Eat your toast and come out here for a minute,' Max said.

'What's it mean, anyway?' asked Dotty, but they had both gone, were now standing outside examining the prints of some photographs they had developed.

Looking at them through the open door, Dotty shook her head and concluded, without knowing why, that it was a nice day, that she was in a good mood. Even washing the dishes seemed mildly pleasant, and as long as Dotty could remember she had been washing other people's dishes.

Emily was all right, she thought, and as for Max—he was a bit more. He must be deep. But no airs and graces. No. But if he just sat quiet, looking round—whatever he was doing—you knew he was there. Those big horn-rimmed glasses when he was reading—it was hard to know whether he was ugly or nice-looking. But she liked him. Yes, though he took Em all over the place with him and taught her all kinds of high-falutin' rubbish, he was deep; he could do all that without looking silly, or soft.

Dot felt something for him that she had no name for, that she had never felt before. She resisted it, and was often short-tempered with him, treating him as she treated Rosen and Lilian and everyone else: the difference was that she respected him.

'Only ten minutes!' she yelled, coming out of her trance. 'You don't want to miss your bus.'

'I just have to see these.'

'It's always something.'

Her morning attempts to be part of the circle of two, her changed way of speaking to Emily were accepted by the girl as part of her increase in value since Max had chosen to find her valuable.

'If it isn't one thing, it's another,' Dotty confided to the dishes as she swished them through the suds.

Some mornings the excuse would be that Gussie—the blunt-nosed, gallant-eyed mongrel who had adopted the house and its inhabitants—needed company. At other times they would have to examine the fruit trees at the end of the long untidy garden to see what particular miracle—if any—had happened overnight.

Now the photographs were left for Dotty's delectation while the executants walked round to the front of the house, to the letter-box at the gate, Emily leading the way to what was the only puzzle in her mornings—the indifference with which Max regarded his few, mostly official, letters. *Her* letters from Paula and, now and then, short ones from her father were, irrespective of content, irradiated by the distance they had covered. That her attitude was at fault she did not doubt: Max's she could not understand.

She was too young to know the sad sensation of late youth and middle-age, when what is yearned for is not news of a kind relation or friend, but a word from the past to say that old, lost opportunities are yet to be had; that the old loves, canonized by nostalgia, still remember, are waiting with all the bitter, heavy glamour still intact to take up again, and lead to a happier conclusion, relationships unhappily gone awry.

She was aware only that he was distant from her and, somehow, from himself. Faintly chilled she waited, until he should return, with what seemed a laborious resurgence of breath, consciousness, and energy, to her un-understanding smilingly apprehensive gaze.

Today, though, when she said, 'It's empty!' he seemed not to care. They continued to walk along the paths around the house, ate two loquats from the tree, talked and were silent; in the end it was she who remembered to think of the time.

Jolting to school in the top of the red double-decker bus she was stimulated to the point of laughter by the memory of the frantic rush—Max quieting Dotty's not very forceful tirade, saying to relax, the world would not end if she was late for once, at the same time doing his best to ensure that she was not.

The memory slipped away. She was in the bus going to school—lurching, swaying.

It gradually dawned on her that a furtive conversation about love and marriage was going on among her uniformed acquaintances. She listened, at first, with a sort of ironic pity, not untinged with complacence. Voices were lowered. Hearts and initials were carved in breath on thick glass windows, and forefingers grew grubby.

'I know how to find out who we're going to marry,' someone shouted, and immediately cases smelling of sandwiches opened, notebooks and propelling pencils came out. Then, with mysterious schemes of initials and numbers it was ascertained again that everyone would certainly marry someone.

Gazing through the window at the prospect of steelworks Emily expelled Max from her mind. It was unbearable that she should so much as think of him in the presence of her companions. She burned with vicarious shame. As a whispered conversation behind her progressed she grew angry, then anguished, and was not comforted to remember that last year she too, had done her share of whispering and speculating.

She slumped. More whispering. Now they were giggling. She wanted to scream at them, to stand up and denounce them and tell them to grow up or keep quiet. Especially to keep quiet. Hideous inhuman pigs. They had ruined everything. And she was one of them. Unworthy, contaminated. She could go no lower, but she stayed at a great depth for some time.

Then slowly, indignation, anger, common sense, began to burn and blow in another direction. She sat up. Her back straightened. How could she have been so witless as to think that they, or anyone, could damage *that*. It was safe from everyone.

Her exacerbated sensibilities recovered just in time to subside completely—for there was the red school building.

Books opened and shut: three-quarter-hour periods succeeded one another in the silent class-room. A series of women, variously shaped and dressed, came and talked, or were silent while the class wrote and noted through eyes in the top of its hydra-head a way of sitting or of speaking that might be branded different from the norm. The imitation of any such discovery—together with sausage-rolls, spotty apples, cheap assorted sweets and the unveiling of family skeletons—occupied its lunch hour.

During the afternoon, facts and energy drained from the teachers and accumulated in the pupils. Their faces took on added colour and shine, and hands grew dirtier than in the morning. Their collars began to wilt. It was as if, in the midst of learning, they made unconscious preparation for the return to private life, though the necessity for competition—never so urgent as here—kept them a whole.

Only on the homeward journey were the morning's voices reasserted, but more noisily, as a protest against class-room circumspection. Round brown and freckled cheeks bulged with bull's-eyes, and fashionably battered school hats spiralled in the air. Between crunchings and suckings, perfunctory, restless attention was granted the favourite girls of the day, but often shrill voices interrupted them.

After the first of their company had split off there was an air of the rehearsal room about the bus, while attitudes were adopted suitable for presentation to—it was to be *hoped* after all they had been through—impressed, devoted parents. After a little nourishment, a little bracing encouragement, an expression of fear for their nerves and strength had been extended, and graciously received, they might perhaps be ready to deflate and go in search of one of themselves to play with.

Emily no longer envied them these once jealously witnessed joys. She never stood with that disintegrating solitude of the past, listening to the chiding, cherishing reminiscences of another mother and child. She felt nothing for her school friends now but pity—for they were young and ignorant.

Encountering her for the first time that day, Lilian said, 'Good God! More work? You'll have to clear these things off the table by five o'clock. What are they trying to do, giving you all this? Now listen, I want you to run over to the shop and get some things for Dotty. A pound of butter, half...'

She ran willingly, exulting in her speed, the sky, the evening air.

A few minutes later on the corner, Patty said, 'Well, it's true you won't go to Heaven.'

(Meeting, they never wasted time on small talk.)

Emily considered this. In spite of tentative requests *her* ear had never been whispered in. It was impossible to pretend that any voices or whispers in her head were any but her own. She knew no one who went to church—except a few Catholics. She said, 'I don't believe in Heaven.'

'You'll go somewhere else, then.'

'You said I would anyway, so...Do you really think only Catholics do?'

Patty nodded. 'But don't you really?'

'No. Just don't.' Emily raised airy eyebrows and added with more nonchalance than she felt, 'You *see*! I'm here.'

'Oh, well,' Patty struggled to say, aware that her side might seem to have been let down by this obvious truth, 'you'll find out.'

Being dead. Not one person Emily knew had ever died. She had *heard* about people it had happened to, of course. But it was an interesting fact that no one...

'Pat!...Do you know anyone who's died?'

The girls juggled their parcels from arm to arm and scraped the soles of their shoes on the footpath.

'Auntie Mavis and Grandfather Flanagan.'

'Oh.'

In a moment Patty asked, as if she were offering an alternative to Heaven, 'Well, can you come to the pictures tonight?'

Max was giving a lecture at the Technical College in town, so Emily said yes.

'There's something good on tomorrow, too,' Patty said. 'You're missing everything these days. Can you come tomorrow?'

'Max's taking me to the dentist and then I don't know where. He's made about six appointments for me.'

'What for?'

'Dunno. Suppose because I had toothache last week. I wish I hadn't told him.'

A penetrating call from Patty's mother, seen irate on the veranda, waving an arm at them, broke up their session, made them run home with their parcels.

Craning over to look at her watch, Emily stumbled and almost fell when she saw that it was five o'clock—time to meet Max.

Not six but nine appointments spread over three months saw a few teeth extracted and more filled. On the corner of the street, nursing a pound of beans and a loaf of bread, Emily opened her mouth to Patty. At once, her tonsils, or some other ancient organ, blocked her breathing.

'Hurry up!' she complained, unintelligibly. 'Can't you see *anything?*'

Patty concentrated. After a minute, 'Yes! Two big ones at the back. I bet they hurt. Your tongue's red.'

'Cherries. Have some. Didn't hurt much. He gave me injections. Oh! I have to go, Pat. I'll be late for Max.'

'Why are you always going to meet him? You like him, don't you?'

'Yes.' Emily was insulted.

Patty chewed, swallowed, spat four stones into the gutter. 'But, why, Em?' she asked, with a kind of inattentive persistence. 'He's old. We're only young.' Four cherry stones in the dust. Tinker, tailor, soldier, *sailor...*

'Young! Young's got nothing to do with it. What's the difference? I'm *me*. What's young got to do with it!' Emily ranted with an adult irritability that brought Patty back from ships and the sea.

'Oh, all right.'

They walked slowly backwards away from each other, talking.

'But I still can't see why you've got a crush on someone so old.'

'If you say that again I won't speak to you.'

'Oh, phooey!'

Turning, heads in the air, they skipped and ran away from each other, looked back, once each, at different times. Emily took her parcels inside.

A crush, Patty said—a funny unworthy word to describe a funny unworthy state of mind. But not hers, Emily thought, almost grimly.

Away from Patty, preparing to meet Max, there was a shifting of key in Emily, a translation to a deeper level of reality, a translation to herself.

By Patty's words she *had* been insulted; she no longer was. It was as if, before, she had responded childishly according to age, according to Patty's expectations: together the two girls were younger than they were apart. Now a kind of mature confidence in her own judgement made it unnecessary to defend herself or her feeling to Patty.

Even those times in the past, the feelings for those other people, she could not dishonour with that word. From most of them, as far as she could remember, there had been little to be learned. She had had to hold them in spite of themselves, had had to admire in spite of her own instinct, had deliberately courted and willed obsession. She had no word for it; she simply knew what it was not. It was not what girls of her age felt for boys or girls of her age, or for their teachers.

At first, to Max, her reaction had been uncomplicated devotion and delight. She was entranced by the diversity of her entertainment. But she had known all along that it was not like anything else that had happened to her.

And one night, for no reason, she knew something more. Her simple belief in simple happiness dissolved as she apprehended almost with alarm the expanding complexities of her life, the perverse emotions, the dangerous strength of her untrained will, full of potential power and threat as an unconnected live wire. She came to a newer understanding of her feeling for Max.

Her feet were nowhere; she was aghast at the immensity she glimpsed. She experienced a sensation of joy, beside which, in inverse proportion to which, she discovered a bright fear for the future. For what was Max to her? What could he ever be?

Max lived, she had inarticulately grown to know, not with happiness, as she had easily supposed, but resignation. That this was all that by *her* side could be achieved, dismayed her. What then could he feel for her?

A tormented desire to know *exactly* what he felt for her became increasingly insistent. Her eyes asked it. In a moment which might before have been the victim of boredom, this question dwelt. She and it revolved together tightly.

Only the most intense perversity—prompted by a relentless desire to *know,* to make someone *say*—could have made her pretend to doubt, against reason and belief, the interest and generosity with which she was treated, or the affection from which it sprang.

She would swerve from a rigorous pretence of hurt and misery to a voluptuous, certain belief that she was seen and felt. What did the reason matter? Whether it was because he indiscriminately liked children, or because he pitied her for being stupid, or neglected, or hideous or awful—anything—as long as she knew. She *would* have affection on any terms.

In bed, in the nights after days of utter contentment, her thought would flicker over conversations, in which she found much that was satisfying, sustaining, if not perfect. But she wanted perfection, impossible declarations. She knew she coveted eternal assurances of love; she knew the impossibility; she knew her age. But that adult balance and proportion that she so revered, she longed to overthrow. It was a serious, honourable thing.

No, what she had was not perfect, but so nearly so that when she made the words and pictures of the day play over, there was still to be found in the midst that extraordinary pang—of love, was it, or gratitude? She often intended, and as often feared, to exercise it further.

Hastily, one night she turned from the memory that induced that heart-felt pang of pain and delight. Tossing round in bed the sensation faded. She held the dammed-up knowledge back a moment longer, and then began to feed again to her slow-thumping heart, the memories of the day, realized anew. She was valued! She was valued! The thumping and the tenseness dissolved in slow, self-conscious, thrilling tears. They fell briefly.

Repelled by a moment of cold insight, she stopped dead, and after a breath, cut contemptuously through the profusion of curiosity, flagellation, and false sentiment in which she had entangled herself. In the darkness her expression became bleak, almost austere.

There were no protestations and recriminations: there had already been too many, too misused. What she wordlessly knew was that feeling should not be tinkered with and too much handled; that warmth began where protestations ended, that hearts and wills and feelings, even adults', were not toys to be manipulated. Protestations were for those others, for Lilian and Paula, and all their world, but not henceforth, for her.

It was Tuesday night. It was midsummer. Emily left the house by the side entrance and walked to the top of the hill. Behind her, below her, lay the last trickle of streets of Ballowra's most isolated suburb. Beyond them was flat marshy country, rich, vulnerable to floods, through which the main road stretched to join the cities and towns of the coast. At the point where Emily had stopped, another road ran at right angles along the crest of the hill. She had walked up from the valley of corrugated iron rooftops and on it now turned her back: on the other side the hill sloped, all pale greeny shiny grass, dry and polished, down, down a long way to the river where the factory stood. Though more than twenty years old it was considered new for a place like Ballowra, had had to penetrate further along the river than was desirable for lack of space in more accessible areas. It was at a distance of three-quarters of a mile, or perhaps a mile, from the top of the hill.

To the right and left the same green slope continued its long downward roll to a river which, under the bluest sky, remained opaque, strangely colourless, its width so flawed by small tree-covered islands that its far bank was invisible, merging at some undetected point with the plain of dark treetops that extended to the hills on the horizon.

Apart from the four brick buildings of the factory there was one other to be seen—or part of one: the old monastery. Its roof, rising from among the trees on the other side of the river, was singled out each afternoon by the sun, and the mellow red flared among the unlit dark blue-green. When sometimes in the evening a wind or a stillness carried the sound of bells across the water people paused at their tasks, or their pleasures, listened as if trying to translate from some half-forgotten language. Women sighed, without knowing why, perhaps at an idea of pale, smooth-faced, black-robed men, dedicated, eyes uplifted.

Among the local men, as tales do, tales did go round, each addition to grow inevitably so lush that credulity was sacrificed and a new story begun.

To Emily the monastery's isolation was poetic, therefore admirable, and, too, it gave a kind of romantic focus to the valley which, in smoke-ringed Ballowra, was to be valued fiercely. Bearing the responsibility for all that was harsh and ugly she nevertheless most relievedly had this to offer Max as a symbol of something fine, as, inexplicably, a concrete symbol of her aspirations in regard to him, to the future, and to virtue in general.

Now she turned benevolent eyes from it and, ignoring the motor-road to the factory, climbed through the wire fence and glided down the hill.

Leaving his laboratory, Max waved and started to walk up to meet her. In a matter of seconds her flight neared its end.

'I'm going so fast I can't stop,' she shrieked, approaching with outstretched arms.

'Look out!' Deftly catching her, Max swung her sideways so that she collapsed laughing on the grass.

'We'd better sit down till you get your breath back.'

The vast sky of a vast unmisted land shone bright and hard in the light of the afternoon sun. The earth was warm. In the far, far distance, touching the sky, were some faint unknown hills or mountains.

Emily coughed, yawned and gasped for air while Max banged absent-mindedly at his pockets in a search for his cigarettes. He took off his coat, forgot what he had wanted, and stretched his arms lazily. He smiled at her. 'Well...?'

Frank, yet guarded, she halted in her pantomime to return his look. She looked at him stilly with a frank expression covering her face. 'Hullo.'

There was a pause. Max said, his voice touched with amusement or perplexity, 'What goes on in your head?'

Released, she smiled slowly, innocently, and said nothing.

'What's been happening today?' Max said. 'What did they have to say about your essay? And *what* are you looking so pleased about?'

She was enveloped in smiles. 'Just pleased,' she said and went on to tell him the events of the day.

They both breathed and yawned and looked at the sky. After a moment Max said, 'Oh, I heard from those college people again today.'

Emily felt a throb of jealousy. 'What did they want?' She looked from her shoes to his eyes, and turned to unsheath a pale round stem of grass with idle fingers. Looking back at him she bit the tender dark green segment of new grass. It tasted sweet.

'They liked that lecture I gave a few weeks ago. They asked me to do a series, but it would mean going along there most nights in the week so…'

Penetrated by the acuteness of Emily's listening silence he gradually slowed down and finally stopped altogether: she was desperately afraid.

Max was appalled by what he could feel of her strain. He went on, 'So, of course, I'm going to refuse. I have plenty to do.'

A single tear of relief eased all her fear. It made a dark stain on the lemon and white check of her dress. 'That's good,' she said, in a constricted voice.

'I suppose it is,' Max said heavily.

Dark swarms of men emerged all at once from doors at various points round the factory buildings less than half a mile below the spot where they sat: automatically they got to their feet and began to walk on.

'I would have hated it,' Emily admitted cheerfully, feeling nothing now that the danger was over, stripped of all the cramping reticence imposed by the emotion of the previous moment.

Max deliberately changed the subject and they kept up a facetious debate which petered out as they reached the fence and climbed through. Waiting for a bus to pass before they crossed the road, they stared at each other in silence.

'What's going to happen to you, Emmy?' Max asked at last, as if by hearing the words he might more easily arrive at an answer.

Thrown back on herself she looked at him in wonder, wondering what he meant. 'Me? When? Nothing. I don't know.'

They went quickly downhill. Approaching the house they saw, to Emily's displeasure and apprehension, that Patty stood at the corner waiting, her hand lifted in a tentative wave. With a terrifying smile Emily flapped back at her to signal that they were not on any account to be waylaid. Thankfully she saw that the message had been received and accepted; after a stationary moment of working-up, Patty skipped off in the other direction, her fair hair bobbing on her shoulders.

'Max? What's the matter? What did you mean up there when you said...?'

This evening had seemed the same as any other: she could examine every word of their conversation without finding one to account for this strangeness in him, this withdrawn, almost angry air about him.

She could not know that the reason lay in her own eyes, in the look she had turned on him, in the emanation of panic that sprang from her and sat between them like a ghost.

That petrified stillness and silence, that look in the unmoving eyes that said, 'I can't bear it if you go,' had been borne with a restraint completely adult; yet the abrupt change to youthfully naïve confession had been equally natural. Now that it was over she seemed protected from a knowledge of the duality of her response.

Max was assailed by weariness and doubt. Until tonight he had not seriously believed that any harm could come to her through him. While not underestimating her attachment because of her youth, he had imagined that what he gave in return was stuff of a kind likely to endure and benefit her after his going, that in the balance he did more good than harm. Yet the fact remained, he thought, that she had looked on his temporary absence from the house as if it were a prospect she could not endure. With others, he knew, she was often dramatic, but not with him, and what had happened this evening had been the opposite of the theatrical.

'Max?' she said.

As they walked along the back lane Lilian could be heard from the kitchen calling to someone in another part of the house. She made it possible for him to say, 'We'll talk about it later.'

But when he said that, Emily remembered what she had genuinely forgotten—that she had cried—and knew that a single tear had taught him what he had not known. But what? She had thought there was nothing he did not know about her.

A vague sensation of dread hung over her and would not disperse, she sensed, until she found a way of assuring him that whatever he had learned tonight was wrong.

'Here's the whole damn family!' cried Lilian.

Wearing a new black dress, her hands shining with diamond rings, supported by the drinks she had had with Billie during the afternoon, Lilian was feeling at her best. A certain quantity of alcohol brought out in her a kind of mellow fruitiness that was the nearest she ever came to any kind of charm. It had misled more persons than one.

'Come on,' she said with an arbitrary wave of her hand. 'I heard you coming so I got out more cups and saucers. Come in and keep me and Billie company till our old men arrive. We're off out to dinner tonight. *Yours*,' she said to Max, 'is in the oven.' Her tone was peculiarly familiar, implying an intimacy between them that had never existed.

Catching a tentacle stretched in the direction of Max, Emily looked at her from under level brows and silently warned her off, but Max, feeling it advisable to stop Lilian's humour from declining, said, 'Some tea would be just the shot!'

When he followed Emily into the shadowy sitting-room five minutes later the two women braced themselves in their chairs as if, in their black dresses and thin suede shoes, they had been challenged. Lilian widened her eyes and shot a significant glance at Billie as she introduced them.

Balancing one knee carefully on the other, Billie raised a hand to be shaken, and under the windows, in a corner of the sofa, seeming to survey the tea-leaves in her cup, Emily watched the swaying leg, the languid hand.

Billie, imposing her preconceptions on what she saw, saw a tall youthful man with a pleasant smile and a clever head. She saw a lonely man, lonely for Billie, and she said, 'Isn't Ballowra quiet after Melbourne? You should've been coming with us tonight. It's just a small party. We'd have found someone for him, Lilian, wouldn't we?' She laughed and was about to threaten that she would take him on, herself, and send Fred packing, when she looked in his eyes, and saw with an alarming diminution of confidence that she was being looked at. He seemed friendly enough, she could not have said why she wanted to wriggle.

With a resurgence of confidence Billie decided to take what she had seen as no more, and no less, than a considerable interest in herself. She began to talk more freely.

Lilian's smile grew stiff; she fussed over Max's tea, and planted herself in a chair between her friend and her boarder.

Obliged to answer Billie, Max responded with a conventionality that pleased Emily. It antagonized Lilian—for why was he so patient with her if not attracted?—and satisfied Billie.

Silent, as she was expected to be, Emily studied Billie Duncan. She was forty-five, an old friend of Lilian's, short, with a pale thick-skinned face, dark moist eyes and a prominent nose. The piercing soprano she raised at parties was understood to be her most prized asset, and had won her much applause. Emily did not like her.

Billie was saying, 'Yes, but aren't we dull for you after Melbourne? Don't you miss the night-clubs and the races and everything? All the shops and picture shows?' She hesitated coyly. 'And your friends?'

'I'm fairly used to moving about, the company sees to that. When the job came up here I hadn't much choice. Actually I wanted to come: Greenhills is near enough to being country to be a pleasant change.'

'Well, I don't know,' Billie said vaguely. 'My Fred shouted me a trip to Melbourne—by coach—two years ago. What a place it is! If he knew the half of it he'd want his money back this minute!' She gave a scream of laughter.

Emily's eyes skidded from Lilian to Max. That he was depressed, more than anything, she guessed, without understanding why. But having solved his reaction, she knew how to adjust her own.

'You think we're all country bumpkins,' Billie mused into her tea, interrupting a short innings of Lilian's. 'But I get all my clothes in Sydney, don't I, Lil?'

'That stuff,' Lilian looked at the bottles on the table, 'is stronger than you'd think.'

Max got slowly to his feet. 'Thanks for the tea, Lilian. I hope you have—'

'You must think it's funny,' Billie said, gazing moistly up at him, 'that I'm going out with my friend Fred, instead of hubby, but we don't get on, you see. Though we live in the same house we don't get on. He's not kind to me. Country bumpkins,' she said, sounding argumentative, 'can have their troubles, too.'

She seemed to expect an answer so Max said, 'They're not easy to avoid anywhere.'

'My God, that's true!' said Billie heavily. 'Too true. All alike. Country and town. Troubles, troubles.' She said to Lilian, 'I like Max. I don't know why you haven't made him come to some of our parties. I do think you're selfish.'

The irrelevance, to what had gone before, of the information about her friend's married life, made Lilian uncross her arms and beat a fist against her thigh in a movement of unbearable impatience. The experimental flirtatiousness she had tried in the kitchen was soured. Now, Billie's presence, her determination to win not only attention but admiration, suddenly freed her from the tangle of deference that hindered her dealings with Max. For being male and resisting her, for Billie's interest, hypothetical success and actual failure, she hated him. That he was not at once aware of it made her hate him more. Her eyes took on a glitter that heralded the provoking licence of which she was mistress.

To Billie she said, 'Shut up! You don't know what you're talking about. He's been asked often enough. He'd rather stay home with Emily.'

Billie rolled her eyes in amazement and turned in her chair to look at each of the strange creatures she all at once found herself with. 'Oh! Oh, I see.'

'They're always at their books or games,' Lilian said with a suddenly vicious smile.

Emily sat between fury and bewilderment. How the conversation had turned out like this was more than she could understand. But Max was not surprised. Domination was natural to Lilian. An attempt by her to overcome him had been inevitable from the first.

'We're dull company for you, Lilian, I quite agree. And I don't blame you for losing patience with me. On parties, people often do.'

And Billie, entirely discomposed by his composure, giggled and glanced at Lilian nervously.

Hearing the formal breaking-up, Emily left the sofa and walked slowly round the far side of the room to the door, already several minutes ahead to the time when, away from these extraordinary artificialities, real life might go on again.

As Max turned to go, Lilian leaned forward in her chair and held his eyes compellingly. She smiled and said to Billie, 'There's one thing I didn't tell you about Max. You two have a mutual friend—or had. Max used to be a very good friend of Thea's. You remember Thea who used to live here? She had the room he's in now. Isn't it funny?'

She had determined with an inflexible will that she would strike a hot reaction from him; if not passion—which was unthinkable between them—then anger, hurt, something. She would make him recognize her as a power. If he had behaved himself she might have let him alone, but he had to spoil himself, she thought. He had had to annoy her today. Well, he would see now, he would see. Like some insane despot she nodded her smiling head and watched his face.

At the sound of the name, at the revelation of this unknown connexion Emily stood hypnotized, stared at his back, her grandmother's face.

Powerless to have those words, the implications of tone and eye retracted, Max looked with numb curiosity—even with fascination—at the woman who revealed in herself so strong a desire to wound. He wondered, with part of his mind, what could be the matter with her.

Billie was wide-awake to innuendo. She said, 'Oh! So you knew Thea!' And her big dark eyes examined him with insolent freedom. 'I've often wondered what happened to her,' she said untruthfully. 'You don't know, I suppose?'

'I'm afraid not.'

Apart from the fact that his voice might have been heavier than usual, Lilian could detect very little reaction. There was certainly a frozen expressionlessness but that hardly amounted to the kind of success she had aimed at.

Baulked, she pressed her lips together in a tight little smile, and thought of saying, but merely thought: you'll know soon enough. I'll get you together, my friend.

Emily pushed against the wooden frame of the door, looked at the three still figures. 'Come on, Max,' she said in a small voice.

'Get out of here this minute,' Lilian said. 'And if you keep on interrupting grown-ups I'll just have to see you're sent where you won't bother us any more. There are reform schools for girls like you, you know.'

Emily's ears were hot. She closed her trembling lips and bitterly went up to the end of the hall to watch the door. She had wanted to help, that was all, to get Max out of the room. She had not meant to attach herself to him. Certainly she meant not to intercept him. He had not even turned when she spoke to him.

Like someone lost she stood and waited and tried to link those two names in her mind. Max and Thea. She could smell furniture polish, see a pale reflection of herself in dark wood. Suspended, she stared at, into, through it in an effort to find the face of Thea, her Thea of long ago, who now appeared to be Max's Thea as well. She stood like an image with the concentration of experiencing again all that she had heard and sensed in the past minutes.

That Max was vulnerable, that Lilian knew it, she had learned with despair. Reasons, reasons, lay complete inside her and she approached reluctantly.

With a swift movement she gave the bracelet on her wrist—Thea's bracelet—a violent tug, but it held firm and would not break. Max appeared in the hall and she jumped guiltily and moved back.

Out of sight of the women in the room he paused in the semi-darkness for a blind, distracted moment and then walked slowly to the back door and out of the house.

He'll never come back! Emily thought. Then, breathing again, she thought: his things, his books, *me*. And reassured that he would not desert she turned her head sharply, let her eyes roam blank and birdlike while she considered the justification for her next act, which was to run silently to the adjoining room and listen at the door.

Lilian was saying, 'No, what she said to me was that he and his wife were Catholics and couldn't divorce, but that was just because she didn't want me to know the truth.

Oh, she was sly. Do you know, I was in her flat once. Once, mind you. She never asked me, and I'm not a great one for visiting, anyway—but there you are.'

Billie made clicking noises with her tongue.

'Do you know I didn't even know he'd been living there with her till Mr Watts came and asked me to take him in.'

'How did you find out? Why didn't you tell me? This is a spicy bit of news to keep to yourself. I'm interested.'

That was the answer. Lilian had suspected that it would make Max too interesting, and, somehow, more accessible to Billie. Obscurely, for no reason she could think of, she had not wanted that to happen. Until today she had contrived that they should not meet.

'Well, you see, Watts tells me the name of this man who's to have the room, and I say, "I know that name," and he says, "Well, he was here a few years ago." So I said, "Did you know him?" (not letting on whether I did or not, you see) and he gave me a funny kind of smile and said, no, but he'd heard a bit about him from a few fellows who worked with him before. Then I said, "He used to be a good friend of a friend of mine," and I told him her name. Well, he *laughed*, he couldn't help himself, and when he saw I'd more or less been having him on, he laughed all the more. So then we had a little cup of tea and he told me all about it.'

'Men are worse gossips than women,' giggled Billie. 'But how did he know all this?'

'How's your tea? Cold? Well, this firm he's in seems to have plants and offices all over the place and these top men are always travelling round. Someone up from Melbourne told them about his wife, and they told him about what he'd been up to here.'

'Poor soul! His poor wife!' said Billie sanctimoniously. 'Sometimes I think hubbie'll do that to me, you know. Drive me right off my head.'

'*She* went of her own accord,' said Lilian pointedly.

After a moment Billie said, 'Imagine him going back to her, though. Why, do you suppose? She can't have been all that mad, can she?'

'Well, she is now,' Lilian said. 'Maybe she had money or something.'

'Ye-es,' Billie conceded that that was a point. 'Maybe, though, he found out he loved her best.'

'Ha!' was Lilian's comment, and Billie's chair squeaked as she dragged it closer.

'Well, what do you think?'

'I don't know. But he and Thea had this flat for two years—bold as brass. Watts said they just didn't care if people found out. Watts said that none of the people in the flats would speak to them. People won't put up with that kind of thing, you know.'

'No,' Billie said. 'Well, this is a decent town.'

'Great city folks, them!'

'But fancy you not knowing, Lilian, all that time.'

'How was I to know?' Lilian sounded huffed. 'After she left this house I saw her three times in two years. Once the day I went there, once when she came here, and the last time just before she left. She had Emily off for a few picnics or something—when he was away on business, I suppose.

But how was I to know? I don't know anyone who lives in town, and I don't suppose they went out much. Anyway I never saw them.'

There was a pause, then Billie said, 'You'd never think it to look at him, would you? You know that kind of distinguished...'

'She was secretive about it,' mused Lilian.

'I thought you said...'

'I don't like secretive people, do you?'

'Oh, no!'

A ruminative pause followed, during which they seemed to think it over, and try to decide at what point to pick it up again.

'Of course, I never liked her,' Billie confessed.

'No,' said Lilian, without expression.

'Of course, there was something about her! Though, I don't remember her very well...'

'Good eyes. Very good eyes...'

'Do you think he cared? Just now, I mean. When you said that.'

'He cared, all right.'

Lilian's manner became increasingly dry as the conversation progressed. It stimulated Billie and had the effect of preparing her for the climax towards which Lilian unconsciously worked.

Billie gave an agitated titter. 'Romantic, isn't it? Do you really think he still...?' Apparently in answer to a look from Lilian, she protested, 'But it was years ago. She must be married now. She must be getting on, too.'

'He's thirty-four. She must be about three or four years older.' Then very casually, 'And I can tell you another thing. Not married.'

Worked up to exactly the state of receptivity that Lilian demanded, Billie shrieked with anticipation. 'How do you know? You've got something up your sleeve, I can tell. Come on!'

It was clear that they were enjoying themselves.

'Wait till you hear! At first I thought I wouldn't, but today I just thought, what the hell!'

Here Lilian went off into a laugh which, as it prolonged itself, found competition in Billie's high giggle. Together they laughed till they were breathless. When Lilian could speak again it was, with renewed spasms of laughter, to compare Thea and Max to two characters in a dirty story.

The laughter rose again, and as it did, there slowly rose in Emily's heart an overwhelming wave of anger. She was submerged in bitter anger.

She got stiffly to her feet. Tears streamed unnoticed from her eyes. She stood looking at the door, bewildered by the intensity of her anger and disgust.

A last shout of laughter from the other room pierced the mass of undirected feeling that burdened her, and she kicked the door violently to make them stop.

'Shut up! Shut up! Shut up!' she screeched.

There was utter silence.

Sightless, weeping helplessly, she made for the front door, ran down the path, round the corner and up the hill. She climbed through the fence, in the hot light of the setting sun, and half fell, half ran, down the slippery deserted hillside she had lately climbed with Max.

'I didn't follow you! I didn't know you were here!' she gasped, affronted and defensive to come on Max at the river's edge.

An uneven line of trees and bushes had prevented her seeing him until it was too late to retreat. Now, hands tensely raised, she paused, the alertness of her pose suggesting that she might at any moment decide to turn and run back the way she had come. Yet she knew, through all the confusion of surprise and resentment, that she would not go: a marble pillar might more easily have uprooted itself and moved of its own volition than she.

She said, 'I didn't follow you!'

Max looked at her bright defiant eyes. 'All right. I believe you.' He took a few slow steps along the narrow path of trodden earth that ran parallel with, and two feet distant from, the edge of the river, towards the spot where Emily stood transfixed on the downward curve.

'Come down. What's wrong? Have you been in trouble?'

She felt herself shut off from him: she felt he scarcely saw her, but at his voice she dropped her hands, shook her head. 'No,' she said.

'Come down...' When she was silent in front of him, Max said, 'What's the matter, then?' But she twisted away and flung to the ground at the very edge of the river. She plucked restlessly at the long withered spikes of grass.

'Oh, Max, I hate them!' she cried, suddenly still. 'And you'll hate me now, too.'

He sat down beside her. He was neither pleased nor displeased by her accidental intrusion. Simply, there was an empty abstracted detachment in his manner that he could not shake off.

'Why should I hate you?' He heard his voice, hollow, rhetorical. 'Why should I? You'd better tell me what's happened.'

'I *listened*!' she sobbed. 'I listened at the door to hear what they were saying about you and Thea and everything.'

He was made weighty, concentrated, feeling, subject again to natural laws—an instantaneous transformation brought about by a word.

'Did you?' he said flatly. 'Well, I don't want to know what you heard. And, as it could have been nothing but—to say the least of it—ill-informed, I'd be glad if you'd try to forget it.'

But now that he was no longer looking at her, Emily got to her knees and hysterically addressed the side of his face.

'Be quiet! I don't want to hear. I don't *care* what they said.'

Voice and tears checked by his hostility, she stared at him for a moment, and then she burst out, '*I* do! They said horrible things. They laughed and laughed.'

Max gave a sigh and roughly rubbed a hand over his face. With the other he felt for Emily's head.

'Stop crying,' he said at last. 'You'll make yourself sick. Here—wait a minute—I think I've got a clean handkerchief somewhere.'

He gave it to her, and let his eyes rest on the sluggish dark-grey water in front of him. 'So they laughed...Well, why not?'

Emerging from the handkerchief, Emily, still on her knees, sat back on her legs and looked at him with blood-shot eyes. Her lashes stuck together in frail, damp clumps. It came to her in a sweeping wave of regret as she looked, and caught the echo of his words, that in order to relieve herself she had inadvertently done what Lilian could not do.

She put a hand on his shoulder and shook her head drearily as the tears started again. 'Oh, no, they didn't, Max. They didn't laugh. Truly, they didn't. Please, Max. They didn't.'

There was a pause. Beside her Max was thin, hunched up, drawn—in pain, because of what she had said. He seemed young, and dreadfully human, as easily hurt as she. Emily gave a little moan.

Trying to respond to the girl's abrupt attempt to undo the damage, and protect him, Max said in a brisk, automatic voice, 'No? Didn't they? Well, it doesn't matter.' Then he looked at her. 'Hey, what's this?' he said gently, catching her by the shoulders to prevent her lying face down on the grass in an abandonment of remorse. 'Stop it, Em, or I'll have to treat you like a little girl and give you a chocolate to make you behave.' He felt in his pockets and added, 'In fact, I would if I had one.'

Finding something, under his fingers he exclaimed, 'We're in luck. If you're good I'll give you something.'

'Oh, really!' Emily deprecated through her tears, smiling, embarrassed that he should carry out his threat. 'What is it?'

'A walnut, of all unlikely things.' Max held it between two fingers and gazed at it with vague pride.

'Oh, a walnut! Oh, really!' They both laughed.

'Where did you get it?' Emily asked, blowing her nose, laughing weakly.

'From whom, rather? The why still escapes me.' Max polished the shell on the sleeve of his coat. 'From that queen of the kitchen, Miss Dorothy Brown. Remember the cake?'

'The one that had the hole?'

'*This* should have been in it.'

He wandered away to crack it on a stone, and Emily, watching him, heaved a tremendous sigh in the direction of calm. She leaned over the low bank of the river and trailed a corn-coloured weed through the water.

But Thea, she thought darkly, feeling her heart pound. He loved Thea. More than me, more than me. She was grown-up. They lived alone together.

Calmly and deliberately she undid with her right hand the thin gold bracelet on her left wrist. Had it ever been undone before? No matter, the catch worked smoothly. She held it in her right hand, swiftly glanced over her shoulder, turned again to the river and dropped it in with a little smile of triumph.

Triumph? It dropped from her fingers so willingly, unprotesting; its shining length now made a hummock of gold on the river bed, sank into the river mud.

She felt it was her heart she had thrown away. She felt she had vomited her heart out through her mouth into the river.

'What's the matter?' came Max's voice.

'Oh!' She lay back on her elbows, sat up and touched her head. 'Nothing. Nothing. I felt a bit dizzy...I leaned over too long.' Silently, to the river, or *something*, she apologized: I'm *sorry*...I didn't mean to...I didn't know...

'Sit still for a moment. You'll soon feel better. Look! Eat this up and you'll be as good as new.' He smiled at her averted face, rallying her.

Limply she took the shell. Her hands felt powerless to lift the kernel out, to so much as support its weight. She had no breath. She was conscious of having sinned, of irreparable loss.

'I'm eating mine,' Max said, trying to make her smile by keeping up the pretence that she was a child.

Her hand went obediently to her mouth and she nibbled at the nut like an exhausted mouse: she held it to her lips to satisfy and silence the voice that talked to her.

She endured the curious, hollow sensation in head and chest, and thought: I did it myself. She had damaged the root of her earliest memories of good. She had forsworn an old idol: one from whom she had received benefits, to whom she had given affection. And she herself had become lighter, of less value, the victim of a small self-murder.

With a new direction of vision opened up by pain and experience she understood for the first time that it was she who had by far the greatest power to damage herself.

She sighed profoundly and looked at Max: he said, 'I think we ought to go. It's getting dark.'

He put an arm round her to help her up the hill and she leaned against him, silent and tired. But when he began to speak she moved carefully away and trudged beside but at a small distance from him.

'When Lilian and her friend talked this afternoon they probably meant no harm. What they said can have no effect on anyone they mentioned, but the thing is...Do you remember Thea?'

'Yes.'

He hesitated, then said, 'It may be wrong to involve you further but I think, as you know so much, that you ought to know the truth.'

Briefly, dryly, he told her the facts.

When he first came to Ballowra he had been legally married for four years—though, in fact, less than four months. His wife, Irene, disappeared as she had—he then learned for the first time—after an earlier marriage which had been annulled.

He saw her before she left for a trip abroad to discuss arrangements for a separation, but for various reasons, he said, among them his own reluctance—at that time—to have the subject debated at length, nothing was done. His wife was indifferent.

She came back from her prolonged stay in England shortly before Max left for Ballowra the first time, and they met again. She looked ill. He thought she had been taking drugs. This time it was she who spoke of divorce. She wanted to remarry, but her prospective husband was too prominent, she said—in what sphere Max never learned—to marry a divorced woman. She, she insisted, must be the innocent party. She would start the proceedings at once. Max agreed, and left for Ballowra.

The following day he met Thea. Adult, intelligent, feeling, the opposite of frivolous and yet not earnest, she was the opposite of the popular ideal of her place and time. Then and there, in the cities, great wealth masked a naïvety one would hesitate to call childlike. A contradictory striving after perpetual adolescence, sophistication and an accumulation of wealth were the motives of action. The chief conviction was one of superiority; this was brought about by the Pacific isolation of the continent, and, contrariwise, by trips to a Europe where all the famous treasures were old and frequently dirty, where there were peasants, and the city-dwellers were peculiarly poor. What the fuss was about Europe few Australians could imagine. Not all of them believed in its existence.

To be one of the self-critical minority was to be not so much politically unsound—for there was very little, it seemed, to be political *about*—as thoroughly, disagreeably, un-Australian.

Two members of the small minority, meeting, could not easily part without a promise of further meetings, letters, communication. The opportunity was rare.

For *these* two, only together, it seemed, were they able, for the first time in their lives, to be completely themselves. To share a common attitude, for them uncommon, was to be led to a love from which, once acknowledged, no retraction was possible. Aware of this, they hesitated, and until the letter came from Irene's sister, Christine, eight weeks after Max's arrival in Ballowra, nothing was said.

That day Max showed the letter to Thea at lunch-time, sitting by the river, not far from the place where he and Emily had talked.

The day was cloudy and windless. The river was grey, the grass straggling on to the path cold round their ankles. Seeming to create and stand in their own shade the tattered gumtrees were dark and still.

Thea read. The letter was short. Irene's friend, it said, had learned something about her past, discovered that she was taking drugs and broken off the relationship. She had attempted suicide, and was at present in hospital under treatment. Bartlett, Irene's lawyer, had suspended work on the case. There was no possibility of anything further being done while Irene was in her present state. 'For your sake,' the letter ended, 'I'm sorry about all this.'

After a long silence Max said, 'She didn't like her sister.'

They looked at each other, and a shock of profound physical dismay bleached Thea's face. The final admission of love cannot be without shock, and melancholy for the past. She said automatically, 'Why not?'

'Irene tried to break up her marriage.' He paused, and they were speechless, seeming almost wearied by precognition of all that must be said, once silence was broken, before they could again simply look, simply know; wondering perhaps if so much as that would again be possible. They stared at each other.

It was thus, after two months, that their first day as lovers began.

Towards the end of two years, when they were making plans to return to Melbourne, Max had a letter from the doctor who had been treating Irene. He knew the past history of their marriage, he said, but believed that his patient repented her behaviour, and was sure that, if she was given the opportunity to prove this, and to take up a normal life with her husband again, her chances of being restored to full mental and physical health would be incalculably greater than they at present were. She had expressed her willingness, even anxiety, to be allowed to join him.

The letter had a bare dry look about it, as if it had been sent out as a circular many times. There was the feeling that, turned over, it might reveal its purpose in a single line: Use Our Matt White Paper, followed by a list of sizes and prices. A machine, not a man, had dictated that bald, bland ultimatum.

Dead-white, Thea said, 'No one has the right to ask that. It's brutally unfair.'

'Considering the facts, it's grotesque. I'll refuse, of course; I don't know what he can have been thinking about to suggest it.'

They moved slowly together. They looked at each other a long time in silence, destitute, dry.

For days it kept them strained and silent. Then one night Max said, 'I can't believe that it's the only way she could be helped. To him, it's no more than an experiment. If it failed he would have to think of something else. It was purely accidental, I suppose, that he thought of this.'

Tonelessly, Thea said, 'If we parted...even if we parted we would bear it somehow. In some curious way it's that that makes me most despair. I don't want to be tried. I want what we had.'

'Why do you say "if", Thea? There's no question of it.' Urgently Max stared into her face. He touched her cheek and she closed her eyes. Presently she said, 'We both know so well, don't we, my darling? What did he say? A mind. A life. Whose doesn't matter, does it? That we don't care doesn't matter either. The strength of my not caring amounts to a passion. I don't believe in self-sacrifice...And yet...'

In the end Thea left two days before Max was due to go to Melbourne, and it was over. With heavy, numbed incredulity they parted, scarcely aware, at the very last, of the rending of heart and spirit. Helpless as lead figures in the sun they watched the separation of the indivisible and felt nothing.

The doctor's experiment failed, but not conclusively for eighteen months. During that time Max, his wife, and her nurse lived in an atmosphere of hospitalized isolation. Life became a mechanical routine; a circular pantomime through which the characters, ground very small, drifted painlessly.

When a series of relapses took Irene to a mental hospital Max did not write to Thea to tell her, and risk smashing, perhaps to no purpose, whatever calm she had found for herself. In watching the weak, ineffectual struggle for sanity, he had not been unmoved, but he was drained, hardened by the effect on his own life, and Thea's. As he was, he would not approach her.

A further eighteen months of rigid adherence to a programme of work that left time for nothing else ended in his return to Ballowra. He had expected never to be there again, but he accepted the necessity, and later bowed to the irony of Watt's choice of a dwelling-place. It seemed that whether he would or no the dark tunnel of the past three years had ended.

Some of these facts he now related to Emily.

Her over-taxed spirit plunged to exaggerated depths of pride and humility at this proof of his confidence. She could have wept with gratitude. Inside her head, slowly, with the threat of added momentum, a merry-go-round of sensation began to lurch and turn. His words seemed to make the ears that heard them ache with pity. She had never loved him so much. For Max's Thea she *would* feel a kind of exalted admiration and compassion; for her own—there was still a deadness, a breathlessness at the centre, as if she had not yet recovered from shock; the body falling from the cliff, the irretrievable loss, the error, the sin impossible to undo.

When Max had finished speaking they walked on in occupied silence. Once he looked at her in a reverie, seeing her not as herself but as someone who had known Thea. When, caught by his concentration, she glanced round inquiringly, he realized his fatuousness and was disgusted.

He remembered how, earlier in the evening, his concern had been for the danger to which he might unintentionally have exposed Emily, and could have smiled, for it had become apparent since then, in his reaction to Lilian's gossip, what effect his efforts to bring her into touch with life had had on his own life. Emotions moved, however lightly, attitudes rethought, stirred memories, and that almost comfortable resignation that had been his chief support was suddenly seen to be in jeopardy.

Comfortable resignation. He looked at the idea of it. It had not always been that, but the change had been slow and subtle, worked in him secretly. Now the metamorphosis was complete, surprising, disagreeable.

Emily's blue eyes scanned his abstracted face. The silence had been long, long, long. If she spoke now, said something striking to catch his attention back from—back to herself, it would surely not be indelicate?

Her censor left the question unanswered, and when she spoke it was with an artificial force that made her sound everything she wanted not to be—insincere, childish, coy, lacking in understanding.

'Oh, I *hate* them!' she cried emphatically, leaping under the fence, looking back to see what Max made of this declaration. 'When they said something awful at the end I said, "Shut up! Shut up! Shut up!" and kicked the door.'

She smiled at him but a twinge of fright made her shiver at the sound of her own voice. What had been spontaneous, became with re-telling shoddy and self-conscious.

Max fought down a sense of alienation and said, 'None of it's your fault. I know. You did it for me. Don't worry.'

The house was empty and in darkness. Max switched on the light and Emily looked in the oven to see what was for dinner.

'A casserole,' she announced, and began to set the table.

Feeling that something ought to be said about her fervent declaration of hatred for Lilian, Max contrived during dinner to establish a list of positive and negative virtues which Lilian could be said to possess. Emily listened to him obediently and seemed literally to take over his views:

in any case, with each nod of her head his own conviction of Lilian's worth diminished.

Pointing out one of the many instances of Lilian's quite genuine generosity—a handsome gift of money to Dotty's mother when she was recently ill—as final and conclusive evidence for the defence, he wound up. It had been a tasteless, even farcical conversation, but he felt constrained to convince the girl that there was reason to respect the woman with whom she might yet have to spend years of her life.

Emily turned with some relief from the burned saucepan whose interior she had been studying and said with serious, almost technical interest, 'But is that so important? Money?'

'Very, when you haven't got it. Mrs Brown could tell you just how important, I don't doubt,' Max said, feeling atrocious. 'But right now all *I'm* trying to tell you is not to go round saying or thinking that you hate people. You don't at all, and it's not a particularly good habit of mind to get into.'

Emily was meek. Perceiving that Max was not angry with her, simply trying to improve her, she was happy. They went to the sitting-room and sat listening to music.

Doubting if his lecture had had any effect, doubting its veracity, Max wandered off into a maze of speculation. What place should any action, unaccompanied by a degree of feeling, have in an absolute scale of values? he wondered, thinking of the charity of an organization, of necessity acceptable, of necessity impersonal and nourishing as a rock. And then Lilian's generosity had to be seen beside her 'easy come, easy go' attitude to money, beside her total incapacity to understand, and complete indifference to, the mental suffering she induced in others.

For Dotty's mother, Mrs Brown, he realized that such questions would have no meaning. Her urgent appeal for a loan had been met by a gift and that was that. No other solution would have been so immediately beneficial, no amount of feeling have been adequate substitute, or seemed in the moment of need so admirable.

The difference between their points of view might be merely, he thought, that she had been the object of Lilian's generosity, and he, tonight, of its opposite.

How unsurprising, how very much to be expected it was, he thought, that he should adopt the standpoint of the ideal and use it as a platform from which to illustrate, albeit to himself, Lilian's shortcomings, and that Mrs Brown, the beneficiary, should praise and admire. Or did she entirely? The antipathy felt by receivers for givers was as old as history.

But he knew the whole premise was false. It was no subjective reaction to a single event in which he himself was directly implicated that had shaped his opinion of Lilian, or his definition of good.

Feeling and motive, he believed, could not be over-estimated. Tonight, though, for valid feeling and motive, he had had, by implication, to depreciate both to Emily.

Yet, he was aware that she had taken his lecture lightly enough. He could not pretend he had done any damage by, for once, saying less and more than he thought true. His concern seemed disproportionate. He knew it was.

He knew that he was pedantically occupying, and continue to occupy, himself with every implication of the evening's scene—moral, metaphysical, sociological, psychological—that he would consider the effect on Emily, on Lilians relations with her, on his own with Lilian; that, in short, he would do anything to postpone that inevitable flooding of his consciousness by the futile, insistent desire that the catastrophic emptiness of the past years should not be allowed to continue into the future.

From the bedrock of resignation—and there seemed no other vantage point from which to view the universe—it was possible, he believed, to live a life of dignity; even, for individuals to establish a sphere of order, and to extract great happiness from it, open-eyed, in the face of all. But not alone. Solitary resignation, circles and chimes of utter loneliness: to be alone…

The thing was—and it came on him savagely—where was *she*? What was *she* thinking? What changes had taken place in *her* life?

It was inconceivable that he did not know.

'What do you want to play next, Max?'

The music had stopped. Emily, her head on the dark table beside the gramophone, looked up. Another record was substituted and the music began again.

What a horrible, and kind of wonderful day it had been, she thought. And how strange it was, what she had learned. Oh, Max, you're awfully quiet, she silently said, gazing at the table between her arms. Don't be different! Don't think about what I said! Don't think about her! Don't love her more than me! Don't wish I wasn't here!

The music swelled, washed through the big dull room, over its pale walls and dark furniture out through the open windows into the black oblongs of night.

That day of upsets was followed by calm. The episode was not mentioned by Lilian to Emily or Max, nor did they discuss it with one another.

And while Emily's days were occupied by Max, mathematics, syntax, Shakespeare, French and picnics at the beach, Lilian passed her time with a small amount of housework, many cups of tea with Dotty, much gossip, sufficient alcohol, and more than enough Rosen. She tried in a thousand ways to use that surplus energy which was at the same time her greatest attraction and her greatest defect.

She had not abandoned her plan to get Thea to the house, but it lay in abeyance: she was dimly conscious that it was there to be brought out on a boring day to provide entertainment. She thought of it as someone else might have thought of a sketching block in a cupboard.

At night she and Rosen were never apart. Whether they stayed home and read or played cards, or went driving through flat familiar streets in search of novel sights and a change of temperature, whether they joined up with Billie and the rest of their friends for a party, Rosen was always beside her. He was her tame bear and she treated him with condescension.

With everyone else Rosen was pompous and haughty. He hated Max, whom he could not reasonably regard as a rival or usurper, but whose presence in the house he believed acted as a hindrance to his aims.

His presence acted, in fact, in precisely the way that Lilian had hoped. It gave an air of respectability to the arrangement of her household; it annoyed Rosen; it relieved her of all thought of Emily and bore possibilities of future amusement. No, it was really *more* than she had hoped.

Her relations with Rosen were at this time equivocal. Would he or would he not ask his wife for a divorce? His wife wanted him back, but Lilian knew what *he* wanted. Wouldn't she say the word? He didn't want to go to all the trouble and expense if she'd made up her mind against it.

Lilian taunted him happily, saying that she could understand that he wanted to tie himself to her. She was a moderately wealthy woman; she would be quite a catch for him, wouldn't she? If he could catch her. But he was no particular asset. What did he think he had that made it worth her while to be stuck with him for life? Say one thing. One thing.

Wanting to cry, Rosen said nothing.

CHAPTER SIX

'I KNEW! I knew!' Billie's head came round the door and she gave a little scream of laughter. 'Lilian said, "They'll be away for a walk or something," but I guessed you'd be here. This is Fred. See, they're playing ping-pong, Fred.'

Fred came in after her and grinned sheepishly at Emily, half raising a hand in salute. To Max he gave a wary nod. 'Yeah,' he said slowly, staring at the table, net, bats, and ball with apparent absorption.

'Here we are,' Max agreed, not sounding amused. 'Were you looking for us?'

He waited with an air of tolerant curiosity to hear why they were sought out, while Emily, after an indecisive moment spent watching the spangled apparition leaning against the solid Fred, commenced to bounce the ball up and down, obviously waiting for them to go.

Billie turned from Max delightedly, seeming not to hear, and looked up at Fred as if to say, 'What did I tell you?'

But she said, 'There's a party on tonight. I said to Lilian if we had her birthday party at home you couldn't get out of coming, so you're caught.'

'Lilian's birthday? I didn't know that. In that case I—'

He was not allowed to finish. Running up to him, Billie grabbed his arm with drunken determination. 'No! You're coming whether you like it or not.' Laughing and gasping she clung to his arm. She smelled disagreeably of wine and cheap cosmetics.

Fred and Emily exchanged a look and he advanced a step or two. 'Aw, let him alone, Billie, if he doesn't want to come.'

'He's got to,' she panted. 'Come and give me a hand with him or I'll yell for the others to come out and help.'

Max detached himself from her, but like a child who will not allow the game to end, Billie put her arms around his waist and, bending double, tried to tug him from the garage by force.

In the hard shadows cast by the single unshaded light over the table, the tussle looked grotesque: the neutral colours of the men, the rough blackish walls against which leaned two bicycles, the dark vacancy at the far end, normally filled by the car, the waxy wood of the long table, Billie's lilac silk back, dark head, and spangled stole.

Max removed her to arm's length where she elected to stay, submissive and arch.

'If you give us ten minutes to finish the game, I'll come in to see how the party's getting on,' he said, and Fred, rightly taking this as directed at him, led Billie backwards by the elbow to the door. 'Oke!' he said.

Convinced of her success, Billie tilted her white face at a provocative angle. 'I'll be watching for you, Max.' She was unaware of the cruelly unflattering light: the three who listened were made despondent by her confidence.

Max signalled his agreement and Fred apologetically turned her round and led her down the three cement steps to the path, and back to the house.

'Oh!' Emily groaned, leaned over the table and dealt it several sharp nervous raps with her bat. Her head still down, she turned to look at Max.

'What was the score?' he said, smiling faintly.

Ten seconds later, searching behind a bicycle for the ball, he said, 'I didn't know it was Lilian's birthday?'

'It isn't,' Emily said. '*She* made it up.'

In the sitting-room were assembled about twenty-six people. Most of the furniture had been removed; what was left—chairs and sofas and a small table or two—was pushed against the walls. The gramophone played; everyone was moving, talking, waving glasses, reflected three times over in the mirrors so that the room seemed grossly overcrowded.

Lilian's voice rang out above the others, over the music, cheerfully inciting her guests to all manner of reasonable excess. That there was more to a successful party than a large number of bottles was an idea conceived by very few of those present—certainly not by Lilian—and she responded with a blank whoop of laughter when Gladys said, 'You're in great form tonight, Lilian!'

Fortyish, a hairdresser who had lived in the city, Gladys was known as a hard case. Self-conscious in a way that was unusual for a member of Lilian's circle, Gladys was able, when she chose, to manipulate the impulses of her friends into patterns as intricate as those her fingers created on the violet, copper red, and white blonde heads that Emily now gazed at from the door.

Seeing Max come in, Rosen nudged Lilian. 'What's *he* want?'

'A drink!' she said, with a soft flash of menace. 'Go and get him one!'

But before he could make his way across the room, Billie and Fred had hailed Max and taken him off to their corner. Emily stood by the gramophone and watched it all unblinking.

The din was now so great that—as if it were caused by some external natural force—everyone had to shout to be heard above it. Della Griffiths sat sobbing noisily in an armchair by the windows. On the sofa, Gladys and her friend Jack were in a tight, and, as it were, explanatory embrace from which they disengaged themselves to make a point to the couple who stood over them, and then resumed. Rosen had dropped a plate of potato crisps on the floor and was in disgrace.

After fifteen minutes, Max started to work his way across to the door; and as he reached it, caught a story, coming from a group of men, which it was impossible that Emily should not have heard.

She followed him down the hall to the kitchen.

'I always went to these parties before you came,' she said, before he could reprove her.

'So I believe. Tonight, though, I asked you not to come.' He sat down at the table and abstractedly fingered some of the papers he had brought home.

Emily pulled roughly at the bobbles on the table-cloth and gulped back her tears, cast down as much as anything by the knowledge that it was her youth that occupied him.

She wanted to explain to him how accustomed she was to most of the things he minded; how drunkenness, occasional violence, smutty jokes, biliousness and hard-breathing demonstrations of what was alleged to be love had been part of the common scene all her life; how she watched it with scorn and boredom if she watched it at all.

'I'm sorry,' she mumbled, then looking up, leaning her cheek on her fist she added, 'But it was just an old party. I don't take any notice. They're all mad.'

Clearly this had not been the right thing to say, but a speechless look that asked forgiveness for whatever it was that was wrong made Max say dryly, 'All right, all right. Now what about some work?'

After lighting his pipe he took out his pen and wrote steadily, covering long sheets of paper, while Emily went over history dates for a term examination due to start in two days' time.

The door from the hall was closed but even so, subdued explosions of sound penetrated from the other room and occasionally someone new to the house would blunder in in search of the bathroom, the end of a laugh still hanging to his face. A stagger of surprise at the unexpected studiousness of the scene, a prolonged explanation of how he had come to open the wrong door, an apology, and then he would lurch out and turn in farther up the hall.

At eleven o'clock Rosen put his head round the door and called Emily out.

'What do you want?'

'Listen!' He leaned over her and breathed spirits in her face. 'We're all going out soon, and you're to go to bed, but not in the front room. You're to sleep in the dining-room.'

'Who says? Does *she* say so?' It was some time since she had been turned out for the night and Emily fixed him with a suspicious stare.

'Yes, yes, Lilian says so,' he said hurriedly, glancing over his shoulder. The noise of the party seemed to make him nervous. He started to go away. 'Now don't forget. The dining-room.'

'I'll ask her myself,' Emily tested him.

He came slowly back. 'You'll do what I say, you little—'

'What's the matter?' Max appeared at the door.

No one answered.

'You should've been off to bed before this, Em. It's late.' She went at once. 'No, don't go away, Rosen. I want to talk to you for a minute. Come in here.'

With the patient, exasperated air of one humouring a lunatic, Rosen followed him. He folded his arms. 'Well?'

'I heard what you told her.'

'Well, what about it? What the hell's it got to do with you?'

'Nothing. What's between you and Lilian is entirely your own affair. My complaint is that you involve Emily. Damn it all, Rosen, she's only a kid. You ought to be able to arrange things without that.'

The older man's face turned a purplish-red. He sputtered, took a step forward. His loose, undefined lips opened and shut. 'What's it to do with her?' he blustered. 'What's it matter to her if she's all that innocent?'

Max stared at him in silence. Eventually he said, 'Did Lilian ask you to tell her?'

He was answered by a change of colour and clenched fists.

'I thought not.'

'Do you think she hasn't?' Rosen sneered, smiling, raising his eyebrows. 'You're making a mistake if you think that, you bloody Boy Scout. She's been moved a few times without your permission, I can tell you that.'

Max regarded him through narrowed inscrutable eyes. 'It seems an extraordinary arrangement from everyone's point of view. It can hardly be satisfactory.'

'Huh!' Rosen muttered gloomily. 'You don't know Lilian!' After this confession of weakness he moved closer to Max, and with the drunken necessity to emphasize speech by physical contact, poked at his shoulder with a plump forefinger. Max stood impassive. 'Have it your own way. Go on, go on! Don't think it'll make any difference to me. Tell your little friend to stay in her own bloody little bed. That's fine. That's all right. But just take a bit of advice, Mr Max. Find yourself somewhere else to live. I've got a feeling you won't be here much longer. I can do *some* things with Lilian, you know.'

When, with many backward glances and muttered threats, he had taken himself from the room, Max went outside to get some air. The noise of the party spilled out through the windows. He was angry.

There was an unhealthy pervasive quality—almost viciousness—in Lilian's relations with Rosen; in the inconsistency of her attitude, and in the feeble, constant pressure of his. They made the climate of the house too close, too strained, too charged.

If Emily's presence was considered at all in respect to the situation between them it was by Lilian, as useful, adding to the tension, by Rosen as obstructing.

Truly she was the responsibility, primarily, of her parents, but, having agreed to accept the charge, Lilian rendered herself liable to criticism if she neglected to provide a minimum of attention.

Liable to criticism from whom? Max asked himself. Not, apparently, Paula or Harry Lawrence. Not Rosen or Dotty or Billie. According to their standards Lilian did very well indeed. Emily was housed, fed, and clothed; she was not expected to do housework; she was allowed to go three times a week to the pictures and had done so, before he came. She was irregularly given by Lilian some pound notes or a pile of silver. Witnesses at these ceremonies, without moving their too-bright eyes from the pile of money in the girl's hand, exclaimed on Lilian's generosity, Emily's luck. Very soon. 'She's lucky' was 'She's spoilt'.

What did it all prove except that their standards were not his? If they had looked after her in *any* respect, he thought, he might have found their reasoning easier to follow. But it was...it was as if, being young, her connexion with the human race was very simply discounted.

No external excuse, no lack of this or that fine feeling could be counted as justification. Nothing could undo the harm these casual people had done. Yet, Max argued, they were themselves and lived as they could, and had not been wisely treated either, very likely.

It made no difference. Tonight he could not convince himself that they mattered so much—not so much as Emily. It was not possible that they had ever been what Emily was, or that she would grow to be what they now were. The principle of equal rights was denied before birth when the limits of capacity and human quality were set differently for each separate being. If, following that line of reasoning, no one was to be blamed for his behaviour, and impartial justice to be administered according to the capacity and quality of the individual, why was there the implacable sense of outrage, of deep dismay and reprobation when pain was inflicted unthinkingly? It was too easy to exempt from responsibility those who felt no responsibility for their actions. Too easy, reductive, wrong.

Remembering the scene in the kitchen his anger stirred again. He was aware that Emily saw the loveless tension between the two; that she accepted it calmly in no way exonerated them in his eyes. He knew that she had little time and few thoughts to spare for Lilian and Rosen now, whatever it had been like in the past. What troubled him was the knowledge that the present was the interlude, and the past and future the bulk of her life.

Slowly he climbed the steps up to the veranda, and passed across it, disturbing an amorous couple.

Knocking at Emily's door, he said good night and told her to stay where she was.

A week later, on the way back from the hotel, Rosen had stopped the car, the better to answer Lilian. Now, in spite of her repeated requests that he should take her home, he sat stubbornly clutching the powerless wheel, monotonously asking, 'But why? Why? What have I done? What's wrong?'

Through the grey stormy evening light Lilian looked at him with detestation, tightly crossed her arms, clenched her teeth and after a sharp breath of exasperation said, 'Because you're a great loafing bastard, that's why! You've had all the gold watches and signet rings and suits you're going to get. You've just been a bit too damned smart once too often. Making up to her in *my* house! Talking big to *my* friends! Feeling so grand in all the things I've given you! Trying to tell me what I should do!' She shook her head and snorted with irritation. 'Well, you've made a mistake.'

Rosen blew his nose and she smiled. He said, 'I've told you I was only having a friendly conversation with Glad. Don't talk to me like this, Lilian. I've helped you, too. Be fair to me, Lilian.'

She gave a contemptuous laugh and looked consideringly at his fleshy, U-shaped face, the pale mournful eyes, and bald shiny head across which a few strands of gingery hair were draped in parallel lines. 'Remember the night you came to my door with your case? "Please let me stay. I've left my wife. I'll be good to you. Just to be near a woman like you would make a new man of me." Then you had a little cry, didn't you?'

Even by Lilian, Rosen's protest was felt across the narrow space that separated them and she stopped.

'Oh, Lilian!' He blew his nose again noisily and long.

'You've helped me, did you say? When? How? What could someone like you do for me?'

He was silent, so she turned away and glared through the open car-window at the park by whose side they had stopped. A row of dusty palm trees looking like overgrown pineapples enclosed the rapidly darkening square of grass. It was the only park in Greenhills and Lilian had never been in it; its sterile attractions were—even to inexperienced eyes—so far from what might be expected in a park that it was shunned. Children preferred to play in wide cement storm-water channels and lovers to find back-lanes, quiet beaches.

'Well? Can't you remember?' she asked too pleasantly. Politely she waited. 'No! Because you've done nothing for me but take. You're good enough at that, all right.'

'Presents, Lilian! I didn't ask—'

'You didn't ask! You didn't say no! Oh, I know, I know all about you. I've heard about the way you go on at your office telling them all what an important fellow you are. Showing off the things I've given you.'

'It's not true. Who said so? I swear to God—'

'Oh, what do you know about God, you baldy old heathen! Swear your head off for all I care. I said you're to go, and go you will, right out of my house.'

Rosen's oyster-eyes overflowed. The street lights came on and flashed on the tears, on Lilian's diamonds and her yellow hair, and as if moved by the same switch her finger came up to point at his face and she gave a squawk. 'Ha! Look at that! Ha!' She stayed for a moment silent, her hands clasped at a level with her throat, her mouth twisted ironically.

It seemed that nothing could provoke Rosen to retaliate. Solemn, almost dignified, he removed his spectacles and wiped his eyes. With painstaking care he readjusted the thin gold wires over his ears. He sighed. 'You can be very cruel. You know how to hurt a man.'

'Man!'

A group of anonymous figures passed along the footpath close to Lilian, hurrying because of the cold wind and threatening black sky. She screwed up the window and lost some of her zest for the game. God, you'd think it was winter, she thought. She suddenly longed for the cosy fire, a cup of tea and a salmon sandwich.

'If you don't take me home this instant I'll call a policeman and have you arrested,' she said through her teeth. 'And don't think I couldn't do it!'

He did not for a moment doubt her powers. The car slid out into the road.

One night some weeks ago Rosen had worked overtime and Lilian had gone to a party by herself. There she met for the third or fourth time the cheery, gossipy, portly Mr Watts who had told her about Max. Since then she had seen him frequently, though not alone, and while there was nothing between them except a certain complicity which was the responsibility of their eyes Lilian knew there was more to come. It was inevitable. She would never marry Rosen. He bored her. If he had not been so soft he would have forced a decision from her long before this. But where was the man who could force her to anything? His grievous absence from her life, the lack of that hard hand and will inspired Lilian to ride over her own and other lives with the mindless destructiveness of a hurricane. Whoever the superman was, or was to be, it was not Rosen.

Financially he had done well. Even emotionally—for he was a man born to be dominated by a woman—his wants had been satisfied. And his wife would take him back.

Feeling her temper desert her, Lilian guessed that this would not be the show-down. He would not go this time, nor, when she thought it over, did she wish it. With her mind firmly settled she could have a little fun with him before the end, and then, some visible competition would do that jolly Mr Watts with his wicked brown eyes no harm at all. He was a bit of a hard doer, Mr Watts.

Rosen, who had been following his own thoughts, went morosely behind her into the quiet house. He had it all worked out. He knew who it was he had to blame for this. He had had back there a moment ago a sickening vision of Max wearing his new gold watch. Lilian would never let him take it away, back to his wife. It was far too expensive. But his suits, made by the best tailor in Ballowra—she couldn't keep them? He was broader all over than Max.

Yes, that must have been what happened. Max had talked to Lilian and got her worked up about decency and Emily and God only knew what. After all, she was impressionable; she was only a woman, full of fits and fancies. Oh, he would not believe she meant what she said. Spurred at the thought of all he stood to lose, he lumbered quickly after her. She was trailing through the house, calling instructions to him, switching on lights, leaving her scarf in the hall, her coat in the sitting-room, her handbag in the kitchen.

There, catching her, he chanced a reproachful expression, seeing that, anyway, her grey eyes were no longer hard, but mild and blank. She had quite abandoned her fiery mood. He was reassured, and smiled at her sheepishly. Her new look must mean apology. In fact, Lilian thought about salmon sandwiches. She filled the kettle.

'Where's Emily?' Rosen asked, inspired.

This was so unusual a query as to cause Lilian to turn right round to see what he meant.

'What do you mean?' She held the tin-opener poised.

'I asked if you knew where Emily was,' he repeated, with visible patience.

Lilian looked at him, turned back to the table. 'She's out with Max, I suppose.'

Behind her back Rosen mimed his sad concern at this news. He cleared his throat. 'I don't like all this business.'

Lilian had just dropped the salmon into a bowl. Now she turned with a rather more incredulous expression on her face. 'All *what* business?' she demanded. 'What are you talking about?'

'Lilian...' Suspecting that this was one time when he might safely play the master, he waved an authoritative finger at her, and sure enough, she responded, came over to him, heavy and erect in her smart blue dress. 'Well?'

‘I know I’m no relation—it’s nothing to do with me—but I tell you I don’t like the way Max hangs round her. Emily. That’s all.’

‘*What*? ‘Lilian screwed up her face and waited for patience. It did not come. ‘The way Max hangs around her! Oh, you’re—’

Rosen had expected this reaction, and was consequently so calm that Lilian halted. He gestured again to establish his probity. ‘All I say is, have you ever asked yourself why? He could be her father, but they’re never apart. It’s not natural. What does he want?’

Lilian was transfixed. When she was able, she gave him a look that was infinitely withering. With the quietness of exhaustion and pity, she said, ‘Don’t be so bloody silly. “What does he want?” What in hell’s name do you think he wants? Ask him yourself what he wants. My God, if he’s queer, so are you. You’re a good pair.’

Trying to cover his chagrin with an air of righteousness and impartiality, he said, ‘Laugh! Laugh! You’ll be sorry, Lilian.’ He strolled over to the table where she had begun to butter some bread. ‘It’s what I said—unnatural.’

Mildly, she said, ‘Shut up before you start to annoy me. Here. Make the tea.’

Straight-faced, she was amused by the martyred air with which he accepted rebuke and task. Looking over her shoulder to see how he would go about it, she noticed more, his height, the width of his shoulders under his white shirt.

Great hulking thing! she thought, divided between desire and exasperation. She cut the sandwiches, washed her hands at the sink and frowned.

Together she and Rosen set the tray. When it was completed Lilian said abruptly, 'He only likes to talk to her, don't you think? She's company.'

Rosen eyed her dispassionately.

'There's nothing wrong with him. Nothing like that,' she insisted. He was still silent. 'Well, if they can't play their chess and go to the beach without...Oh, you're just a nasty old man.'

Made by her uncertainty invulnerable, over-confident, and having easily convinced himself of the truth of his cause, Rosen became less than wise. He said, magnanimously ignoring the jibe, 'My advice to you is to send him away—now—before any damage is done. You'll be sorry if you don't, mark my words.'

'O-oh!' Lilian cried on a note of complete comprehension. 'That's it!' And she and the tray were suddenly gone, borne swiftly from the room on a surge of relief.

Rosen was taken aback by the speed of her withdrawal. He needed to see from her face what she had inferred. Charging after her, thrown a little off course by his bulk and his urgency, he knocked against a small table which, its claw feet catching in the thick pile of the carpet, could but topple over, carrying with it a vase of carnations and maiden-hair fern. He was, as Lilian had had reason to know, an incurably clumsy man.

When at length they were established by the fire, drinking the too-strong tea, she remembered and waved a half-eaten sandwich threateningly. She swallowed, drank, and said, 'I know what that was all about. You've been looking for some way to get rid of Max ever since he came into the house. Why, I wonder? Now, I wonder why?' She smiled. 'You're jealous.'

Rosen would not meet her eye. Instead, he gave some fussy attention to a morsel of pink fish which had fallen from his plate to his grey flannel knee. His intention was to be very distant with Lilian in order to prove her wrong. She was nothing but a misjudger of men, of him in particular. He was a victim of that common human failing which is to lie, grow angry that the lie is recognized for what it is, and fume with disinterested rage to imagine that *thus* it would be received if it *were* the truth. Outraged that the truth should be outraged, he ate the piece of salmon.

'You're jealous,' Lilian repeated. 'Yes, you are. That's what your trouble is. You'd like to be the only great big man for miles around. You should have been a sheikh. You should have had a harem.'

He blushed. 'I was talking about him with Emily, not...'

'Yes, I know you were. And don't do it again,' she said, suddenly hostile, conscious that she was a grandmother. 'Just because he's not like you you think there's something wrong with the man. Well, I know for a fact he's had a wife and a girlfriend, and if he hasn't got someone else tucked away right now I'd be surprised.'

'How could he? He's always with Emily?'

'Not every minute of the day and night! Anyway, shut your face! He's a very clever man. He's a good twenty years younger than you and he'll have more money at the end of every week than you'll see if you live to be eighty.'

Diverted, as usual, by Lilian's illogical course, hurt, Rosen said, 'It's not so hard to get on if you've had attention and good schooling when you're young. I've had to make my own way, Lilian. I had to leave school to help my mother and go—'

'Oh, not again!'

There was a silence.

Lilian thought of nothing, but Rosen's insinuations were in the air. She disbelieved, but she was disturbed.

All at once the idea of summoning Thea to the house was pricked to life. Without giving in to Rosen, it would settle everything.

'Fetch me the Sydney telephone book,' she said in an other-worldly voice and, eager to ingratiate himself, Rosen went.

Lilian stood up involuntarily and let her not over-supple imagination rest for a moment on the implications of what had been suggested. She ran restless fingers over the curves of her ears and finding pearl earrings attached to the lobes she unscrewed them and tenderly pressed the soft flesh.

She thought of Paula; she thought of the telephone book. Her wandering unfocused eyes met their reflection in the round wall mirror, rosewood framed, and she was drawn, perhaps by an echo of her reference to age, to examine her face in its bright surface.

She saw the special enigmatic face of self-communion. It made her tired. It had looked out on fifty-three long years. It was lined, heavy at this moment. Her mouth was smaller than it had been. Tightly drawn, it radiated lines. And as for her neck...

Her mother had died, she remembered with an astonishing pang of fear, when she was fifty-one. Died. Broken apart. Putrified. And there was no God.

She lifted a hand to her cheek.

Finding her thus, strangely still, Rosen came up behind her and not very hopefully put his arms round her. She clutched at him, turned to him, and did not send him away.

Lilian stood on the footpath outside the back gate, waiting for the car. It was three o'clock on a hot Saturday afternoon.

Above, the sky was drained of colour, the sun so glaring that no cloud survived to float across its face and bring an illusion of relief. In a world so hot it seemed that the sun might dissolve and merge with the spaces of the sky without a lessening of that fierce power whereby it drew up moisture from the earth, and life and virtue from plants and mortals.

Lilian shivered. She sneezed as another blast of wind from the furnace of the west struck her. The light silk of her dress clung to her clammy skin.

Fifteen minutes earlier she had lain on the leather sofa, her face covered by a rapidly drying cloth. Under a newspaper tent, Rosen sheltered from the flies and tried to sleep. In another room, flat on a strip of uncarpeted floor, Emily was eating a peach and reading *The Mayor of Casterbridge*. Gussie the dog, gasping in the humid air, was taken by Lilian to lie on the tiled floor of the bathroom and given an ice-cream in a saucer. His head between his paws, he occasionally whimpered, causing those in the sitting-room to bestir themselves in the midst of lethargy to identify the sound.

Driven desperate by this and the persistent buzzing of imprisoned flies, Lilian had demanded suddenly to be taken to the Horizon Hotel where there were high ceilings, a view of the ocean, and air-conditioning. 'Air-conditioning!' Though hers was not a voice accustomed to yearning and pathos, she now included so much of both in her plea that Rosen jumped to it.

Not a man, or a dog, or a bicycle intruded on the grey cement paths, the roads of sticky tar, and clay. Under the sun's curfew, all Ballowra remained indoors.

Preceded by a pant of transparent blue smoke, the car crawled on to the road: the noise it made, its bulk, was an affront to the boring vacancy of the scene.

As Lilian climbed in, Emily came through the gate and said listlessly, 'Hullo. Here's a letter for you. I just found it.'

She retired into the shade of the garage and watched while Lilian tore open the envelope. 'From Sydney,' she added, and she sighed as she leaned against the blistering dark red paint of the door. She wore a white seersucker dress without sleeves, and white sandals. Her feet were powdered with the dust of her short walk down the path. 'Where are you going?' she asked Mr Rosen uncuriously.

'Town,' he said, wiping his face while Lilian read, and they both waited, for nothing in particular, completely passive, until Lilian cried, 'I said so!' and looked sharply from one to the other as if to exact acclamation.

Emily gazed back with a mild lack of interest but at that moment, suddenly, her head was turned by a distant sound. Her arms rose like wings, she cast the swiftest smile over her shoulder at the car as if to say, 'Rejoice!' before she cut noiselessly away, running to meet Max who had appeared at the top of the hill.

'What is it? What's the matter? Where's she off to?' Lilian asked, assuming a testy air of mystification.

'Him,' he said, without turning his head to look. 'I wish I had her energy.' And as if to illustrate his weakness he let the car coast downhill.

Lilian held before her eyes for a moment that expression of Emily's. She tapped the letter in her lap with moist fingers. Gusts of dusty air beat against her flushed face and added to the chaos begun by the melting of her make-up. 'Energy?' she repeated vaguely.

With a groan she peeled herself from the leather of the seat and resettling at a different, though hardly more comfortable angle, said, 'Anyway, this is from Thea.'

'What does it say?'

'She's supposed to be coming here for a conference soon and if she does, she's coming to see me. She will. I know she will!'

And momentarily forgetful of their discomfort, Lilian and Rosen beamed through the shimmering air at the blue-black surface of the road and the burning silver of the bare tramlines.

In the pale shade of the plum trees Max and Emily stretched on the grass and drank lemon and iced water from glasses on whose surfaces moisture had condensed in a cold mist. The air weighed oppressively on them.

Emily swept her long brown hair away from her neck and glanced at Max. He was studying the dissolving cubes in his glass. Scarcely able to contain her enchantment she looked at her ice, too; then, so that she might not exclaim aloud, she put a hand behind her back and smoothed the surface of the tree-trunk against which she leaned. It was real. Her isolation here alone with Max was real.

Oh, but I'm only twelve, she thought, with a fall of exaltation, and I'll be young for years. All at once she was imprisoned by her youth.

With a flutter of panic she looked at the garden to reassure herself that it was no mirage. We're here *now*, she thought, and she leaned slightly forward, taking her weight from the tree, almost imagining that pressure anywhere was pressure on time, pressure on the sun, hastening its descent.

'What time is it?' Max asked, and she looked at her watch, 'Quarter past three.'

'As late as that? Fine time to get home on Saturday. I ought to resign.' He finished his drink and put the glass down on the turf where it became, for an hour or so, the wonder of the ant world. 'It was a meeting. I was reporting progress.'

Reporting progress to Macmillan, being told that they wanted him back in Melbourne as soon as possible, before the year was up—this instead of the extension he had half expected.

Emily had forced an unspoken agreement never to mention his going. Now he wondered how he might best approach the subject. The silence between them, while not in itself unusual, seemed to demand that he speak and speak to the point; instead he said, 'You didn't want to go to the beach?'

Emily shook her head. 'Too hot.'

'So it is. Happy here, then?' he asked, looking at her quizzically, searching, almost appealing, for some sign of boredom, of that childish desire to be for ever moving, running, going somewhere.

'Yes,' and she smiled at his ignorance of her.

She had to restrain no other, youthful impulses in order to fulfil a more insistent one to be with him. There was no choosing, no indecision, however slight: there was no subjugation. With him her need was filled: she was content.

Presently Max said, 'You haven't told me how you're getting on with Darwin.'

She was amazed to hear it. She sat up and proceeded earnestly to tell him what she thought about the origin of *homo sapiens.* Now she was in Asia, now in Africa, now she was a monkey. And why weren't monkeys daily turning into men? Where—no—*what* was the missing link? No, not what—*how?*

Max groaned, summarized a few theories which left her dissatisfied with, and critical of, the world's scientists. He concluded, 'And if you ask me *why—today...*'

She laughed. She had meant to.

Smiling, he said, 'Tell me what you think.'

'But I don't know.' She was suddenly very young, uncertain of everything—including him.

That crushing uncertainty had been, when he first came, the most noticeable thing about her. She had had a quite extraordinary lack of confidence. That had not surprised

Max for long. Even now, occasionally, he saw her crucified by Lilian's sarcasm, when, provoked to stammering rage by some piece of hypocrisy and ruthlessness, she sallied out, wordless, flashing-eyed, her whole nature pressed rigid against what she could sense of Lilian's underlying motive. It was a motive recognizable to Max, for Lilian was not subtle and hid nothing of herself. It could often be placed no higher than sadism. In microcosm Lilian was the world. She was the majority, and had its qualities for good and evil. Living with her was practice in bloodless warfare...

What in Emily *had* surprised him, was the discovery that under the ingratiating smile and the puzzlement, was a basic, unshakable belief in the rightness of a life that did not sin against intelligence and kindness, and she saw these qualities he knew, as high, august, and including all virtue. She desired for herself and for others that they should live to principle when it hurt.

Max shifted his position restlessly. He lit a cigarette, smoked it without enjoyment, and tried to concentrate his thoughts on the meeting with Macmillan.

At that moment he would not think of her reaction to his going, of its effect on her, or of his own regret.

It was as well for his peace of mind that he could not know of the way in which her time was spent when he was out of sight—of the entranced inspection of his room, the mathematical straightening of bedcover, curtains, shoes; of the strict order of precedence with which the table was set, the dishes dried, with his identified and treated, as were all of his possessions, with a reverence usually reserved for the bones of saints.

And he was not sufficiently vain to imagine the enormous power her memory attained through the strength of her desire to lose nothing of him; the conviction with which his standards were adopted; the impetus he lent to that yearning to be good, just, and true.

But if the situation between them was one that could have deteriorated into something ugly, no one was more aware of it than he—though from the first he had felt it would not do so. Emily responded to his attention with a nervous sensibility that was, in its lack of childishness, as well as a signal of her character, a pointer to the extremity of her deprivation and, to Max, a cause of anger.

They had fallen silent. Now they were returned to themselves by an increase in the intensity of the heat. It seemed too hot to breathe. The air withheld itself, suspended motion, was suddenly felt to have withdrawn into the upper regions so irrevocably that the two under the lattice of gnarled branches and leaves were roused to turn their heads and finally look up to see where it could be.

There appeared at that moment in the glaring deserts of the sky a single cloud—a small untidy mass inconceivably composed of moisture and coolness, inconceivably designed to shade and dampen. Watching it, they were forced to sigh.

Emily moved her upturned hand to and fro, played with the luminous patterns printed by the sun, curled her fingers in an idle attempt to capture a piece of living light, then, tiring of a game that had unconsciously imposed itself as an aid to concentration on she knew not what, dropped her hand to the grass. There it plucked and plucked at the short dry blades until, her eye coming to Max's hand which lay as if sleeping, it was directed to touch it, identifying, claiming it with drowsy satisfaction.

'At least,' he said, turning on one side and leaning on his elbow, 'at least we must try to see that you get to university. You're nearly thirteen. That means, four, five years here before you could go...But if you had that as an objective—I'm sure you could get a scholarship. What do you think? It would be worth some hard work, Em. You'd never regret it.'

The intent, unseeing gaze with which his grey eyes had imprisoned Emily's blue ones changed, swept the suspicious face in front of his with entirely conscious attention. He smiled.

'Don't you think you might like it? Remember how interested you've been in all the things we've talked about. And they are only the beginnings of what you would learn...'

Her heart seemed to open with pain. She could not believe he had so misunderstood. Made vocal by shock she cried, 'Oh, Max! It wasn't *what,* not the *things*... I mean—Max—I liked the things, but it was the *way, you...*'

He frowned at her. 'Of course it matters that we like to talk together, but you're not being honest to suggest that—to you—the subject is unimportant. And in fact I know that isn't true. You couldn't argue me down if you didn't care. You, the defender of the Spartans!'

'It's just that the historians aren't fair to them, Max. It makes you have to defend them. They go from one extreme to the other on Athens and Sparta. You know they do.'

'So do you,' he said, smiling at her, 'on all kinds of things.'

'But they,' she explained patiently, 'are prejudiced.'

'And you're not?'

'No.'

'All right, then. As I was saying: if it's possible to get you to university, we must try. Don't expect it to be the answer to everything. It can do the wrong people positive harm by misleading them about themselves. They count up the facts they know, and if they amount to a great many, they decide that they are rather wise.'

Emily could not help a smile of fellow-feeling.

'Often then,' Max said pointedly, 'they proceed to say and do a number of dangerous things that they'd have lacked confidence to do but for the mystic wisdom they feel they have had conferred on them.'

'How?' She stubbornly followed him.

'By three or four years spent in the same square mile as a lot of books and a few old men, who are perhaps quite wise, but do not think so.'

Trying to make this out, Emily looked at him, solemn. 'I better not go,' she said, at last.

'You only listen when you want to.'

'No. All the time, Max.'

He believed her and he sighed. Then he grinned and ruffled her hair. 'For you, I don't say there's that much danger! I think you might just avoid it. You would learn. You would have a chance to meet other young people who— Now what?'

He saw that she suspected him of trying to pass her on to a chilly crowd of strangers. Sitting up, he clasped his arms loosely over his legs. 'I'll start again. We'll forget about the people.'

'I only want you,' she said in a low voice.

'The point is,' he went on, 'that you have it in you to be a good scholar, and I can see you don't believe me now, but you'd *like* it.'

She looked at him doubtfully. 'Did you?'

'You know all about that.'

They both smiled and Emily said cautiously, 'It might be nice.'

'It would be.'

Emily looked at him steadily, listening, not caring. Inside herself at this, as at every demonstration of his concern, her heart beat with a heavy melancholy joy; she wept, moaned soundlessly, could have died peacefully in the sheltered happiness of the moment. Wrapped in a cocoon of warmth, the reason for his solicitude mattered not. He cared. Someone cared. Max cared.

Sensing her distance, Max said, 'This is important, Em. If I speak about it to your mother, will you back me up?'

He had hesitated to put his idea to Paula, foreseen objections from her husband and Lilian. He was aware that his suggestion would amaze them. They had no time for education. It was not one of the things that they, or anyone they knew, had ever gone in for. It was eccentric to dwell on it. They would not allow that it was for those in a world above theirs, but it was for those with a great deal of money. It was something that happened to city socialites. University was a place where they went to meet husbands and wives. Quite what a degree was, no one Lilian knew in Ballowra knew.

Max remembered the few references to Emily's future: 'She's got long fingers, she'll probably be a famous pianist' (this from Paula in a cheerful mood, in the face of the fact that there was no piano and had never been lessons); and Lilian's equally airy, 'She's tall, she might be a famous mannequin.' Almost impatiently he said, 'You will, won't you?'

'Yes, yes,' she protested. She looked down at the ground and exclaimed, 'Oh, look at all the ants in the glasses!'

'What's the matter? What's wrong?'

'Nothing...Oh, Max! Where will *you* be? You won't be there. Where will you be? I only want to be with you. That's all I want. Don't make me leave you. Don't go away. Don't leave me with them.'

She leaned forward and put her head on her knees, racked with sobs.

Max got to his feet and waited.

Presently, Emily blew her nose and said indistinctly, 'Where are you? What are you doing?'

She blew her nose again and Max held out a hand and said, 'Stand up.'

In front of him, abashed, she roughly pushed her hair back from her face and eyed him in silence, frowning.

'We'll go round to the other lawn; there'll be more shade.' He took her arm. 'What would you think about a swim this evening?'

'The baths? They'll be floodlit. That'd be nice.'

It was not far to the other side of the house, a little over a hundred yards, but they went slowly, curiously in need of the sun's benefits.

Max felt the warm walk in the sun to be a kind of convalescence for the girl who walked beside him. Her tears disturbed him. She wept as someone else might have succumbed to a recurring fever. When he saw her cry he could not escape the idea that she was sick. At these times, Emily was taken over, banished; *something* wept, something deep, universal. It was not pleasant to see.

He started to talk. His was now the task of stimulating into full life the confidence and self-reliance in her which had, over the months, been increasing in strength. Though it was contrary to his aims, Max spoke at first in personal appeal—sure there of her response—of what he hoped and expected of her; mentioning too, what she had always known, that his time with her was limited, and growing shorter. But the truth was that Emily needed one person, one human. He at present was the person, and he was going. Independence did not exclude loneliness, lovelessness. And Emily was young. She had known too much of both; she had too few memories to sustain her in an empty time, and no reason to look to something better in the future.

Listening to his comments on the morning's novel, the state of her bicycle bell, and again, university life, Emily was interested, cheerful, as forgetful of the past half-hour as if she had indeed been hypnotized into oblivion. She asked him what time they should leave for the pool, and mentally made a perfect dive through the shining black surface of the water.

But catching sight of her expression in repose, Max thought, what have we done?

CHAPTER SEVEN

ABANDONING FRED to Lilian and Rosen, Billie went in search of Max. She walked on tip-toe down the hall, face uplifted like an antenna, arms extended slightly to balance her teetering progress. A forgotten cigarette in her right hand shed flakes of ash as she pushed at the kitchen door.

The room was empty and marvellously neat. The big unshaded globe set in a socket in the wall burned steadily, giving the silent room the look of a shrine dedicated to the domestic gods. Billie, at least, gazed into the halo of light as if she believed herself to be in the presence of *something*. It was several seconds before she could accept the idea that she was quite alone.

Then a ball of amusement began to unwind in her chest. She knew he was in the house. His non-appearance gave her the nerve-scraping sensation that he was playing a game, teasing her.

She gave an excited giggle and touched the wickerwork of her lacquered hair; noticing her cigarette, she stubbed it out in the sink; then, smoothing her red and white floral dress, she went out into the hall.

'I'm fed up with Fred,' she had confided to Lilian recently. 'He thinks more of hubby than he does of me. He wouldn't offend him for anything. He comes to call for me, sits down, starts to talk to hubby, has a drink...I come out and say, "It's time we weren't here, Fred."

'They both look up like a couple of stunned mullets, and, I might add, make just about as much noise. I suppose they're really jealous of one another but they've got a queer way of showing it. I don't want them to be fighting or unfriendly or anything, but wouldn't you think that once in a while they'd flare up? But no. Sometimes he stays so long that hubby has to say, "Isn't it about time you two shoved off?" It makes me feel so small. And Fred knows it.'

Lilian listened without sympathy or indignation to this tale of suffering. She felt very little for Billie but mild contempt. However, a subsequent conversation, during which she had been driven to reveal her own irritation with Rosen, made a bond of mutual discontent and Lilian had advised her friend to follow her example and look around for something better.

Billie's journey to Max's room tonight was in direct response to this advice, though, as she well knew, Max was not precisely what Lilian had had in mind.

A line of light showed under the closed door of his bedroom and Billie stopped dead, listening, wondering whether that pest of a kid was with him. Defiant, she refused to knock but suddenly pushed open the door and stepped into the room.

'Surprise! Look who's here!' she cried, oddly out of breath. 'All alone, Max?'

Abruptly deported from Europe, Max looked up from his book. His abstraction merged into impassivity when he saw what the situation was in the Antipodes, and was to be, according to Billie's plans. She meant to stay. He rejected the five or six most appropriate answers and said, 'Hullo, Mrs Duncan. Another party?'

Carefully not meeting his eyes, she slid into the green upholstered armchair he had just vacated. She crossed her legs and draped the soft folds of her skirt consciously while Max, after switching on the centre light to supplement the lamp, found a packet of cigarettes and offered her one.

Released at length from the elaborate business she made of having it lighted, he sat down opposite her and leaned back.

'I wasn't disturbing you, was I? You were only reading.' She flashed him an almost nervous, embarrassed glance. But if she counted on disarming him by a show of diffidence she was unsuccessful.

'As a matter of fact, I *was* reading.'

'And *I* only came to have a chat,' she told him, widening her eyes, defensive, aggrieved, and ready for battle.

From himself to Billie Duncan, there was nothing to be said, but eventually, to break the silence, Max said, without great pretence of interest, 'Was your party successful the other week?'

The effort of asking, the premonitory boredom of hearing a lengthy answer, was so acute that, temporarily drained, he leaned back in his chair and tried to draw some strength from his cigarette.

But tonight, nothing he said was to connect with what Billie had to say. 'Your little friend isn't home?'

'Emily? No. She's gone to see Pat.' Reluctantly, in response to his wishes.

'I'm not exactly sorry, are you?' Billie muttered, staring at the bright tip of her cigarette.

'I don't believe I've thought about it one way or the other.'

Aware of his gaze, Billie became less happily aware that she was exposing herself at close quarters to a man several years her junior. She admitted it—ten years. For the first time she confronted the idea that the liaison that had lately filled her daydreams might not, from his point of view, have so much to offer.

'Oh, by the way,' Max said suddenly, 'is Fred here? You remember he asked what the chances were of making a change-over to our firm a few weeks ago? I must have a word with him about it.'

'What's Fred got to do with it?' she said sulkily. Max looked so young. His skin was fine and tanned. More temperately she said, 'What were you reading? You've got two books there.'

'I should have been looking at this report; I have to speak about it tomorrow, but—'

'I'm keeping you back?' she said, getting hostile.

'Instead, I was reading this novel.'

Her attention was nailed down. 'Novel? Story, you mean?' She turned on Max the besotted expression a woman gives to a baby. 'Detectives? Cowboys? A love story?'

'Not really—'

But she would not listen. She knew *exactly* what it was. She shook her head sagely, half lifted a hand to show him it was useless to demur. His secret, she seemed to suggest, was discovered. She crowed as if it were the most delightful thing she had ever heard. 'Well, fancy that! Fancy you!'

Max dared not speak, and if he moved he would be bound to speak. He stayed in his chair, surveyed the room. He noticed the way the black night air seemed to enter through the open window and penetrate for a short distance before submitting to the lights.

Billie was still talking, but her voice dropped now to a note of throbbing alcoholic seriousness. '—read poetry, too.' She had lifted an open book from the shelf and was looking at it as if it were a sacred relic, and at Max, the possessor, with something of the same awe.

'Read poetry?' he said. 'Yes, occasionally. Not so much as I used to.'

'It was open! It was on top! You must have put it there!'

'Perhaps I did,' Max agreed.

'Can I look at it?'

'Do.'

How is it possible, Max wondered, giving way to moody generalizations, that the idea of progress can survive in the face of the evidence supplied by human nature? If it were suggested to Billie, for instance, that human nature had not only not improved, but had not changed in the last two thousand years—what would she do? Laugh. Something. Anyway, disbelieve.

Not exactly cheered by his conclusions he moved, and disturbed Billie, who had been running a finger along the broken lines of verse and wondering how she looked from Max's chair.

'What's the matter?' she said, noticing his expression. Leaning forward at an angle of forty-five degrees, she looked like a not very well-carved figurehead.

'Matter? Do you like it?' he asked, glancing at the book in her hand.

'Oh.' She relaxed and gave a little smile. 'It's beautiful, just beautiful. It does you good, doesn't it?'

'Take it with you. Keep it as long as you like.'

'*Could* I?' She appeared overcome at the thought.

Leaving her eyes on his, she could be seen to retire: seconds later, in tears, her voice pitched high, she returned. 'What's the good of it to me? *I* can't read it. You know how to. You can,' she insisted wildly. 'Max, I never knew another man who did. I never knew anyone else like you. They've all been rough—not like you...'

She reached out to touch his hand, but the chairs were too far apart. 'You've got to help me. You've got to be nice to me. I'm so unhappy. If you knew—'

When Max stood up she was immediately silent, watching him, tense and expectant.

'I honestly think you shouldn't say any more. It would be a pity. I think you would be sorry. If it's something between you and Fred—'

She made an angry movement to shut him up.

'Forget about Fred! You don't have to keep going on about Fred! I'm talking about you. And me. I know what I'm doing. You teach that kid all kinds of things. You talk to her, Max. But I need you. You could tell me things, too. Teach me. Be nice to me. And I could do more for you than a kid like that...Couldn't I? Or don't you like me?' Her voice dropped a tone.

Max stood listening—hands in pocket, head bowed—with a complete absence of feeling. Yet when she asked that last question he winced. She was uncertain. She was vulnerable. Even Billie. Next to someone who felt something—if temporary, mistaken, unadmirable—he was obscurely ashamed.

Sitting down he said, 'I think it's not so simple as that. I'm in no position to give or receive help, Billie. And if I were, I must say frankly, that I wouldn't be the right person to help you find what you want. I know that in another mood you'll agree that I'm right. You'll wonder how, from your own point of view, you could have thought so.'

He held her eyes steadily, and his voice, with its rough undertone of resonance, was serious. Mistaking the flicker of angry fascination on her face for an acknowledgement that the scene was over, he said more lightly, 'Is Fred here? I spoke to the foreman about him and he thought there was a good chance of something coming up next week that might easily suit him.'

She looked at him quickly, exhaled a stream of breath and cigarette smoke and stubbed out the butt in an ashtray on the shelf beside her. In her left hand she held, and with her long fingernails penetrated, the lace edge of a small scented handkerchief.

'No.' Without expression she dismissed his last remark. 'Why?'

It was evident that she threw the question at him from some stubborn prearranged position along the course of her own inner argument.

'Why?'

'Wouldn't you be the right one?'

Her unabashed persistence seemed to convey an awful blankness at some centre of her being. Max said, 'I think it would take too long to tell if I haven't already made it clear.'

One could not talk to, reason with her: yet she was human. She looked at him with animal blankness, then she was suddenly penetrated, changed colour, grew human.

Even in her humiliation Max felt relief.

'I know.' She smiled and the corners of her mouth turned down. 'I'm nothing. I'm not good enough for you. I'm just a housewife in a small town. Say it!'

There was a strong impression in the air that Billie saw Max and herself on a screen, in black and white.

The situation was ludicrous. Max had to try to make her admit it before she went away. 'You don't believe that for a minute.'

But she held her position, staring, venomous. 'It's just that you like them younger, I suppose. Well, that's your own peculiar affair, isn't it?'

For a shocked moment she waited, then, alarmed by the sound of her words, and his rigid silence, she retreated sideways to the door. Even so, through her fright, she was suddenly insanely angry.

'I hope you won't be too lonely if I leave you to get on with your poems and love stories,' she said shrilly, stretching her mouth in imitation of a smile, 'but there's a *man* waiting for me out here. Maybe your little playmate'll soon be back to keep you company, though. Ta-ta.'

Breathless with agitation she opened the door and slid out into the passage.

Max rubbed the back of his neck. With a suppressed exclamation he went to the door and locked it. Striding across the room he threw the window open wide and stood there, looking out, seeing nothing, for some minutes. Finally he pulled on a coat and left the house.

Billie rearranged her expression on the way to the sitting-room, and released a final sharp breath of chagrin before she presented herself, looking quite unnaturally mild, to the inspection of three pairs of eyes.

Fred, idleness and boredom personified, uttered an inane, 'Wha' d'ya know?'

On the table in front of him was an erection of playing-cards—a pagoda, perhaps, but of a style belonging to no known country.

Billie gave a brittle laugh. With a flip of her fingers she finished his game and turned away without seeing the blight that came over his face. He poked a dejected finger among the ruins.

Lilian and Rosen sat on either side of the cold fire. Next to Lilian on a small carved chest was an electric fan whose blades were still.

'Well?' the two women said simultaneously, looking at each other with vague inward attention.

Dyed blonde hair and grey eyes—colourless, Billie thought. And Lilian shook her head slightly with pity at the sight of her friend's dyed black hair and great cow eyes. So ageing, she thought.

'Can I park here?' Billie dropped to the arm of her chair.

'Where were you? We thought—'

Suspecting an unsanitary joke, Billie snapped, 'It's none of your business,' and Lilian laughed behind her hand.

'We're one up,' Rosen said, giving her a glass of wine.

Not looking at any of them, Billie drank. When she had put the glass down, she said, 'I think that Max is funny.' *That* Max, she said, as if she were isolating one particular Max from many others. 'I ran into him in the kitchen just now and he started going on about how lonely he was with Emily round at her girl friend's. I think he's off his rocker.'

As at a signal, she turned to Rosen, and for the length of a breath their eyes held together.

'I didn't hear you in the kitchen,' Lilian said smoothly, turning in her chair so that she could fix Billie with her formidable eyes. She asked Fred, 'Do *you* think he's queer?'

Fred looked at Billie, looked away, 'He's all right.'

Lilian's laugh, scornful and comfortable, mingled with Billie's unconcealedly bitter one.

'You can laugh. You just don't want to see what's going on under your nose.'

'That's what I keep telling her,' Rosen put in self-righteously, but the next instant he was floundering for apologies, shaken by a look of contempt from Lilian. 'Well, all I meant was...'

Brusquely to Billie she said, 'There's a chair over there. You'll break the arm.'

And to Fred, who was eyeing them all with a lazy benevolence that appeared to cover any number of judgements on the situation, she said, 'What do you say they've got their reasons, Fred? Eh? Not too hard to guess, are they?'

'Well, if you're going to get nasty...' Billie said, while Fred reiterated to the cards on the table, 'He's not a bad cove.'

'That's all you know. I tell you he's rotten,' she cried hysterically. 'It's got me worried sick when I think of him near that young girl. It shouldn't be allowed.'

Smiling, Lilian watched the performance until Rosen brought himself to her side and blocked the view. 'I swear I'm only thinking of you,' he said in a low voice. 'We're speaking for your own good.'

'Shut up!' she said with a tight little smile and gave the side of his face a malicious pat with her open hand.

He retired to the windows.

Rising, Lilian pulled down her dress, saw that she was firmly balanced on her high heels, and gazed round as if she were master of ceremonies. She rubbed her hands together and called, 'Shut up! Shut up, all of you!' Everyone attended. 'Well, now, what about some bridge?'

'No, thank you, Lilian,' said Billie primly, staring at the carpet. 'I've got to go home. Are you ready, Fred?' She had become so distant that her vision seemed to have been affected. She was intensely vague.

At this set-back, Lilian consulted her intuition to gauge the amount of energy necessary to save the night. A moment later she called in the same cheerful tone, 'Get out the car, then! We're all off to the Horizon for a prawn supper and a dance.'

It was irresistible. Within ten minutes they were ready to leave the house.

Across the shady black veranda they passed down the steps into a blaze of moonlight that gave to houses, fences, and telegraph poles the sharp transparency of a negative held close to the light. The moon floated in a sky made pale by its brilliance.

The two women went down the dark gravel path by the side of the house with caution, clutching each other's arms, pointing out, in the friendliest manner, the hollows and rises to be avoided. While they chatted their lovers plodded after them, sombre, stolid, deaf, and—when the procession to the garage was abruptly halted—bewildered, as if wakened from a deep sleep.

The path beside the house approached at right angles the bone-white path running from the back gate to the back door. Sheltered from sight partly by shadow, partly by a bank of overgrown hydrangea bushes, Lilian and the men were pulled up by a dramatic barricading movement of Billie's arm. Wordlessly she pointed to the gate where Max, returning from his walk, had been seen and hailed by Emily. He stood waiting for her.

Angry, but held to the spot by a kind of fascinated curiosity, Lilian submitted, and the four crowded together against the wall.

Emily ran to Max as if she had been shot from a catapult. Her arms went round him and, before the watchers had time to register emotion, dropped again. They stood talking for a few moments in clear voices which the horror-muffled ears by the house could not understand. Emily said something and Max laughed and put a hand on her head.

This time Billie drew in a deliberate, and deliberately audible, breath.

Slowly the two walked down the path. Yes, they were almost touching, the narrowed eyes made out. Oh, God, there was her hand in his. Yes, they were horribly intimate. In the moonlight their faces were extraordinary: the onlookers were appalled.

By watching, they had themselves provided the necessary atmosphere of stealth: easily transferring it to those on whom they spied, they were convinced of evil. And that Max and Emily supposed themselves alone and were not seemed, inexplicably, to give further proof of guilt.

When they had passed out of sight, Billie hissed, 'What did I tell you?'

'Shocking! Shocking!' muttered Rosen.

Confused, Lilian turned from one to the other with an apprehensive uncertainty as to what she was expected to do. As she became aware of their alarm and exultation she knew what must be done. They felt they had been proved right: they were crowing over her. Her task was obviously to smash their victory, to astonish and overawe them by the severity of her pronouncement. Accordingly, she looked at the three dark faces and said, 'I'll send for her mother and father. He'll leave this house.'

Rosen's voice was stifled. 'Yes.'

Billie said, swallowing noisily, 'Oh, isn't it awful! Oh, imagine!'

Only Fred, who screwed up his face and looked round at the eerie beauty of the black and silver night, said nothing.

'Not a word to anyone,' Lilian cautioned them, from her distant stronghold. 'Nothing's to happen till Paula and Harry get here.'

Her two disciples had no other thought than to chorus: 'Oh, quite right! Of course!'

'Well, come on,' she said roughly. 'We can't stand here all night. We might as well go and have those prawns.'

Fred followed Rosen into the garage, and the two women waited outside at the gate, X-rayed by light now, as Emily and Max had recently been.

'They're in the kitchen,' Billie said. 'Do you think we ought to see what they're doing?'

'I've seen enough for one night,' said Lilian with grand indifference.

'I hear music, though. Do you think we ought to leave them by themselves?'

'Why not? They've been alone for months. Well, he'll soon have his walking papers. It won't be much longer. He's a dirty little rat if ever there was one.'

Fervently Billie agreed. She felt that until tonight she had not properly appreciated Lilian.

CHAPTER EIGHT

WHEN LILIAN left the sitting-room to refill the teapot and put the roast in the oven, Emily flew after her.

'What's he want? Did you know he was coming?'

Receiving no answer, she followed Lilian about the kitchen asking, 'But why is Mum coming to see him? Is something going to happen?'

'Nothing that concerns you,' Lilian said, obviously lying, just not obviously enjoying herself. 'This is for grown-ups so don't go bothering your mother and father with questions.'

Emily grimaced. As if she would ask them anything. As if she cared what it was. But she shot a calculating glance at Lilian and could not prevent herself from wondering.

For all the normality of the scene—the efficient way in which Lilian handled the meat, the way the kettle steamed, the way Gussie pounded in at the back door and put his muzzle in her hand—Emily felt a current of critical excitement in her grandmother that was anything but normal. It made her peculiarly uneasy. She leaned against the wall and studied Lilian's face with a kind of half-conscious wariness. She saw pale powdered skin, rouged cheeks, busy, glittering grey eyes and a mouth held set. She gave herself up to brooding speculation.

A minute or two later the sheer offensiveness of the lump of raw meat in the baking dish on the table brought her back to herself. Repelled, she dragged her eyes away from it, and volunteered, 'Oh! Max won't be in for dinner. He asked me to tell you. He's working late. He's going to get something at the canteen.'

Lilian slid the dish into the oven. 'Is he now?'

Taken aback by the edge of sarcasm in her voice, Emily felt another jolt of dismay. There was no need to pick on him just because there were visitors, she thought. But then she told herself that maybe it was just that she was boring Lilian by saying Max's name, or that she was thinking of something else and was just not interested.

She scratched a bare brown knee, gave a philosophical sigh and stretched her arms up to the top of the door.

'Well, they'll—Mum and Dad'll still be here tomorrow, though, won't they? Because Max has to see them, and he didn't know they were coming. But if he's late tonight, I'll tell him in the morning.'

Flabbergasted, Lilian slowly turned her head to look at her granddaughter. The utter astonishment of her pose caused Emily to grin, and her eyes to shine with wicked amusement.

'What do you mean, he has to see them? What for?'

Success! Electrification! Emily was overjoyed.

'It's for grown-ups, I can't tell you,' she said pertly, but she grinned a shade less joyfully when Lilian started towards her with a threatening hand raised. 'I can't. It's a secret,' she protested, dodging round the table.

'You little monkey!' But Lilian halted. There was a guilelessness about the girl that made her feel foolish and repent her panicky speculations. Of course it could be nothing important. She would not have anyone know what she had imagined for the world.

Walled-up by her reaction, she filled the teapot and hastened from the room without a word, unaware that her failure to laugh, to persist, to rebuke, raised Emily's eyebrows and choked off her small victory with apprehension.

When Rosen went at five o'clock to meet Paula at the station Harry had offered to go with him, but Lilian insisted that he stay.

'Rest!' she had said. 'You must be tired.'

Naturally he was: he very seldom was not. So he stayed. Besides, it was what he was obviously meant to do.

It was Friday afternoon. Lilian's cryptic telegram had reached him the previous morning; by the early afternoon he had arranged leave, packed, and booked a seat on the only long-distance train out of Coolong for twenty-four hours. Now that he had arrived and been assured by Lilian that no one was dead or dying, he wondered rather pettishly why Paula, who had not half so far to come, had not been there to welcome him.

But in fact, though he criticized, he was pleased to have time to himself to ponder on the alternative crises that could account for the unprecedented summons, and to prepare attitudes to meet them.

He was more relieved than resentful that Lilian had determined to say nothing until Paula arrived. He had no wish to face alone what must presumably be a joint dilemma—if dilemma it was.

Ostensibly waiting for the car to return, he stood at the gate, smoking, looking up and down the road, thinking of neither Paula nor Emily. His hazel eyes gazed blankly at the scene in front of him. Characteristically he had soon abandoned the effort of conscious thought and waited now for events.

From the steelworks to the north came the familiar shuddering of machines; the thunderous roll spreading across the built-up plain was of less note than a clap of natural thunder, or the cry of a bird gone astray in the wilderness of wood and corrugated iron. But Harry had grown unused to it, and turned his head to look at the reverberating sky.

At another point in the garden Emily was talking to Patty. She and her father, intent on avoiding each other, found that by a small restriction of head and eye they could seem to be unaware of each other's presence. Apart from a few minutes in the sitting-room over afternoon tea, when both Rosen and Lilian had been present, they had not been together.

'I'd like a big pot of paint,' Emily said moodily to her friend.

They stood inside the fence eyeing the three provision shops on the opposite corner.

'What for?' Patty asked, idly chewing a leaf.

'I'd slosh it all over that,' she said, pointing to the blue and silver advertisement that covered the outside wall of Sim's shop. 'And that, and that.' Pointing a finger, she ruthlessly obliterated red-painted declarations of ownership, yellow and green caricatures designed to encourage the consumption of porridge.

'What for?'

They were untidy: they caught the eye. Huge printed letters under a sky of blue crystal, smoke-streaked; printed letters with real air blowing on them. She could not convey how peculiar it seemed. 'Oh, I don't know. I just would.'

Out of the corner of her eye she saw that her father had moved, was going back into the house. Why?

'Well, what colour would you use?' Patty persisted, abstractedly picking bits of leaf from her tongue.

Emily gave an exclamation of mingled irritation and misgiving. Her hands met nervously behind her neck, twisted her stream of hair into a rope and let it go again.

'Huh? What colour, Em?'

'Oh! I think I hear the car. I'll have to get tidied. See you later.'

She was off up the steps before Patty had time to listen, look, and contradict.

Simultaneously entering the house at either end of the long passage, Emily and her father stood for a moment transfixed, eye to eye, till with the bound of a startled rabbit she made for the bedroom and, holding her breath, closed and locked the door.

She tore off her school uniform and fought her way into a dress, occupied by an artificially stimulated fear that he might come banging at the door, demanding entry and audience; complacent in the knowledge that he would not.

Just the same it was immensely embarrassing to have a stranger as an intimate relation. She did not feel, and would not act, like a daughter, and Harry's half-hearted attempts to play the father shocked and mortified her. He was so obviously an amateur. And anyway, it was gruesome, she felt, to see grown-ups pretend anything.

If it did nothing else, concentration on this old grievance dispelled the vague feeling of dread that had come on her again in the garden. She now tied the belt of her dress, fixed the buttons, and brushed her hair with complete forgetfulness of the intangible strain, the mysterious unease that she had earlier in the day apprehended. Brushing mechanically, she even forgot the awkwardness of having her parents come together under one roof, of their making claims on her.

With a smile she pressed her cheek to the cold silver mirror. 'Hullo, Max,' she whispered. 'I love you, Max.' The blue eyes were unwavering. The room was dim, blinds and curtains drawn against the sun. Her smile faded as she regarded herself.

And I feel so old, she thought heavily. I'm not young. I'm not young.

At dinner she sat between Paula and Harry; Lilian and Rosen sat opposite. They were in the dining-room—an ominous fact in itself—surrounded by pieces of tall furniture which stood round the high dark walls. There was a sense of being overshadowed, hung over, watched. All that was horizontal in the room, apart from floor and ceiling, was the sofa where Emily sometimes slept, and the table at which they sat—two who knew, and three who were mystified. Lilian would wait till they had eaten to speak.

'When are you going to move to Sydney, Harry?' she now asked, jolting them all to life, more than hinting at what she expected to be the outcome of their meeting.

Harry said soon, and suddenly meant it, and Paula, quickly taking a spoonful of hot apple dumpling, scalded her mouth.

She wondered if her mother was going to marry Rosen, but the next instant she dismissed the idea. What would have been the purpose of summoning Harry to hear that news? Not simply to arrange for Emily's removal, surely? Perhaps. Her mother might, on occasion, do anything.

Paula prepared to accept the latest arrangements that fate (she had never been able to separate her mother from fate) had fixed for her.

Harry was, with added maturity, a changed man. She herself was not what she had been. They found it surprisingly easy to talk together. There was no other word for it—before dinner tonight they had actually flirted. She had difficulty in remembering why they had parted, and stayed apart so long.

And both thinking that Lilian's intention was simply to force them together for their own good, she and her husband mentally assumed that her arguments would be, indeed, had been, won. Occasional glances exchanged behind the head of an immobile Emily helped to bring about the conviction that the assumption was mutual.

'You won't ever be as good-looking as these two blondes,' Rosen said suddenly to Emily, beaming, pleased to have complimented both women at once.

And Harry, feeling an unfamiliar rise of pride in his possession, looked across at Paula—she *was* nice-looking—who had turned a curiously gratified smile on her daughter.

But Lilian would have nothing to do with smiles and compliments. Though Paula and Harry strained to convince her by every means except actual *words,* that they were in happy accord with her intention to reunite them, she was grim, her manner portentous. She seemed not to notice; she would not respond. They thought—even Paula thought—that she was dense.

The heavy central light shone on the white table-cloth. Emily moved her head slightly from time to time to catch a new glimpse of the woven pattern. Shiny bits, dull bits. It was infinitely boring, frighteningly boring...Oh yes, she was frightened.

The conversation—the talk about Sydney, about the future—she disregarded in a way that ought to have been impossible. It concerned her deeply. But she knew. She knew that this was not it. She had heard Lilian say, 'Later,' meaning later, when *she* was not there. And without that she would still have known with clear cold certainty, and her knowledge would still have made her heart beat with foreboding as it did now, slowly.

At the end of the meal, abruptly Lilian said to her, 'Go out and talk to your friends for half an hour while we do the dishes and then come in and stay in your room with a book.'

No one ever told her what to do. Everyone looked at her. She extricated herself from the tight wedge of chairs, from their solemn-eyed presence. She had no will. She went like an automaton.

Patty was at the gate. 'Hullo. That's your best dress.'

'Yes. I have to go in in half an hour because they're here.'

What did they bring you?'

'She brought sandals. He gave me a box of chocolates.'

'You get a lot of things.'

Emily breathed.

They walked up and down the short stretch of footpath between their respective homes. They walked hand-in-hand, looking now at their shoes, now earnestly into each other's eyes, as they talked.

The sun jerked below the horizon and it was night. Streetlights came on, and the lights at the windows of the bungalows. Curtains and blinds remained undrawn on the summer night. A scattering of stars appeared.

Patty said, 'I know why people get married. You don't, do you?'

Emily had not known she did not know. 'Why?'

They scuffed along, voices low and constricted. Patty told.

Complete silence, then, 'What?' Emily screeched. 'Oh, I don't believe it!'

'Well, it's true! Someone told me who knows. But I don't *get* it, do you?'

They had stopped walking, now they moved on again in silence.

That men and women went to bed together was old history. Some notion of the purpose had been conveyed to Emily at seven, when she had shared a bedroom with Audrey, a girl who worked for Lilian before Dotty came. Audrey's boyfriend got into bed with her the nights that Lilian went out. They used to wake Emily up. At first she had been obscurely terrified, but after a while she took no notice. It was simply something else that grown-ups did. Events had never conspired to convince her that there was any connexion between this habit and marriage, still less, love. Even the baby business, as she thought of it, was a mechanical matter of cause and effect. Weird. Loveless. And now this.

At length she said gloomily, 'Good heavens!' Then again, overcome by the preposterousness of Patty's claim she said, 'Well, I knew about *that,* but I didn't think that was why...Oh, there must be more to it than that—liking one another and being friends and being interested in things and talking...Don't you think so?'

'That doesn't matter at all,' Patty said firmly. 'It's just the other.' Borrowing the tone of her informant, she was convincing.

'You would have thought—' Emily began, and shook her head. She had meant to say, 'You would have thought they would have loved each other,' but in view of the truth it sounded too naïve. 'Heavens, Pat!'

'That's what *I* said. I wouldn't believe her for ages. I don't care though, do you?'

'No.'

Shaken, they spent the following fifteen minutes cheering one another with avowals of indifference. But each felt the world to be colder, flatter, less explicable, for the loss of passionate, but chaste, romantic love.

It was time to go.

'Incredible!' called Emily from the veranda, and Patty lifted a hand at the gate, 'But true!'

How wise, how disillusioned, how philosophical they felt! And somehow, how marvellous they were! So that was life!

In the split-second of turning in at the front door, reality, the present moment, forced itself back on Emily. What did she care about all that? This was tonight, this funny night. She had eaten less than half an hour ago and been afraid. There was only this moment, this suspicion. She listened to the sounds of the house. The washing-up was finishing in the kitchen; the men were in the sitting-room.

The thin belated squeak of the gate and sudden footsteps jerked her round in time to see Billie and Fred advancing up the path. Billie looked up at her with the kind of serious glitter suitable for royal occasions, seemed to stare at her as if it meant something.

Doubtful, Emily looked down at the skirt of her dress. It was her best one, and worth a look, she supposed.

She smiled at them and Fred mumbled hullo, then as Billie swept past her into the hall, her mother and Lilian left the kitchen—Paula to join the men, Lilian to come forward to meet her friends.

Mutely, she greeted them, her eyes making signals so obvious as to be almost audible. Billie clasped her hands and watched while she gave Emily a little push on the shoulder.

'I was just coming to call you. Into the bedroom this instant, and stay there, do you hear me?'

Furious, Emily stalked away from them. 'Yes, and you don't have to push me! I was going anyway!'

It had only been a token push, but still! What for? And in front of Billie who didn't like her!

Unhappily Fred fingered his jaw-bone and looked at the wallpaper.

She heard Lilian say, 'They're all waiting.'

I want a glass of milk.

She rehearsed the unmeaning words of justification several times before going to the door. There was no sound.

I want a glass of milk.

Very lightly, very slowly, she crept out into the open space of the hall. Had they all gone?

But then, at once, she knew the house was occupied. The silence on which she had opened the door was a prolonged pause—nothing more—in a turbulent conversation. It began again with a kind of restrained vehemence, ran swiftly, skirting hysteria. The voices combined in a sound that made Emily shiver with fear.

This was what she had heard an hour ago, more faintly though, for then she had not moved from her room. Now she went close to the place that had quite suddenly become the source of panic. Her back pressed against the wall, she stood staring at the door, impaled by a sense of impending calamity, incapable of distinguishing words or voices, simply apprehending in tones and echoes, a fear and intention that left her cold to the heart.

All at once Lilian's voice rose above the others.

'Why should *I* have the responsibility? You'll just have to make a home for her. And you've to see him in the morning, Harry, and tell him to get out by lunch-time. These people—these people will tell you what's been going on...'

A chorus of mixed voices interrupted her here, but in a moment she went on, '...not her fault, but I can't be always watching...always round her...got a bad reputation...Thea and him years ago...get the police on to him...Anyway, *I'm* not, I'm too...Well, they'll tell you, and it's time you...'

'...get a doctor...' came Rosen's voice.

'Shut your mouth, you...'

Someone gave a cry and again the voices rose, clashing with alarm and hysteria; the voices split, and Rosen and Billie could be heard shouting each other down. Her mother and father in lower, less steady tones explained and apologized into the unlistening air. Over all came Lilian's voice, strident, dogmatic, hot with accusation.

Confirmation had touched off the climax of horror and grief, an explosion of horror and disbelief. Now Emily's lungs were full of lead. She went back to the bedroom pursued by a raucous cry. The next instant, a profound silence, the suspension of which she did not hear, settled over the house.

She sat on the sofa and played the hem of her dress through her fingers, not thinking, looking pensive, taking a spasmodic shallow breath. She sighed.

And then the inadequacy of any outward gesture to relieve or express what she was as yet too numb to feel made her shrug, as if at some other, frivolous self who had come along saying, 'You're upset! Make a noise! Bang your head against the wall! React so that you can be sure you're unhappy.'

She sat thinly alone. Tonight for the first time she was united with herself in desolation, and the solitude of that unity made her turn her head slowly and look round the walls in helpless wonder. Tonight the customary split between actor and commentator was bridged, there was nowhere to retreat, no demonstrative companion to say, 'Yes, this is sad, but bearable. Yes, you're right to moan, but it doesn't matter very much, does it? Calm down and stop kidding. You don't really care about anything.'

At other times since she had known Max, the wry and imperturbable adviser had vanished and she had wandered out alone in happy country where she simply *was*, and questioned nothing. This was the other side—the far side—of that country.

Looking at her, slumped forward on the tight blue sofa, one would not have thought her capable of so immediate a return to life as she displayed when a sound warned that someone was coming.

She leapt behind the sofa, stood gripping the back. Paula came in, silently weeping, her hands to her face. At the sight of her daughter, she stopped, and was stared at with wild accusing eyes.

Following her a moment later, Lilian looked from one to the other impatiently, made tutting noises with her tongue. 'Well!' she exclaimed.

There were about her still, traces of high excitement; her cheek-bones, her eyes, were brilliant with colour.

'You'll have to come out and say goodbye.' She touched Paula on the shoulder. 'They're all waiting. I told them to wait for you.'

Heavily Paula looked at her. 'Do I…? Oh, all right.' Wiping her pale lips she went to the dressing-table, fluffed some powder over her face without seeing her reflection, combed her hair.

Watching, Lilian could not help the wave of stimulation that swept over her at the sight of Paula's tears, her puffy face. It was not that she hated her; there was merely an obscure judgement somewhere in her mind that made her feel that it served Paula right. She had been too placid, too untroubled. *This* was what happened to fine people from Sydney.

'I'm ready.'

With another wordless look at Emily they went out. She heard them cross the wooden veranda, walk down the stone steps, crunch along the gravel.

So this was it. It was all over. All over?

Rubbing her hand along the polished wooden frame where it found itself she came out into the room and stood. She stood in the centre of the room. Suddenly she flung herself over to the windows, with trembling hands sent the curtains flying, jerked at the window and sent it shooting up with a crash so that the six people in the dark garden turned in surprise and saw the subject of their conversation outlined against the bright light of the room.

Eyes flashing with tears, she stared out into the darkness. Her chest heaved. When she tried to speak she gave a groan. A curious human groan came to block her voice.

She clutched at the window-sill. 'What have you done?' she screamed. 'You're all mad! You don't know anything. I hate you all! I wish you were dead!'

Her voice cracked. Choked with tears, she turned slowly away and leaned against the wall.

The curtains fell across the windows. The people in the garden gasped; someone said, 'Ignore it. She's delirious. She'll be all right in the morning.'

She was running through the house, calling Max, looking in every room, biting on the back of her hand in an effort to stifle the sobs that threatened to incapacitate her.

Coming up from behind, Lilian caught her by the elbows and, relying on superior weight, started to steer her to the bedroom.

With a quick wrench the girl escaped. Her tears stopped. 'Don't touch me!' She backed away. 'Don't you touch me!'

Nonplussed, Lilian hesitated. 'Well, get yourself off to bed this minute or you'll be touched whether you like it or not. There's places for girls like you, you know. Blubber, blubber, blubber. It's all you're good for.'

'Oh, Mum!' said Paula, distressed. 'Don't talk to her like that.'

Harry and Rosen looked on with expressions of mingled satisfaction and dislike.

‘Oh, well,’ Lilian excused herself. ‘*You* tell her to go to bed. I don’t know. I don’t know. She’s given us enough trouble for one night.’

The adults revolved to watch Emily go, baffled by her, by her extraordinary attachment, by her expressed (though undoubtedly hysterical) dislike of themselves.

At the last moment Lilian could not restrain herself. She shouted, ‘She’s a little blighter, though. If she worried more about her own mother and father instead of getting worked up about old married men old enough to be her father, it’d be more like the thing.’

Harry smoothed back his hair and frowned at Paula disagreeably when she tried to rise to a placating smile. He told her plainly that in his eyes she bore sole responsibility for her mother and her daughter and that he, for one, was fed up with the lot of them.

‘Would anyone like a cup of tea?’ she said timidly, gazing at him, but Lilian cried, ‘Listen!’ and, electrified, they obeyed her silencing hand, heard footsteps on the path outside.

‘It’s him! It’s him!’ she hissed, eyes dilated. ‘It’s up to you, Harry. Catch him now. We’ll all go to bed out of your way. Come on. Quick. You know what to say, Harry.’

After a confused moment during which the four milled, crashed into each other, and generally panicked, she and Paula fled towards their room. Rosen, standing at the entrance to his, finally saw it and melted round the door, leaving it sufficiently ajar, however, to catch Lilian’s *sotto voce* message from the top of the hall to Harry, who stood irresolutely scratching his ear.

'No fighting, Harry! I won't have any fighting. Keep your head with him.'

He nodded glumly and disappeared into the kitchen where his adversary could be heard moving about.

In the front bedroom Lilian and Paula lay side by side, listening to the silence. A few feet from them on the sofa, Emily lay with her face pressed between the pillow and the hard shiny brocade of the back, her red-rimmed eyes closed tight.

She knew what they meant, and what they meant to say to him: she understood that she was helpless to prevent them. She wanted to die.

At half past six, chinks of bright daylight ran down the sides of the window blinds. With infinite stealth Emily lifted the blankets and slid to the floor, hot with fear, not moving her eyes from the bed where her mother and grandmother slept.

Crawling on hands and knees to the door she anticipated the despair of a final deprivation. If they could prevent her seeing him, they would, and if they did...

Outside, she tugged on her dressing-gown, and paused again only when she reached his room, her fingers on the white china handle. She was all at once sick, shy, guilty, afraid of Max. She was beset by memories, too, of the long succession of other mornings, the entry into Max's life, understanding, understandable life.

She went in. He was sitting on the edge of his bed, dressed, smoking. Around him were scattered open suitcases. When he looked up she ran to him.

Clinging to him there was no necessity to look, no possibility of being seen; but weeping, clutching him desperately, her voice muffled by his shirt, his arms, she had still to smile because she was with him now, could feel the warmth of his skin, the vibrations of his voice.

Yet an instant later, separated from him, she could have blushed. They had been made strangers, self-conscious strangers. There seemed suddenly no reason why they should address to each other a single word. What could they possibly have, or ever have had, to say to each other? Even so much as goodbye would be superfluous.

Indeed, it seemed to the girl that Max had already gone from her, that this calm gentle stranger who had allowed her to sprinkle him with tears, was not Max. She wiped her eyes and blew her nose. She glanced up, and they exchanged a painful look. She saw that he wanted to be kind but hardly knew how to go about it.

She whispered, 'Won't I ever see you again?'

With the last exhalation of his cigarette, Max sent up a smokescreen. He leaned across to the ashtray. 'I had to leave soon, Emily. The firm is sending me back to Melbourne. I meant to tell you before. I should have.'

Then he gazed at her and, when he saw her bewilderment, frowned. She looked up and he went on briskly, 'I'm sorry I won't be able to write, or hear from you, but I'll be very busy and so will you, and your father thinks it best not. On the whole I quite agree. But wait a minute.' He extricated himself from the barricade she formed against his legs and going to the dressing-table lifted a card. 'These will be my addresses when I get back, at work and at home. There seems to be no particular reason why you shouldn't have them. Sometime, later on, if your mother and father don't object, you might write if you have some important news. And I could do the same. But for a long time, anyway, you'll be hard at it at school and so on, and as I said, I...'

Emily took the card. Unnoticed, it fell from her slack fingers. She understood he did not believe what he said.

'Oh, Max, don't hate *me,*' she said in a small voice. The desire that he should be compensated fought with her perception of the affront apology would be and closed her mouth. She smoothed her cheek along the side of the bed as if it were a kind of weight which would hold them both to the room, hold time.

Max, who had been emptying the shelves of books and stacking them into the open trunk, turned at the sound of her almost inaudible appeal. At that moment the big square window filled with sunshine: the room was lightened, warmed. Sunlight fell on the young girl curled up on the floor against the bed, kindled the brilliant dark-blue of her gown and hung over her uncombed hair: her right cheek, her right hand, were touched by it. And he, too, was covered in light, made suddenly round and whole, brought back to recognizable life, made again her kindest friend, breathing, brown-skinned, looking down at her, leaving her, sent away from her...

'Oh, *Max,*' she cried, as if a door had opened for a moment again on feeling.

He helped her up to sit on the bed and stood in front of her, holding her hands.

'Well, Emmy...It's hard to know what to say all at once, isn't it? Try to cheer up, Em. This does no good.'

Her eyelids rose. She looked at him and he smiled, not very successfully. She had no thought of smiling. Her eyes stayed on his, confident that something would come that she could hold on to, that she would not be left without hope. They seemed even to implore him to deny what the room around them proclaimed—that he was on the point of leaving. Today.

'It seems that you'll be going to live with your mother and father in Sydney now, and I think that's a very good thing. I was glad to hear about it.'

She tried to tug her hands away but he held them tight.

'It would please me to think that you'll really try to be happy with them, and try to get the most out of the new kind of life you'll be living there. I won't be there to see how you're getting on, but I'll depend on you to do your best.'

He had never spoken to her like this before. He was treating her like a baby. She gave him an almost contemptuous look and stared stubbornly at the ground. She felt as if the blood was draining from her body.

'I hate them. You know I do.'

'I don't believe that, Emmy. And I wish you wouldn't say it. They...' But he found it difficult to talk about them.

Still holding one of her hands he sat down beside her but she immediately slipped from the bed and knelt in front of him.

He said, 'For the time being, at least, you'd better forget all I said about university, Em. I was mistaken in mentioning it to you before I'd talked it over with your parents. In any case—' he paused for breath. This morning, breath, speech, thought, were things to be achieved laboriously, actions to be performed with the dull persevering abstractedness of someone half drugged. 'In any case,' he began again, 'that's all a long way ahead.'

Hardly taking this in, Emily clasped blindly at his hands, feeling them as if to learn by heart the texture of skin, the firmness of bone, the particular shaping and grouping of atoms that made these hands, that face, unique in all the world, the hands of Max, the face of Max.

He continued to speak, and her mind recorded and discarded his words, for these were not the important words he had to say to her, not the words she would want to remember and be supported by.

'Oh, I don't care. It doesn't matter about that,' she said, shaking her head from side to side. But when he said dully, 'I suppose you're right,' she said, 'Oh, if you think it matters, I do care, Max. I do. But what good does it do if they won't...?'

'None, none, of course,' he said. But it had been something concrete to discuss, if not what she wanted. She was asking for some blindingly honest statement, a synthesis of what this year had been not only to him, but to herself as well. In ten minutes she would have him put into words a blue-print—which would be a promise, too—for the future. She would have a crystallization of his feeling and his hopes for her. She would have it visible, tangible. She believed it could be done.

He said, 'Will you remember the things we've talked about these months, I wonder?'

And now, at last her heart began to beat. There was a kind of humming in her ears which she heard through the sound of her own voice. 'I won't forget anything ever. My Greeks and Romans, I'll never forget. I'll keep on reading till I know as much as you.'

A stray reminiscent flash of enthusiasm surprised her face and was extinguished. But she had seen the flickering response in Max's face so she plodded on, more slowly, looking now at the pattern on his tie, the buttons on his shirt. She swallowed.

'After the death of Alexander I'll go right on to—wherever else it goes. And all the experiments I did. And how to ride a bike and how to dive. And amoebas... And, oh, what else? A lot of things.' She briefly met his eyes and gave a strained embarrassed laugh. 'All the poetry. And all you told me about the stars. And all the other things...'

The things, the things. Now *she* talked about the things.

'Not to be afraid the way I was of the dark, and speaking, and people...'

Max put his hands over her ears and she closed her eyes for a moment to feel them. When he spoke his voice sounded in her head like a memory.

'About people—it's still true, Emmy. Don't spend your nights being afraid of murderers and your days being shy, but at the same time, remember—'

He hardly knew how to voice a warning without frightening her, her reaction to his least word was apt to be disproportionate. He said, 'Learn from people, but don't be dispersed by them. And remember that the bad times have compensations. Unhappiness is not all loss. Not by any means. And as for us—you and me—we've both learned a great deal. A great deal,' he repeated heavily, letting his hands fall.

Words were lame symbols. Speech now, with time passing, was almost a dangerous indulgence. It was too late to meander and qualify. But then he saw by Emily's face that she had hardly heard him.

After a pause he got up and began to move about the room.

As Emily turned on her knees to watch him searching through his books, the urgency of her longing, her necessity to keep him, broke over her.

What use memories of eyes and voice? What use books, ideas, theories—anything—when he was gone? She had almost expected—so fevered was her brain, so virulent her fear—that a miracle might occur. Indeed, for a short time she dreamed that it already had. She had so felt the impossibility of their parting, had so sent the concentrated passion of her need for him to her eyes, had so searched his eyes and *wanted* to keep him, as to have consumed him—not in memory or thought, but in fact. An easy change had been to be consumed by him, to disappear as a person in her own right, for ever, and safely with him, safely *Max,* to go away with him and never return.

But as she blankly rose to her feet, the descent from desirable illusion began. Incredulously she said, 'You're really going.'

Several seconds later Max said, 'I'm leaving these for you.' He indicated a pile of books which he had stacked on the chair. 'Some of them you probably won't look at for years, but I think you'll get round to them all eventually.'

She said nothing but they automatically went to the chair and stood handling the covers of the books.

'You'll need them,' Emily objected, staring blindly at the cold weighty oblong she had lifted.

'No, I'll replace them.'

Slowly they moved away from the chair and stood facing each other in the middle of the floor.

'And now...' Max said, and they heard Dotty letting herself in at the back door. 'I'll be going at half past nine, Em. Harris is sending a taxi round. I'll be at the Promenade till I leave Ballowra in about three weeks' time. Perhaps sooner. I may have the date pushed forward.'

At her uncomprehending look he turned away and went to the window. She followed him in a trance.

'I see now that I may have been wrong in all this... I never meant to do you any harm. I think you know that.' He spoke stiffly. They stood at the open space oblivious of the sun, the morning wind.

Emily waited patiently, arms hanging limply by her sides, a kind of trusting, short-sighted earnestness and confidence about her face, as if, even yet, she would not believe.

'I'll miss you very much. I know you'll miss me, too. We've had a lot of fun—a very good time, together, haven't we?'

The weight of her expectations made him speak lamely, inadequately, even—as he saw it—insultingly.

She had lifted an almost impatient hand as he spoke. Now she said, after the slightest pause, 'I *love* you.' There was a note of incredulity in her voice.

Max took her by the shoulders. 'I know you do. I'm very honoured. In a way, a very good way, I love you, too. And so I should.' He gave her the gentlest shake, tried to make her look up. 'You've done more for me than you know. It's been far from one-sided. It's been a real friendship, hasn't it? And I don't believe we won't meet again. One day, quite soon, I'll see you, and you'll be grown-up and able—'

She had been standing in his arms, lifeless as a puppet, but now she pulled away and stared at him, hostile.

'You don't *care*.'

The smile faded from his face. He looked at her so gravely, so kindly, that her heart threatened to break. Her eyebrows rose in a kind of puzzled entreaty.

And then she imperfectly received the idea that she was young, that Max's past, the life he had lived before she was born, had really happened, was not simply a story told for the exclusive pleasure of her emotions. He had really *lived* longer, and this had happened to him, perhaps, before.

But she did not believe it, any more than she believed that the utter familiarity, the current of warmth, the common language, of their single friendship could so simply remove itself from her.

'You know that's not true, Em.'

She looked at him sullenly, accusing him of evasion. She felt she hated him.

'For my sake—no, don't look so sceptical. You can do better than this. Listen, Em. I must go today—very soon. Nothing can change that. You can make it better for both of us by accepting it, by trying to. It's not easy, I know. Remember that I don't like it either...And Emmy, don't fight your family off because of this. Don't blame them... I'll be seeing you again this morning before I go, but now we must say goodbye. Friends. If we don't we'll be unhappy to remember it. You've been so good and sensible. Don't spoil it now.'

She stepped back.

'I won't. I won't say goodbye. Max, don't make me say goodbye.' Her voice came in a whisper. She moved farther away from him, cringed against the wall.

Max stood quite still. He gave a profound sigh. Seconds passed, and he stretched out a hand. She was in his arms.

There was a knock on the door. It was the signal that breakfast would soon be ready.

Very gently Max kissed and then released her.

In a nightmare, she wandered to the door, drifted out into the hall, found herself in the kitchen watching Dotty who, seeing her, exclaimed, 'Not dressed yet?'

She was turning the toast on the griller, turning an egg in the pan.

'He's going away, Dot.'

She switched off the gas under the milk, reached for the pot holder. 'I know. They told me the other day.'

'Why?' A spoilt, querulous note.

A gas jet was turned off. 'They thought he was too fond of you, they said.'

'Mm? What did you say, Dot?' Her eyelids fell.

'He was too fond of you, they thought.'

And Emily, going away to wash and dress, passed Max on his way to the kitchen, and was ashamed.

CHAPTER NINE

PATTY CAME up eating an ice-cream. She shuffled to a stop at the gate. ''S hot,' she complained. She licked her ice-cream and looked up and down the road. The earth was powdery, the hedge covered with dust.

Two women passed on the other side of the street. Patty stared and licked, stared and licked, turned a complete circle to watch them out of sight. 'Mrs Baker and that Mrs Redfern,' she said. 'Gee, she's fat!

'Mum says I ought to get my hair cut,' she told Emily. 'She says it's using all my strength. Makes me hot, too.' She lifted a languid arm and piled the blonde curls on top of her head for a moment. 'But the boys like it,' she suddenly confided, laughing, showing all her pretty teeth. 'Nutty things call me Goldilocks and Curlytop, but I don't care.'

Cars could be heard coming up the hill. Emily turned a look of such concentration on the corner where they must come into sight that Patty glanced from her to the corner and back again, licking in double quick time.

Four cars and a van streamed in a line past them and up the hill. The projection of despairing hopefulness that had gone out retreated disabled, sank back into the girl. She placed her forehead carefully on the top of the gate.

'Waiting for someone?'

'No.' The brown head stayed on the gate.

'I'm going,' Patty threatened, munching quickly through the ice-cream cone. She looked round for a diversion. She licked her sticky fingers and waved them through the hot air to dry. 'Well, I'm going,' she gave final warning, challenging Emily to try to make her stay. Glancing up at the veranda she said, 'Here comes someone for you, anyhow. See you later.'

'Emily!' called Paula, looking out over the roofs of the shops. 'Emily!' she called. 'Come in and have a glass of milk.'

Unresisting, the girl trailed up the red stone steps. They were all in the sitting-room when she went in, having morning tea, eating square biscuits, looking at newspapers and talking.

Paula, unlike the others, who lolled back among the velvet cushions of the sofa and armchairs and scattered crumbs on the carpet, sat at the table. She was apparently occupied with her handkerchief, giving it rhythmic tugs, pulling it through her fingers, sometimes rolling it into a ball as if the game had ended, only to devise, in the next instant, some new trick for it to perform.

'Well, I always say that Murphy is one of the best little riders we've got. What do you think, Harry?'

'Horses?' He licked a cigarette paper expertly. 'Don't know much about them, Lilian.' His eyes flashed to the doorway where Emily stood watching them.

They all sat up a little: Paula turned in her chair. An air, at once propitiating and self-congratulatory, came over them. They looked at her consciously, positively seeing her in a way usually reserved for her birthday, or Christmas morning.

'Here she is!' cried Lilian, and she and Paula rose together to give her the glass of milk.

At this the two men looked away, looked down at their knees, slightly disgusted and jealous, but when Lilian and Paula turned their brightly smiling faces on them for encouragement and support, they, too, smiled broadly, and Harry cleared his throat to ask, 'And what's on the programme for this afternoon, Emily? Are you going to the pictures with your friend?'

She looked at them. False expectancy emphasized their indifference, made them incredibly alien. She thought: I hate them, and there was hatred in her. But she felt only a profound desire not to see or be near them.

'No. Nothing.' She put the glass on the table and left the room.

Harry said, 'My God!' and clamped his mouth shut with rage.

Rosen gave a laugh that might have been scornful, might have been deprecating, and picked up the newspaper again. He smoothed down the few hairs on his head with the palm of his hand, every slow studied movement, the deliberate sliding of his eyes across the printed page, expressing too clearly his contemptuous amusement at the scene just past, and his extreme personal satisfaction that justice had earlier in the day been done.

For *he* had gone—gone quietly without words or fuss. Officially he had not been seen to go: in fact they had all watched his departure—Paula from the bedroom, Lilian from the dining-room; Harry, in the sitting-room, had seen the taxi when it turned the corner. Rosen had been in the garage. Emily carried a coat for him and a brief-case. She stood at the gate, waving.

As his name had not been mentioned to her since the arrival of her mother and father, it had not seemed possible—even Lilian would have been embarrassed—to forbid her to say goodbye. So Emily and Max alone had freely used the house that morning, while *they* had been constrained to dart from room to room, eyelids lowered, after listening behind closed doors in the hope of avoiding him.

A certain surreptitious enjoyment of the absurdity of their behaviour made them feel a little coy, a little distrait, and, too, rather flat, when they met immediately after his departure—popping out into the passage as if an assembly whistle had blown.

There had been a jittery moment—on the part of the men—of relieved nose-blowing and trouser-hitching, an air of coming to the surface after a deep dive. Lilian tugged purposefully at loose straps of clothing, pushed at her hair and said, 'I think we'll have some tea!' At that they laughed, and rather noisily making free with the spaces of the house, they had adjourned to the sitting-room.

Lilian began to wonder about her bets for the afternoon races. Over the tea the men decided to go down to the shopping centre to have their hair cut and Lilian gave them a list of messages to execute. Only Paula had not laughed. Silent, she fiddled with her handkerchief and paid no attention to what was said. Suddenly she had gone to call Emily, but now, again, Emily stood at the gate.

His face had been grey—grey as that paling fence, grey as that twist of smoke. And he had gone. Finally. Irrevocably.

Almost carefully she led herself back, away from that thought, and as if she was pretending something, drew a shallow sigh from her lungs and tonelessly said, 'Oh, dear!' And she saw the black and yellow taxi drive away. Again she said, 'Don't go!' Again it went away.

Yes, but was it over? Was it? Anything could happen yet. It was only—what time was it?—twenty to eleven. Well, just think, only twenty to eleven. Quite early.

It had all been some kind of terrific joke. You just had to think how they loved to tease people to see it. They'd all got together—though why?...Oh, why was beyond anyone. But that was it. Any minute now the taxi would come back, out would come all the cases—and Max. It was really a stupid thing to have done, but when they all stood round laughing and smiling and saying, 'We had you fooled! You believed it!' she'd play up to them, give them their money's worth, and then she would want to laugh, too.

Max would say—for obviously he must have been in the plot—'We were wondering how long we could keep going without giving it away. You took it so seriously.'

She felt herself straining to smile at this—for coming from Max it did hurt a bit; it wasn't really what you expected from him. But still! What did it matter? Even Max you couldn't expect to be perfect. He'd said things before today, accidentally, that had...

But anyway, there they stood: Max and her mother and father and Lilian and Rosen, all smiling and smiling, and deprecating her youthful gullibility.

They stood in a circle, and their faces gradually set like stone. The picture held, held fast, would not be jogged. Belief could not be counterfeited even in imagination.

For there, inside, a few minutes ago, she had held a glass of milk and looked at them. *That* had not been the direction of their pretence. Silently, insistently, they had said, 'You've lost. Make up your mind to that. We've had our way, so let's be friends and forget all that...You belong to us.' No joke.

> Will you come into my parlour
> Said the spider to the fly,
> It's the neatest little parlour
> That ever you did spy.
> There's a something in the...

She trod deliberately on an ant and looked up, looked suddenly round as if to identify the nature of her own murderer. And it was everything and everywhere. Polished pale-blue sky, white streaky clouds, grey smoke—relentless. Painted wooden houses overlaid with grime; gutters, telegraph poles, insensate wood and brick—relentless: all part of what was opposed to her, what was cold, implacable. And the pale-skinned people in the house behind her, to whom she was, she felt, no more than a troublesome force to be held in check by will—what they had done to him…

Some tears slid down her cheeks and fell on the mottled paintwork of the gate. She paddled a finger in them; spread them out neatly till they soaked into the wood, brought her shoulder round to wipe her face against the short sleeve of her dress. Leaning forward she pillowed her forehead on her arms. The sun burned her back.

The black and yellow taxi drove away. 'Don't go,' she said.

Somewhere over to the left, the garage doors ground open and the car came out. Rosen and her father. With a zoom they went down the hill, throbbed out of sight.

Other noises came then to offend ears drugged by the perpetual humming of machinery—a thin hooting of horns, the rooster-like throat clearing of a solitary bicycle bell as a boy sped past. At Emily's side the uncut hedge scraped its twigs and leaves monotonously under the tutelage of a small monotonous wind.

Across the street a pale-green van pulled up under a veil of swirling dust. A man jumped out, jerked open the doors at the back, lifted out a tray of cakes and ran with it into Sim's shop.

In the house Dotty switched on the wireless. For a moment, unadjusted, it sent the inhuman clashings of a brass band out into the hollow Saturday morning. Someone could be felt to fly to modify it. Lilian's reproof was followed through the window by a song so old that one could only conclude it had been requested as a treat for some elderly relative. 'Look for the Silver Lining.'

Sweeping the steps, Dotty jerked her head at the window as she called to Emily, 'This is for you, love.' And inside, hearing, Lilian and Paula exchanged shocked smiles. There was no answer from the garden. Lilian snorted a little, Paula sighed and they resumed.

Free of the men, they had dropped relievedly into the velvet cushions hollowed out by them on the sofa, and gone again over dates, finances, clothes, aims, and resolutions in regard to the now much-favoured reconciliation with Harry—he returned to Coolong that afternoon to press for the transfer he was confident of obtaining.

On another level, Lilian, at least, held herself ready to be at any moment besieged by *his* return. (None of them—even in thought—allowed that Max possessed a name.)

His quietness, apart from having left her with a quantity of unspent bluster, had not so much convinced her of the truth of her accusations, as concerned her about his intentions. Someone—she had forgotten which of them—had said, 'Sue.' Whether he could, whether he would, whether he thought of such a thing she did not know; she simply felt—she could not have said on what grounds—that it would be just like him.

She bit her teeth together, clasped and unclasped the band of her diamond wrist-watch, and accidentally said aloud, 'Too damned clever!' making Paula, who had been stolidly setting out the advantages of being again supported by her husband, flush, and say, 'Me?'

Later, after a meal which gave the curious impression of having been achieved in the face of difficulties, Paula changed her dress, climbed into the car, which smelled still of the concoction poured on Harry's head by the barber, and went to the station with him. Rosen, as usual, drove.

But the horses were running at Randwick this afternoon and Lilian stayed at home. Emily could not be found even to say goodbye to her father, though five minutes after they set out, she was at the gate, leaning over it, occasionally pulling from the hedge a green-black leaf which left dust in the whorls of her forefinger and thumb.

When the black and yellow taxi drove away with Max, she said, 'Don't go. I don't know what to do.'

Though she trembled, she watched it go feeling little more than weak surprise at the extraordinary power that was able to overcome the very essence of her will. She *loved,* but he had been taken. All her willing, all her concentration, all her promises to unseen gods—unheeded, unheard. She was a very little animal.

And even he had been defeated, could be defeated, in spite of all...

With widened eyes she looked at her dusty fingers, along the quiet street, at the corner round which he had gone away—and the scene was ordinary, familiar. Yet somewhere in the midst of it her intangible opponent had suddenly unveiled himself to her, disported in her tears and weakness. And he was very big.

Thea left the bus and walked along the road on the crest of the hill. It was deserted and, when the bus had disappeared, very quiet. At this point the road ran in the cleft between two crumbling, yellow cliffs, one of which supported a wooden railing, a footpath, and a row of old but rather more elaborate than average bungalows. The other was thin and sloped quickly down to a bank of trees: these trees as yet hid the valley, the river, the factory, the monastery.

At the edge of the road the tar had come sluggishly to life, trickled warmly over sharp stones, held itself in plastic readiness to accept the imprints of a tyre or sole or paw.

And up from the river the summer wind blew, humming its almost peaceful song of distant industry and clamour, smelling ever so faintly of water and weeds and trees, making itself known to Thea's senses, bringing with it such a pang of nostalgia that she had to smile even as it made her heart quake.

For Forrester had asked, when she declared herself finished with the conference after one and a half days, 'What the blue blazes will you find to do with yourself in this dump for a whole afternoon?'

'I'm not sure,' she said, 'but at least I do know what I'll be missing.'

He pressed, 'Oh, come on, stick it out! We'll probably break it up by three o'clock and then we'll all do something together. God knows what! Swim. Have a drink. See the sights.'

Blake said dryly, 'Sounds irresistible. But Thea used to work here for A.C.I.L.' He nodded to Forrester. 'There's your answer. She's off on a sentimental journey to see the old galley, and maybe discover some state secrets from our rivals. Which reminds me. Wasn't it a bit queer that they didn't send their head boy along?'

'No obligation,' Forrester said. 'He sent the stuff, all right. Hear he's leaving any day now. You used to know him, Thea, didn't you? Wasn't a social type, they say.' At her expression, he said humourlessly, 'Oh, sorry, sorry. Mustn't stop the sentimental journey.'

And both men half rose, Forrester dabbing his pale Air-Force moustache, as she left the table and went to her room.

Fifteen minutes later she left the hotel and caught a bus to Greenhills.

Now she emerged from the tunnel of cliffs, walking slowly, her hair, her dress, beating back under the waves of wind: she emerged on a magnificent panorama of sky. Leaving the road on the right, she crossed a few feet of rough ground and reached the fence below which everything lay, serene, familiar, looking exactly as it had when she went away.

Her fingers pressed the top of a grey weathered post which had once been a sapling. Now, grey-blue wire passed through two small holes inexpertly bored by someone long ago. Leaning slightly against it, Thea felt the warmth of the wood. She was so stirred by what she saw, by what she had been told, by her isolation on this particular hill on this hot Saturday afternoon—most of all by memories—that she could have embraced the post, would have been relieved to weep against it, sleep beside it, waken healed and unmoved.

A sentimental journey.

At half past ten in the morning, coffee had been brought into the conference room. Delegates and observers had circulated, formed and re-formed in small groups, talking shop, gossiping, holding cups and saucers high as they edged in and out, and fought their way to some familiar face on the other side of the room.

It was then, quite accidentally, that Thea had heard his name, learned, from a slightly dazzled young man, that Max was in Ballowra, still with A.C.I.L. at the old factory.

She was jarred and sick as if she had fallen in a faint.

When she was able she had been obliged to say, 'Do you suppose we could reach those chairs by the window?' and her informant had eagerly rushed to clear a way, racking his brains to think of something else to tell her—approximate date of arrival in Ballowra, approximate date of departure for Melbourne...

He noted with disappointment that his companion was less interested than he had at first thought. He was himself with A.C.I.L., he told her, but new, and he didn't know where his chief lived, except that he boarded somewhere in Greenhills. However there was someone over there, that chap in the dark suit, who would be sure to know; he would find out for her like a shot.

She seemed mildly puzzled, or amused, by his insistence, and blushing, he subsided in his chair. A moment later he took her empty cup with unnecessary force and clanked it on the table behind him. Just the same, he stayed, and very soon he was talking about himself with rare fluency. How glad he was that he had taken science. And it had been the purest fluke!

It was very likely, Thea thought, that this nice young man would not remember where their conversation had begun. It was almost certain that he would not mention it—or her—to Max. Her involuntary revelation of their past connexion would never reach him, never disturb him.

Yet that seemed hardly to be borne.

She looked down the wind-ruffled slope, became aware again of its shine, the absence of all human life, the susurration of the grass and trees.

After years during which he might have been—for all she knew—thousands of miles distant, he was now perhaps in one of those square buildings at the bottom of the hill. Or in a bungalow some hundred yards behind her. By the river. Anywhere.

With a shifting of panic, of self-preservation, she felt an instinct to hide: her visibility was made suddenly to seem full of danger, her vulnerability brought home to her.

The extremity of her unwisdom in returning to Ballowra had struck her like a physical blow the moment she left the train on Thursday night. Until then she had allowed herself to believe that some slight official pressure, and, less convincingly, Lilian's letter, had made it necessary for her to come.

Yet that was hardly true. She had never tried to deceive herself as to her reasons for coming back: where she had been mistaken, as she now recognized, was in pre-judging the effect on her equanimity and discounting it. But an hour in the climate of the past had confirmed the impact of that first astonished blow. And *then* she had not known about Max.

Even in recollection the pressure of that temptation to say, 'Yes. Ask the man in the dark suit,' exhausted her, made her mouth dry; exhausted her as in the morning resistance had done, so that she had heard nothing of the young man's story, so that she now turned her back on the quiet slope and its eye-level views of sky, and without volition began to walk away from it.

She could at least visit Lilian in indifference, find there distraction and talk, block up insidious supposition, if only for a time.

Wrapped about by silence and warm winds she walked downhill to Lilian's house, feeling a small comforting response to her entreaty for calm as she drew nearer.

The commentator announced that it had been a photo-finish. The decision would be broadcast in a matter of seconds, and Lilian sat—the racing-guide in one hand, a lead pencil in the other—staring at the small cream wireless set, waiting in suspended agitation for the result.

When Emily came in she was listening tensely to an advertisement for hair-oil, so far removed from the events of the morning that she felt no surprise at Emily's sudden appearance in the room, at the girl's expression, or her evident intention of speaking—merely irritation, and faint panic lest the result of the race should go against her. She held up an arm.

The advertisement ended. The result was announced. At the same time, so that Lilian seemed to hear neither and both, Emily said, 'Thea's here. Thea's at the door.'

Catching the accusation, missing the words, Lilian jerked her head up, looked and saw, with a stranger's eye, the tall girl, malevolent, red-eyed, with at this moment, superimposed on her unhappiness, a look of doubting her own sanity. Lilian took in the eyes, the crumpled dress.

She turned to look at the wireless again and, as if in answer to her appeal, the result of the race was repeated. At that moment Emily spoke again, and the import of her first message was flashed to Lilian. She was on her feet.

Rapidly she stuffed the paper out of sight, switched off the voice and tried to tidy herself. Smiling and whispering with what seemed to Emily an odious mixture of ingratiating humility and excitement, she ran her fingers through her hair and looked in the mirror. 'Thea's here, at the door? Quick, go and tell her to come in. No. I'll go.'

Before leaving the room she gave it a glance of inspection which turned, when it reached Emily, to an excited appeal for support, but Emily's face went blank and icy, and she moved away to lean against the wall, her hands behind her back.

Exasperated, Lilian went up the hall at a trot. 'Well, well, well!' she cried, laughing loudly.

Left behind, Emily heard their voices—Lilian's shrill, breaking constantly into breathless gusts of laughter; Thea's words she strained to hear through Lilian's shouted welcome, and was surprised by their arrival in the room.

'—just the same,' Lilian was saying. 'The carpet's new, and the curtains. Do you know what that stuff cost me a yard? Oh. You've seen Emily? What do you think of her? She keeps growing. I don't know where she gets it from.'

'We knew each other at once,' Thea said, and heard again the peculiar note of relevance in Emily's cry of recognition, remembered the extraordinary perturbation her arrival seemed to set up in the girl.

'Ah. She would.' Lilian's response was just not sour.

Thea said, pausing before she sat down next to Lilian on the sofa, 'If I've come at a terribly inconvenient moment—do say so. I should have let you know that I thought of coming out.'

'No, no, no!' Lilian flapped a hand, shook her head. 'Sit down, sit down. God knows I'm always here just waiting for someone to pop in. You're not going to get away now that you're here.'

Her vehemence was comical but reassuring. Thea sat down, to be studied with ferocious shamelessness for signs of deterioration. Knowing Lilian, she humoured her, and waited.

'Well?'

'You're older, but you're still a good-looking woman. You're lucky. Look at me, I'm putting on weight. Have to go on a diet.' She slapped her body vigorously.

Her tone was so downright, her manner so aggressive, that Thea smiled, laughed, made Lilian laugh, and turned to Emily.

Intently Emily looked at the laughing face. She did not remember, would have denied, that she had ever seen herself in competition with this grown-up woman who smiled at her. Indeed, she was at so great a distance from herself that she was conscious of nothing but dull suspense.

For why had Thea come? Why now? For what purpose? That it was accidental she could not believe. A minute after her arrival her presence had seemed to be an inevitable part of the chaos. That she had been summoned for her, Emily's, special discomfiture had been the girl's first thought. But now she began to wonder.

One of her deepest instincts—an automatic response to the consciousness of a conscious person, strong in proportion to the degree of consciousness—made her begin to wonder. So profound was the insidious charm of its unseen presence that it lifted her, at this moment of extreme distress, to optimism.

Max and Thea, Max and Thea...A small fantastic hope began to grow. She stared at Thea's face as if to extract the truth from it, but it was not a face to be analysed while her head echoed with the reverberations of her new belief, while she was gripped by the vision of safety and beauty that life would be with Max and Thea.

For this was the miracle. Max had sent Thea to rescue her.

Animated, Lilian talked of Ballowra and Greenhills, of Rosen, Mr Watts, Billie and Fred, and Paula. She told Thea about her more spectacular successes on Saturday afternoons for years back. She talked about repairs to the house, parties, minor illnesses, a motor accident she had witnessed, a new cocktail she had learned to mix. These were all stories told so often that Lilian herself hardly participated in the recapitulation. She was wondering, waiting, debating.

Thea listened idly, too grateful for the sheer verve and distraction of the monologue to be bored, or to feel the assault on her memory that the room, with its unutterably familiar air, had in its power to deal.

Without thought, at some time during Lilian's discourse, she knew that she would go to Max. That she would leave this house and on her return to town find someone who could tell her where he was. Knowing what she would do, feeling the certainty of the completed action fall into place, she felt the inevitable lightness of her intention. Whatever the outcome might be she was already at peace. Knowing that she would see him, there was nothing to be desired.

She moved, became aware of Emily's concentration on her, and was led to examine and reject the idea that she had been expected. Her method of arriving—unannounced—had been dictated by her uncertainty, resolved only in the five minutes before she reached the house, as to whether or not she would make the call.

Of course the conference would have been reported by the local press, she remembered. Lilian must have seen it mentioned, spoken of her letter, and, presumably, have said something to account for Emily's attitude of—was it anxiety, or expectation? In either case—why?

A shaft of sunlight crept across her knees and she rested her hands in it. After a moment she raised her left arm and pressed the palm of her hand against her cheek.

Bribing fate with an intense, demented belief in her miracle, Emily watched her, refloating without apparent effort a capacity for concentration and feeling which had seemed, even minutes before, to be irretrievably wrecked. Since this morning she had been kept intact only by her incapacity to believe what was proved now to be a lie. Hadn't Patty guessed she was waiting for someone?

They—it—had been testing her, that was clear now. And she had succeeded, and she would be saved.

Silently she went across the room to a chair which brought her closer to Thea. (She might have to receive a secret message: they might have to run. Anything.) Thea glanced at her with a pleased smile of welcome.

This half of the room was brilliantly lit by the afternoon sun. It coloured everything a rather too rich gold. Emily thought she might feel sick.

Now Lilian asked Thea a few questions about the conference and Emily sat listening to the sound of her voice. She felt utterly soothed, incredibly soothed, to be sitting in the sun listening to Thea. For a moment she could have cried with weakness and relief but just then she caught a glimpse of Max and Thea and herself in their own house, and was tied up in fascination.

They were relaxed, knowing one another, a family. You could tell just to look at their faces how happy they were. At night they were all together, truly pleased to see one another, *saying* so. Sitting on the rug, with both of them in sight, Emily hugged her knees to her chest. With them, her life—the whole of her childhood—would be relived and then, only then, would she go forward.

The telephone rang and Lilian exclaimed in annoyance as she heaved herself from the sofa. Before she disappeared she warned Emily, 'Mind your manners, my lady!'

Emily woke with a jerk.

This was the moment. She was overcome with shyness. She could not look at anything but the floor. She saw the elegant lines of Thea's shoes and could have jumped with nervousness. The sense of separateness from the marvellous woman who wore them increased. But this was the moment when they would have to make plans for the escape...

Thea gazed reflectively at Emily's downcast face. At length she said, 'Emily...' She smiled and laid a hand on the cushion beside her. 'Come and talk to me for a few minutes. I must go very soon and I haven't seen you properly at all. What a long time it is...'

Emily could not move from her chair.

After a moment Thea said, 'Lilian says that you're coming to live in Sydney soon. I wonder how you'll like that? Do you mind changing schools?'

Emily felt a surging tumult of despair. She gave Thea a dumb tormented look and stood up.

'What's the matter? What is it? Is something wrong? Tell me.'

The bell tinkled outside as Lilian replaced the receiver of the telephone. Emily ran past her as she came into the room.

Hands on hips, she halted and raised her eyebrows at Thea. 'Good God! Now what? What's she been saying to you? Blubber, blubber. No wonder she hasn't got any friends. Who'd be friends with a thing like that!'

Delivering this, half to Thea, half to the girl, whom she suspected of being within hearing, she tugged at her corsets and dropped to the sofa.

Lilian gave Thea a bright smile of peculiar unpleasantness, as if defying her to protest, as if to mark the opening of hostilities.

Thea had the impression that she had walked into a trap.

She said, 'You're not very kind, Lilian. I don't know what she's done, or what's the matter, but I can't think it's wise to talk to her like that.'

The smile deepened and froze as Lilian huddled over the sensation of rage and pleasure that this piece of impudence brought her. She could always make the soft ones bite. Now that she had been insulted, she could go straight ahead—and would. Whether he sued, whether she sued, whether the roof fell in.

'What did she say to you?'

'Nothing. Not a word. She seems too unhappy to speak. What's happened to her?'

'You might well ask. If you'd come a bit earlier today you'd have heard it all.' Suddenly tiring of hints, she added, leaning forward, 'We've got a friend of yours to thank for all this.'

Thea was surprised. But feeling herself overcome by a tight, throbbing numbness as some apprehension of danger reached her, she had to feign surprise. 'Of mine? I didn't realize—' she slowed, 'that I had any other friends left here.'

She let her eyes rest, with a show of conventional interest, on Lilian's.

'*Didn't* you?' said Lilian quite gaily. 'Oh, yes. My word you have! But this particular one won't be here much longer, praise be!'

'Is that so?' Thea's voice was uninflected. With an effort she added, 'Who is it? You are very mysterious.'

'Do you know that Max is in Ballowra?'

'Yes. Yes, I do,' she said swiftly, too swiftly, on a quick breath. Then she heard the question, heard her answer, was racked with shock.

'Oh. Maybe you know he was staying here then, with us?'

'In this house?' Her eyes went over the room. 'No.'

'He was sent back to the works where you both used to be—you know that, do you? Well, he came to me one night and asked me to take him in, and I'd never seen him, of course, but I remembered his name and that he used to be a friend of yours, so I said, all right. I gave him your old room.' Lilian contrived to look at once severe and wanton.

After a pause, Thea said, 'How long was he here?'

'How long? Going on for a year. My God, you knew what you were doing when you upped and offed, didn't you? You were well rid of that one. Did you know his wife's been locked up again for ages? Did he ever tell you?'

'...No. I didn't know.'

'Not that he told *me*, mind you.' Lilian was scrupulous. 'I heard it from one of the men.'

For an uncertain length of time there was silence. Unnoticed, Emily re-entered the room. Then, at last, Thea broke away from the dull fascination of watching the quick grey eyes opposite her own, at work on her face.

'I'm sorry. I don't seem to understand you. But, apart from whatever it is you're trying to imply, I take it you intended us to confront each other here when you wrote asking me to come? Why? I find it hard to imagine your motive.'

'Why? Why?' Lilian stuttered, giving herself time to improvise. 'I'll tell you. It was to save this. All this trouble with her.' She flung round, pointed to Emily. 'If you'd come when I asked you, things might have taken a different turn. I knew it wouldn't be anything to you to see him after all these years off by yourself in Sydney. (If you *are* by yourself: I haven't heard about that, yet.) But if he'd seen you, he might have remembered to behave himself and saved us all a lot of trouble and worry.' Her indignation turned to a kind of arch reproof. 'You made your mark there, all right. He's lived like a blessed monk on your account. I often felt like telling him he ought to move to the place across the river. But all joking aside, you're better off without him. If it'd just been that he was quiet and wouldn't join in our parties the way anyone might—well, I'd have said, well and good. It's a free country. But. The thing was...He got too interested in this! And she's just—what?—just about touching thirteen. Wouldn't leave her alone almost from the beginning. So. You see why we had to do something about it. Oh, we've had fun and games this last day or so. You've only just missed it.'

Having committed murders all round, Lilian was suddenly stopped by a sensation of fright. In a moment her face declined from vivacity to haggardness. She was frightened of Thea.

'That's quite enough.'

Having felt too much, Thea now felt nothing but an unwillingness on the part of her eyes ever to see the woman opposite her again. Slowly she roused herself, turned away, stared as it were, from the stage, out into the room where Emily, in a world of her own, wept into her hands, recounting with automatic, sick persistence what was the truth and what was not.

In a hard, dead voice Thea said, 'I wish I could believe you didn't know what you'd done.'

Lilian snorted. 'Believe what you like! I'm telling you. I had to get this girl's mother and father here by telegram. We gave Mr Max his walking papers last night and he was out of this house at half past nine this morning. So!' Her grey eyes flared, she crossed her arms tightly. 'As for *her*, silly big thing that she is, the sooner she's away with them the better. Harry won't stand for any of this nonsense. Mind you,' she added hastily, startled again, instinctively, by the unmoving stillness of Thea's eyes on hers, 'I'm not saying—'

'No. You really have said enough.' Thea stood up. 'You made quite vile, unspeakable insinuations which I feel you know, as surely as I do, to be untrue. Your manner, and the fact that you have chosen to repeat this in front of Emily, convinces me of that.'

'It's a damn long time since you saw him, remember. I'm not saying anything about anyone but I don't know what makes you so sure. I tell you—'

On a high note, pushed beyond herself, Emily cried at her in a tone so imperative that Lilian was stopped.

'Oh!' She banged some cushions about and shook herself into a new position. 'Well, I don't know. The whole thing just had to be put a stop to and now it is, that's all I know.'

Thea walked slowly across the room, away from her, towards Emily. She put a white-gloved hand on the girl's shoulder and said her name.

'I don't think there's anything I can do. I'm sorry. But don't cry. Don't cry.'

Emily said, 'I know where he is. The Promenade Hotel, in town.' She felt a moment's alteration in the slight pressure on her shoulder.

'Thank you for telling me.'

Having regretfully acknowledged that her part in the scene was over, Lilian had been sitting slumped, staring at Thea's back. With an effort she pressed her hands to her knees and stood up.

'Well, what's she telling you now?...Oh!' She studied their faces. 'She knows where he is. Oh, well, good luck to you if that's how you feel. You won't have any trouble getting him back, believe me.'

Then as if the silent Emily had screamed, she said, 'Listen to her! She won't like this. I said you'd put a spoke in her wheel.'

Thea put a hand up to the door. Lilian ducked back. Thea said, 'I ask you, for God's sake, for your own sake, not to say any more.'

They reached the front door.

Lilian said, 'There's the car! Oh, forget all this, why don't you? Stay and have some tea and a talk to Paula. There's no need to rush away because of this. He'll be there for weeks yet.'

Thea turned to Emily, who was clinging to the veranda post. She looked at her speechlessly. Quickly she said, 'Goodbye, my dear.'

She was gone. The gate squeaked shut.

Emily and Lilian exchanged a look. Paula ran breathlessly up the passage to the veranda. 'Was that *Thea*? Did you ask her here, Mum?'

Lilian's eyebrows rose. 'And why shouldn't I? Whose house is it? She's off to see him. Everything's all right. I don't know what you're getting so excited about.'

But her daughter had run back inside to collapse on the bed.

'Place is like a madhouse,' Lilian muttered. Catching sight of Rosen she flapped her arms at him. 'Put on the wireless.'

She gazed out, like a ship's captain from his eminence, at the empty street. Paula was right. Greenhills *was* depressing. Discontented, she gave a sigh. She had meant to make a few conciliatory remarks about Max just to be on the safe side, but somehow things had happened too fast at the last moment, and now Thea had gone.

Biting her lips she went heavily back to the sitting-room, and was cheered as she approached it by the sound of an advertisement. That meant the three-thirty had not yet been run.

Emily stopped at the corner, her knees locking to counteract a sudden desire to give in, to sit down. She could see Thea at the top of the hill. At this longed-for, unexpected, reprieve she hung back, unable to remember what it was she had intended to do or say when she left the house.

Obviously the time for everything was past; only some stubborn necessity provoked her against reason to seek the anti-climax of another meeting.

Thea had walked very slowly, she thought, beginning to run again. She would catch her and tell her—what it was her fevered mind for the moment kept her from knowing. All she knew was that her final desertion, their reunion, their forgetfulness of her, their happiness, her immolation, must be postponed.

And running, she felt the bracelet drop from her fingers, felt again the fall, the loss, remembered the flash of gold in the river. Was this the punishment? She could not deny its justice. *That* had to be told whatever else was said.

Abruptly, at the thought, she slowed to a walk, came almost to a standstill, light-headed, incapable of bringing up the wordless thoughts that surged below the surface, unable to localize the intense disquiet of her being.

But Thea had disappeared, crossed the road, and was out of sight. In a panic Emily heard a bus in the distance and threw herself forward again.

Now she was at the top of the hill. A little to the left a red double-decker bus had halted. She was too late.

As it started up and, slowly, approaching the crossroads, drew level, she walked to the edge of the road and narrowed her stinging eyes at its many windows. She lifted an arm to shade her eyes. She was nothing. She felt nothing.

'*Thea.*'

In the empty bus, at an open window, Thea heard and turned her head. She lifted a hand, and then the bus disappeared through the tunnel in the yellow cliffs.

Emily's arm, bare and meaningless as a vacant flagpole, fell to her side.

CHAPTER TEN

IT WAS late afternoon. Outside, a low sky of clay-coloured clouds hung full of threat. There was a sound of distant thunder and occasionally from the clouds, or above or behind them, came a flash of sheet lightning.

Quick-changing variations of darkness had made it necessary to switch on the lights and the effect was to give to the bedroom the artificiality of a stage-set across which the two girls moved with a certain consciousness.

Interested in the clear yellow of her skin, Patty sat at the dressing-table and examined her face minutely in the triple-sided mirror. Emily, wearing a new woollen jumper suit of hard red, stood over the suitcase and gazed at the harmless pile of clothes that was packed in it.

'That's the lot now,' Dotty said, coming silently in on her felt slippers. She handed Emily a bundle of white silk school blouses, still warm from the iron. 'How's it going?' Pausing to find a shoulder-strap, she winked at Patty, looked uncritically at the suitcase, and sniffed and sighed vaguely.

'All right...But look, Dotty. What can I do with all my books?'

'Oh, are you still going on about that?'

'Well, I've got a few little ones on the bottom, but Grandma wouldn't let me put them all in and now it's full, and she says I can't carry them loose...' Lilian's opposition to her every plan for their transport had been off-hand, as if she knew that she need no longer exert herself to rule.

Dotty said, 'Well, what do you think I can do about it?'

The three of them looked in silence at the books on the floor—Dotty, Patty, stolid and bored. 'Oh, what do you want all them for anyway?' Dotty said at last. 'They're not even stories, are they? Some of them?'

She privately agreed with Lilian, who had cursed Max for leaving a pile of old books that no one wanted as a further source of trouble.

Catching the girl's enigmatic blue eyes on her, she wiped her hands down the front of her apron and said indifferently, 'I don't know. Get them the next time you come up, why don't you?...O-oh! Here it comes, and I've still got things on the line...' And off she fled down the passage and out into the back yard, for, with a tremendous, preliminary battery of thunder the rain had started, came down solid and pounding.

Unnoticed, the spray from it blew in the window and dampened the thin curtains.

Emily put the blouses in the case.

'Don't you ever do your own ironing?' Patty asked, knowing.

'No.'

'Don't you know how?'

'No.'

'You're spoilt, aren't you?'

New red jumper suit, new this, new that.

With an effort, Emily threw up a tinny unconvincing smile. The unexpectedness of this small attack momentarily knocked her off balance, deprived her of another unit of energy, almost, it might fancifully have been felt, lessened her chances of survival.

She took a breath and knelt beside the books. With palms flattened she pressed heavily on the clothes in the suitcase. Nothing gave. It was really full.

Patty said in an absorbed voice, 'My skin's as soft as soft.' She caressed her pretty round cheeks with her fingertips and smiled. Swinging round on the stool she looked at Emily with flattering attention. 'And I like your nice dark shiny hair, Em.'

Shiny dark hair. It sounded like poetry. Emily had to go to the mirror.

'And the way you look sometimes, you know, the way your eyes look—I like that. I think we're both rather unusual and interesting, don't you?'

Solemnly, side by side, they gazed.

Forehead, nose, mouth, teeth, ears, neck, shoulders, red jumper suit, shiny dark hair: it was all there, and all right, but eyes...Emily went away. Eyes knew too much.

Lilian came in surrounded by scent and spirits, bound, squeezed, tied, pinched into her clothes—the general darkness and tightness of her ensemble indicating beyond doubt that she was dressed in her best and dressed to go out.

She said cheerfully, 'Are you nearly ready?'

She had about her tonight something of the swash-buckling air of a principal boy, and when she accidentally knocked over some books she started back, pointing to one in exaggerated amazement as if she were indeed playing a part. 'Good God! What's that? Chinese?'

The girls giggled. 'Greek.'

'Well,' Lilian said, 'that was a queer thing to give you. Fat lot of good. You'd better get these into the other room. You can get them when you're up another time.'

Patty tittered. She could smell whisky. She hoped Emily's grandmother was drunk.

While Emily gathered up the books and left the room, Lilian shivered at the sight and sound of the rain. She gave a small exclamation of annoyance when she saw the open windows and went to close them. 'Don't you girls ever think?'

Patty watched.

It was three months since Max had gone. Since then, Rosen had been despatched back to his wife and son, and the friendship of the jolly Mr Watts had been secured. Harry and Paula had had three weeks alone in their new Sydney flat; tonight Emily was to join them. Tomorrow Mr Watts was moving in as a boarder, and Dotty, whose mother had recently died, was bringing her luggage round, full of relief at the solution Lilian had offered to her homelessness.

'Changes, changes!' Lilian said, scrabbling in her handbag for her wallet. She took from it a five-pound note to give to her granddaughter. 'How's your mother?' She eyed Patty. The two women had an old unsettled quarrel and communicated now, when necessary, through the two girls.

'She's fine,' said Patty soberly.

'And she said you can go to stay with Emily in your school holidays?'

'Yes.'

'Good. Now you'd better put on your coat and tell Emily to get ready. We'll be going in five minutes.' And Lilian dabbed on more scent and went back to the sitting-room to finish her drink with Mr Watts.

Emily put the books on the empty shelves and closed the door of the room. It was all now so tidy, so bare, so devoid—apart from herself—of all that was Max. Had he ever existed?

'Max?' Self-consciously, her lips parted; without breath she framed his name, but somewhere she was betrayed for the end of the word came out with a little hiss that sounded absurd in the empty room.

During these months she had been poised, weightless with expectation of a word, a sign, a catastrophe—the sun and moon colliding with the earth: anything seemed possible, and anything catastrophic, desirable. Like an exile from her homeland she waited for a message from home—a place which must exist somewhere outside the prescribed perimeter of her journey to school, outside the fence around the house, beyond the shopping centre in Greenhills, on the other side of the river where she had never been.

At school she had worked with fanatical thoroughness as though she sought to wrest from the facts some meaning other than the logical, the architectural. In the house she was unobtrusive as a shadow. 'You wouldn't know she was here,' Lilian assured Paula on the telephone. 'She's as good as gold now that—now.'

But under the listless surface was a hot, gushing, weak but uncontrollable animal that lifted its arms and exhausted her with meaningless tears—when she broke an old saucer, for instance; at any sudden noise, or small accident. These periodic spasms of weeping she accepted as freak storms, and ignored.

Her chief preoccupation since Lilian had given the date of her departure for Sydney had been to secure that she should take with her what Max had left and, with less compulsion, the few old toys, the odd dishes she had owned since early childhood. They were the only reliable proof she had of having existed in the past—for no one but she recalled her presence then—and as such they were of value to her. Her desire for them had been instinctive, but now that she was not to have her way, she relinquished them without protest. For of course Lilian had said, referring to the toys and books, 'There'll be no room for any of that junk. I'll give them away, you never look at them.'

The two chipped china mugs, the three small plates with painted figures, Emily had not liked to mention, unwilling to give herself away for so fruitless a cause. And anyway, when it came to it, what did they matter? Now, to her, less than the Pyramids.

Tonight she was going. Not for months or years, perhaps never again would she be in the room where Max had lived, where he and she had talked and said goodbye. She stood at the side of the bed and looked at the rough weave of the yellow cover.

Where *was* he? With Thea? Would they always be together? Were they happy? Did she want them to be happy without *her*? No. No, she did not.

She felt the thing within her rise and fall, rise and fall, rise and fall.

'Crumbs!' Patty said. 'What're you doing—just standing in the dark? Come on. We've got to get ready. We're going.' Patty was off.

Lilian threw on her fur coat and jolly Mr Watts stood behind her helping to adjust it, his pleasantly plump and unwrinkled face looking very clean, very shaved, and rather mischievous.

'Well, here she is,' Lilian half sighed, half sang, seeing Emily. 'Off to the big city she goes. Ah, we've had some good times.' She laughed up at Mr Watts. 'I'll miss her, you know, though she's a little devil sometimes. Always singing, always singing...'

Arm in arm they faced the two girls and laughed affectionately. Mr Watts said, twinkling, 'Someone'll have to look after your grandmother when you're gone, won't they, Emily? Do you think I'd do? Would you put in a good word for me, huh?'

Patty and Emily giggled with muffled hysteria and dared not look at each other. They tried to get themselves out of the room, but Lilian stopped them, saying almost experimentally, 'Why don't you sing a little song for Mr Watts before you go?'

This gave the girls reason to laugh again, and drained off the dangerous surplus of mirth.

Dotty came to say goodbye, and then no umbrellas could be found so they had to run bareheaded through the downpour, through the lurid stormy night and pungent rainy smells to the garage.

There was a moment of elated pattings of coats and hair, a sensation of sparkling eyes and glowing cheeks, of having successfully brought off something potentially dangerous. After that, they deflated, saw the table, the bicycles; smelled, instead of earth and damp wool and hair, petrol.

In semi-darkness Mr Watts struggled round the side of the car with the suitcase, scraping it against the wall, and catching part of himself or his clothing on a handle. There was a noise of the boot being opened.

Bored to be still for even so short a time, Lilian thrust herself decisively forward to squeeze into the car.

'If we wait,' she said to Patty, who followed her, 'we'll only get wet again outside.'

They snaked through the few inches that were all the doors would open, and settled back on the leather seats.

According to custom, Emily stayed to switch off the light when the car had gone. But there was scarcely time for her to look, and none for her to frame a message: going, her wrists ached, her teeth ached, and when her fingers clicked off the switch she sent an apologetic glance into the darkness before she was swept away.

Tonight the future was close, about to be invaded. Things were always happening lately and there never was, would never be, time enough to sit and think about what it was that was so worrying. She seemed perpetually to be looking over her shoulder without time to find the words she ought to leave behind.

At the Horizon Hotel, close to the railway station, opposite a blackness that was the ocean, they had dinner in the grill-room. And while Mr Watts and Lilian sat at a corner table against the wall, Emily and Patty sat on stools arranged round a counter. They stared at the murals—reproductions of aboriginal drawings of hunters, animals, and boomerangs—and carried on a stilted conversation in high false accents, enjoying themselves, exaltedly conscious of their conspicuous position, and the imperative, adult reason for their presence here. But after a few minutes they fell silent, for apart from the fact that neither had much idea of what actually was said when sophisticated women ate out at a grill-room, there was so much that was distracting—the vast stretches of cutlery, the mysterious but delicious food, the waiters, the little hats of feathers and veiling...

Behind, from Lilian and Mr Watts, came low, rhythmical laughter which made Patty turn on Emily a sidelong glance of slightly malicious curiosity, but she, enduring a mouthful of something unrecognizable to her palate, batted her eyelids at Patty, and absorbed her look, remaining ignorant of its cause.

In a state of semi-coma they waited for lemon meringue pie and ice-cream. During this period, familiarity with their surroundings having brought about at least an assumption of disenchantment, they remembered that they were best friends, parting, and gazed inarticulately at each other.

It was too late now to say anything positive about their friendship, and before it had always been too early. A premature reference would have been in excruciating taste: any was now impossible.

On the station platform it was very cold. They stood around waiting for the train to come in. Constantly assaulted by the wild shrieks and blasts of shunting engines, eyes tormented by flying grit, they stood, four in a row, collars up round their ears, blankly and rather bitterly watching the other passengers and porters.

In single file they trooped through the crowd to buy magazines, chocolates, and nuts—large quantities of each, for Lilian, unused to travelling, looked on it as an endurance test—something against which enough precautions could not be taken. It was only after she had stared all round to catch the general opinion that she was dissuaded from plying Emily with cheese sandwiches and date rolls.

'It's not that long. She's had dinner.'

But feeling that she had been restrained from a gesture of affection and kindliness, Lilian closed her mouth tightly and for a few minutes looked at no one.

Unconsciously she revenged herself when the train came in by relaying to the entire compartment, through the medium of her chosen confidante, a bathetic biography of her 'only grandchild'. Not recognizing herself in the wistful—and, she privately thought, weak-minded—heroine Emily went red under the interest of the listeners: she and Patty rolled their eyes at each other and remained dumb. Mr Watts smoked in, and successfully blocked, the corridor.

Winding up her tale, Lilian threw a critical glance at the other occupants of the carriage, smiled and nodded to the middle-aged woman she had been addressing, and briskly kissed Emily. Tapping her on the knee, she bade her be good to her mother, and to write sometimes. Rising, she gathered Mr Watts and Patty and was gone.

It was too sudden. Emily craned out of the window but there was no sign of them—only porters and grown-up people pushing past, eyes fixed compulsively ahead. She sank back. Lilian had said goodbye; the others had had time only to work themselves up to a smile, a half-phrase, a lift of the hand.

She herself had been still taking in Lilian's injunctions, listening in a dazzled, perfunctory way, seeing the row of white faces opposite, thinking, even as she answered: don't think I'll ever forgive you.

But now it was noisy everywhere; the lights on the station began to go past the window. All at once she wanted not to leave Lilian, whom she at least knew, or Patty, or that empty room, or the river.

The station had gone, and all external light. The train rocked and rattled and, it was to be supposed, went forward through the blackness that enclosed it.

The top of the raw yellow stake, around which the unenergetic rose bush languidly grew, drove small indentations into the palm of Emily's hand, and gave off little bits of itself which were to come away on her skin when later she moved from the garden.

One arm lifted to the stake, the other bent across her waist, Emily balanced on the low stone retaining wall in front of the flats, in front of the long rose-garden.

Behind her, the building—a creamy cube of brick roofed with multi-coloured tiles—gleamed inoffensively in the late afternoon sunshine, its windows dazzled to black and gold. It wore the look of a building wherein food is being prepared, steam rising from saucepans.

Back to the road, separated from it by two older blocks of flats, it faced the west: it was the last building on the flank of a hill which, below the wall where Emily stood, was covered still by a rough tangle of bush—stunted gums, scrub, and blackberry bushes over which the strangling tide of convolvulus threw its blue and white flowers—for a distance of fifty yards or so.

With a shocking finality then the slope ended in a meeting with a bare flat plain of withered grass—a park, a playing-field on which nothing was played. To the right and straight ahead the park extended for some way, but to the left, just not level with the flats, a semi-circular wall held back the water of the harbour.

This then was the farthest reach of one finger of the Pacific, this bay, this so small as to be nameless bay.

The opposite land—unbuilt, hilly, wooded—curved low, dark-green, ideally rounded and gentle down to a rocky shore and the water. It was a bird sanctuary, Emily had been told, it might never change. It was certainly not *now* to be touched.

The knowledge that it was meant for birds, sacred to them, peopled the small headland hill, in Emily's mind, with bluebirds, wings, cries; with great colonies of birds, cool and busy under the trees' layered leaves.

Empty rowing-boats anchored in the shallow water of the bay had all begun to swing round with the gentle force of the rising water. And the sun shone on their white-painted, water-wet sides; on the occupied, incoming sea; on the tops of the trees; on the dull playing-field.

Soon it would be gone, soon it would be dark, but meantime the earth gave up earthy evening scents, dampness in spite of heat. Frail pink clouds feathered the translucent sky and Emily clutched at the stake and breathed the air, looked with unthinking eyes, was uplifted, transported, gave herself to the present beauty and the coming night. With cold smoothing hands the moment unfretted fear. She could have sung some wild wordless chant. In a trance she watched a bird soar homewards, disappear.

The climax past, the clouds paled and wisped, lay streaked and sheer across a deeper sky. Her eyes suddenly closed tight, hand pressing the stake, hand clutching her waist, Emily thought: oh surely, surely! Surely, surely, surely...

When Harry said that, Paula giggled and he, deprecating his wit, drew a pattern on the table-cloth with his fork and would not catch her eye.

Paula giggled again, a curious little neighing sound, now frequently to be heard from her, and still throwing over her shoulder at him that awed, so flattering look, turned to the oven.

Then he gave a dry chuckle and cocked an eye up at her, but she was busy. A trifle let-down, his mouth fell into a sour curve—but for an instant only. He saw the electric mixing-machine, white and shining silver. He looked at the modern unit where Paula was working, at the green plants on the small waist-high wall that divided the room.

'Paula! I've been figuring out—' He waited till she came over to him. 'I've been figuring out how much I've saved by getting this stuff wholesale.'

Her expression—intended to convey extreme interest—was apprehensive, and Harry did not find apprehension over money matters amiss.

'Three hundred,' he said quietly, raising his brows, looking down at the cutlery.

'No!'

'That's right!' He bowed his head, then glanced up at her as if to say, 'Make what you like of it.'

'Oh, Harry, that's wonderful!' She laughed and thrashed the air with a spoon. 'And you just say it like that. "Three hundred."' She came round the side of the wall to admire him at closer quarters. She had about her a high excessive air of adulation. Again, it did not seem to Harry overdone.

He said kindly, 'It was old Watkins who got it for me. He knows all these jokers in the furniture trade.'

'Still...!'

'Old Watkins, he'd do anything for me.'

But Paula's big grey eyes assured him that she really would not allow him to give the credit to old Watkins.

In silence, rubbing soft fingers over the golden hairs on his arms, he watched her. Suddenly he said, 'Where's er...Where is she?'

'Emily? In the garden, I think.'

'She ought to be up here helping you.'

'I don't need her. She really doesn't know how to do anything, anyway.'

'It's time she did.'

Paula suppressed a sigh and, her preparations finished, rinsed her hands under the tap. She was supported through this moment of less than contentment by the most stable of her joys—the flat, its gleaming furnishings, its waxy cleanness. Vague peaceful sensations of satisfaction came like small waves to wash away the marks left on the sand.

For both she and Harry there had been greater gain in their reunion than either had thought possible. Above all, there was the prestige of respectability. They were married, together, with one child and a nice home—in a similar condition, that is, to most people of any consequence. Physically they were satisfied. And from day to day Harry rejoiced in a resident audience, and applause. For Paula, he was her master, her unruly child. He was the magician who had saved to produce the flat and all its beautiful contents.

Yes, she liked her new rôle. She liked the costumes and the scenery. Ruthlessly she sacrificed all that was left of herself to the part. She was submissive, eager, impressed. She teased and glorified. She was alert. Harry was a man and no one knew his faults better than she. Her care was necessary to keep the balance. He was vain, touchy, selfish. Sometimes already she had despised him, yet she was able to think of herself as happy.

If there was a flaw—and there was—it was their daughter. For one thing—admittedly not her fault—she was older than they would have chosen her to be. A sprite of four or five with curly hair and nice little ways was Paula's wistful ideal, and Harry's, apart from the fact that he wanted a son, was much the same. And then the incident that had precipitated their coming together had not been an auspicious beginning to a new life. They felt they could not really trust her after that.

'Always mooning round the garden,' her father complained, 'but ask her to *do* anything...'

'She does what you tell her. That digging was quite hard work, though,' Paula excused her. 'She's only young.'

'*You* did it,' he pointed out, 'and she's bigger than you.'

'Oh, well, she's only young.'

Harry shifted his elbows on the table and glared at her aggressively. 'Paula, do you know what *I* was doing when I was her age? *I* was—'

'Oh! Everything's ready, Harry. I'll just call Em and then we'll start.' Smiling placatingly, she went to the door.

Moodily Harry watched her. His marvellous, his glorious announcement had been forgotten. Just like that. Three hundred. She said, 'Imagine that! How clever!' and that was that. What was the saving of three hundred compared with calling her daughter in for dinner? A man was just a machine to make money.

Her hand relaxed and tightened on the stake when the voice sounded. She was called. Her mother was calling from the, from here, invisible back door of their first-floor flat.

Holding on to the end of the exaltation she looked round, released her grip, and leapt across the width of the rose-garden to the lawn. Over the grass, along the cement path, up the cement stairs, hand on the piping rail she went, the surely, surely, surely, going with her, being beaten by her into a self conditioned to resist hope. For she had been on the verge of knowing something tonight...

She and her father looked at each other: Paula looked at both and started to chatter. What she said, neither knew. Emily pulled in her chair and sat down.

Harry said, 'Wash your hands.'

Paula said, 'Have you had your tonic?' (The doctor said she had outgrown her strength and prescribed iron.) Emily took the tonic and went to the bathroom to wash her hands.

In the kitchen Harry said, eating, breathing heavily through his nose, 'If I see that look on her face again I'll give her something she won't forget in a hurry.'

And about the look—a provoking compound of scepticism and understanding, impatience and calm—Paula could say nothing. It was not a good look for a young face: it aggravated Harry, but it seemed so habitual that she did not know how to ask her daughter to change it. She supposed it was impertinent of Emily to look like that. She automatically checked a sigh. Regretfully she watched her husband eat his meal, his whole face working.

She looked at her own plate. 'Three hundred pounds,' she said, but Harry was silent. 'Mrs Downstairs came up this morning and she was in raptures over the dining-room suite. She kept saying, "Mrs Lawrence, it must have cost a fortune!"'

Harry gave a short laugh and tilted back in his chair. He prodded his teeth. 'What'd you say?'

Paula felt the legs of his chair digging into her polished floor. Forcing herself to remember the morning's conversation and to derive, as well as to provide consolation from it, she said, 'Oh, I just laughed, but she was so busy admiring the whole place I thought she'd never go.'

Harry nodded as if he could understand this. He sucked thoughtfully at his teeth, scratched his neck with a forefinger, and said on a deep sigh, 'She'll have something else to look at next week.'

Extravagantly mystified, his wife slowly straightened her back and laid down her knife and fork. Her smile traversed his face. 'Tell me, Harry.'

'Tell you what?'

'What she'll see.'

'Oh, that...Well, I saved three hundred, didn't I?'

'Yes.'

'Well then. Gotta get rid of it somehow.'

'What do you mean, Harry? Tell me.'

Nervously she giggled. Her interest was, as usual, uncomfortably tinged with alarm, and would be, until she heard what he intended. Though her dinner was getting cold, she knew that if she started to eat again, now, before he finished the game of question and answer, Harry would be bitterly offended. She was conscious, too, that Emily had not come back from the bathroom. 'Harry, what are you going to do?'

'Guess!'

The game began in earnest.

Emily dried her hands and looked at her face in the mirror. 'Hullo,' she said. 'How are you?'

For some seconds she and her reflection commiserated kindly with each other. To it she confided her marks in today's test. Did it think, she asked it, that she would ever find a friend at school? Now, she sat alone. The rest were all as good as married. Exactly even. Twos and twos.

Still! her reflection said, as if it mattered.

And it ceased to matter.

Then Emily told her friend, with eyes and thoughts, about the sunset, the sky, the pink clouds, and the birds.

Max, it snapped at her. *Max*, it said. Have you forgotten him? Didn't you think of him tonight? Have you forgotten him already? You said you never would. How does your heart feel when you think of him? Is there any love? What did he look like? What did he say?

The towel between her hands, she turned away. Hanging it on the chromium rail she felt the sparking, sparking in her chest. The thing in her chest was brought to life. With a mixture of panic and relief she felt the old familiar swelling and dying, rising and falling, quicker and quicker, rising and falling in her chest.

Then she made it stop. Then she remembered what she had done. As if she had seen someone fall from a height, her body throbbed with vicarious fright. She had torn up his letter. She had nothing of him. It was her own doing.

Appalled by a deeper isolation here among unfamiliar people and places than she had ever known before, she had written a letter to him—the kind that could not go unanswered. Here she lived under closer surveillance, was brought up against jealousy and active dislike. Drift, drift, up and down the stairs; drag, drag, round the paths, surrounded by silence, the utter purposelessness of her existence, the inconvenience of it daily more apparent, she wrote Max a letter imploring something of him. Anything. At least, a letter.

He had answered quickly, submitted to the necessity of sending the letter to Patty first, to be forwarded by her, covered by her big careful writing on the envelope. With what sensations he had done this, when the letter came, Emily did not concern herself.

Sick with excitement she had locked herself in the bathroom, and, unfolding the long sheets of paper, trembled violently, for they proved he was still to be reached, had existed, had surely felt *some* affection for her. By the window, terrified of discovery, she read.

And what had he said in all that space? She could hardly remember. With a slow, incredulous chilling of her blood, she had read, and seen only what he did not say. No promises. No declarations.

In the intensity of her disappointment she loathed him, was utterly humiliated to remember the past. She felt physically sick with loathing and disappointment. What could she destroy?

Someone had banged on the door. She stared at the pages in bitter hurt. Quickly she tore them to pieces, dropped them in the bowl of the lavatory and pushed the handle.

Remembering, she leaned against the towel rail and pressed her mouth to her towel.

For weeks she had hated him, and to feel hate for him was to feel something worse for herself, to be empty of all past happiness and future possibilities of good.

Then one day she knew, and suddenly said aloud, 'What else could he have done?'

It was as if she had learned the most difficult code of all. She begged forgiveness of his memory. (In spite of the letter she had come to think of him as dead. Such utter inaccessibility could only belong to death.) For she would not write to him again. There was no need. Now she could begin to understand the many inexplicable things he had said to her. Now she was responsible for herself, and knew it. She was responsible for her actions. What had been amorphous and unreliable in her seemed, now, to be solid.

She pressed a cheek against the towel and took a deep breath—a sigh that was not a sigh, something that was more than air. With a breath, she had lately come to accept much that was not easy.

All this being brave, doing what he said, growing up, was all very well, she thought, eyeing the dark shadow of herself on the tiled wall. In the daytime, or the evening, looking at a bright pink sunset it was not so bad, but at night...Any time. It was easy for him. *She* had to live without the kindness and communication, without a movement of the heart—and from tonight, without dramatics.

A sudden shattering awareness of the existence of Max and Thea, a memory of her feeling for them, caused such a questioning of life in her that she stood for seconds without breathing, felt the question expand, the small tiled room contract. For she no longer cared. There were memories, and gratitude, but she *resented* knowing that love ended.

There came a kind of furtive battering at the door. 'Emily! Emily! What's the matter? What are you doing in there? Are you crying again? What on earth are you crying for? Come out here at once and eat your dinner like a sensible girl of thirteen. Lots of little girls would be happy to be in your place, you know. Of all the discontented girls I know... I'm really losing patience with you. Come out this minute, do you hear me? Wait till I tell you what Daddy's going to do.'

Casting a last look at the shining tiles Emily said, I have to go.

Sapped, hollow, belatedly obedient, she opened the door. Paula eyed her sharply.

'Now come out here and have your dinner and behave,' she whispered. 'I don't know what I'm going to do with you.'

At the kitchen door she paused, laughing, with her hand on Emily's shoulder, and looked at Harry. 'This is a wicked father you've got, Emily. Do you know what he's just told me?'

Still she and Harry held each other's eyes as in a trance. 'He's going to get us a lovely new car. Going to sell the old one next week and get a lovely brand-new one. Isn't that wonderful?'

Harry stuck out his lower lip. 'You two'll have to clean it, though.'

Paula giggled and raised her brows, sending a woman's glances to the young girl beside her in the hope that she would respond and join her in the fascinating, necessary game of teasing Harry.

Text Classics

The Commandant
Jessica Anderson
Introduced by Carmen Callil

Homesickness
Murray Bail
Introduced by Peter Conrad

Sydney Bridge Upside Down
David Ballantyne
Introduced by Kate De Goldi

Bush Studies
Barbara Baynton
Introduced by Helen Garner

A Difficult Young Man
Martin Boyd
Introduced by Sonya Hartnett

The Cardboard Crown
Martin Boyd
Introduced by Brenda Niall

The Australian Ugliness
Robin Boyd
Introduced by Christos Tsiolkas

All the Green Year
Don Charlwood
Introduced by Michael McGirr

The Even More Complete Book of Australian Verse
John Clarke
Introduced by John Clarke

Diary of a Bad Year
J. M. Coetzee
Introduced by Peter Goldsworthy

Wake in Fright
Kenneth Cook
Introduced by Peter Temple

The Dying Trade
Peter Corris
Introduced by Charles Waterstreet

They're a Weird Mob
Nino Culotta
Introduced by Jacinta Tynan

The Songs of a Sentimental Bloke
C. J. Dennis
Introduced by Jack Thompson

Careful, He Might Hear You
Sumner Locke Elliott
Introduced by Robyn Nevin

Terra Australis
Matthew Flinders
Introduced by Tim Flannery

My Brilliant Career
Miles Franklin
Introduced by Jennifer Byrne

The Fringe Dwellers
Nene Gare
Introduced by Melissa Lucashenko

Cosmo Cosmolino
Helen Garner
Introduced by Ramona Koval

Dark Places
Kate Grenville
Introduced by Louise Adler

The Long Prospect
Elizabeth Harrower
Introduced by Fiona McGregor

The Watch Tower
Elizabeth Harrower
Introduced by Joan London

The Mystery of a Hansom Cab
Fergus Hume
Introduced by Simon Caterson

The Glass Canoe
David Ireland
Introduced by Nicolas Rothwell

A Woman of the Future
David Ireland
Introduced by Kate Jennings

Eat Me
Linda Jaivin
Introduced by Krissy Kneen

The Jerilderie Letter
Ned Kelly
Introduced by Alex McDermott

Bring Larks and Heroes
Thomas Keneally
Introduced by Geordie Williamson

Strine
Afferbeck Lauder
Introduced by John Clarke

Stiff
Shane Maloney
Introduced by Lindsay Tanner

The Middle Parts of Fortune
Frederic Manning
Introduced by Simon Caterson

Selected Stories
Katherine Mansfield
Introduced by Emily Perkins

The Home Girls
Olga Masters
Introduced by Geordie Williamson

The Scarecrow
Ronald Hugh Morrieson
Introduced by Craig Sherborne

The Dig Tree
Sarah Murgatroyd
Introduced by Geoffrey Blainey

The Plains
Gerald Murnane
Introduced by Wayne Macauley

Life and Adventures 1776–1801
John Nicol
Introduced by Tim Flannery

Death in Brunswick
Boyd Oxlade
Introduced by Shane Maloney

Swords and Crowns and Rings
Ruth Park
Introduced by Alice Pung

Maurice Guest
Henry Handel Richardson
Introduced by Carmen Callil

The Getting of Wisdom
Henry Handel Richardson
Introduced by Germaine Greer

The Fortunes of Richard Mahony
Henry Handel Richardson
Introduced by Peter Craven

The Women in Black
Madeleine St John
Introduced by Bruce Beresford

An Iron Rose
Peter Temple
Introduced by Les Carlyon

1788
Watkin Tench
Introduced by Tim Flannery

Happy Valley
Patrick White
Introduced by Peter Craven

textclassics.com.au